TIGERS QUEST

EMILY ROSE. This is for you.

Thank you for coming back into my life.

Acknowledgements. This is my second book, it is just as difficult and just as lonely as the first to write and yet again I am indebted to others for their help. Mr Roger Paul for telling me about his exploits in Spain and for our hundreds of hours on surveillance together, giving me plenty of ideas for future novels. Mrs Nat Shaw for picking me up when I was down. Miss Kelly Brotherhood for her unbridled passion for writing, the helpful notes she made on a read though and the character 'Hook' Callan. Mr Martyn 'Griff' Griffiths for allowing me to keep the 'Gruff' character and Mr Ade Wildsmith for the author's photo on the back cover. Much more importantly, to each and every person that has ever purchased or downloaded my books. You're beautiful people. Thank you.

You haven't let me down and I hope that Tiger and his mates haven't let you down.

As usual, any errors, geographical, technical or grammatical in the following pages are mine and mine alone.
       Frank Castle. Lincoln. July 2020.

6

~ONE~

Tiger had three seconds left to live.

He was never going to stop in time. He'd left his braking far, far too late and that momentary lack of judgment was going to cost him his life.

Seems like an unfair equation. Simple human error equals death. Tiger was not in the habit of making simple errors though, and he knew how to fight. He was trained well by the best instructors in the world and had practiced his craft in some dodgy little corners of the world, little dark corners of the world with names that a Western tongue found impossible to pronounce and right now, on a well maintained stretch of road in the Wolds of rural Lincolnshire it was supposed to end?

Tiger didn't think so. His right hand was pumping the big front brake lever causing maximum braking under cadence and giving him an opportunity to make slight, but critical steering inputs though the handle bars of his Triumph Bonneville T140 sports motorcycle.

The howling of the rubber from his front tyre actually comforted him, this was the noise of maximum adhesion of tyres to tarmac, despite the fact there was only a three inch circle of rubber in contact with the road surface at any one time.

The ball of his left foot was working hard on the rear brake pedal and despite the thickness of the soles on his leather engineer boots he could feel the muscles in his foot cramping up. Keeping the weight of the bike forward wasn't just the key to the whole process, it was crucial and as the lightened rear end of his machine skipped and bounced he would leak off the tiny amount of pressure needed to control the forward/rear balance ratio.

He was also busy sorting out gears, this involved releasing the throttle with his right hand and pulling in the clutch with his left. His right boot moving forward two inches on the foot peg, poised above the gear lever in order to smash down the sequential gearbox in perfect timing with each pull of the clutch lever with his left hand, one quick squeeze for each of the gears from 4th down into 1st.

It was time. The time when most motorcycle riders would die, panicked and engrossed with the unmovable mass hurtling towards them, that and the primal reluctance to let go of the front brake, it was against every survival instinct of the human brains twisted network of neural senses to do such a thing.

Tiger lifted his boot from the back brake then completely released the front brake causing the front of his machine to rise up slightly on the twin suspension front forks adding a little bit of pressure to the rear one. He snapped the throttle fully open, this forced the inlet butterfly valves on the twin AMAL carburettors to allow the fuel air mixture to explode into the top of the engines cylinders and put most of the available fifty brake horsepower on instant orders to move.

The engine didn't let him down. The rear of the machine squatted down and the whole mass of man and machine accelerated hard. Tiger forced the right handlebar away from him and the bike leaned hard to the right, an action known as counter steering.

Sweat poured from beneath his helmet and channelled around his goggles before being whipped into the slipstream, the colossal concentration required without getting a target fixation on the leviathan sized obstacle in front of him and the strength of his forearms maintaining the steering would have been far beyond the skills of an average motorcyclist.

The motorcycles nearside mirror and Tigers left knee brushed the offside rear corner of the slow moving Combine Harvester with the softest of kisses. A quick correction on the steering and Tiger was howling back down the open road in one piece.

Easy.

TWO~

Tiger throttled back as he entered the pretty Lincolnshire Wolds village of Donington-on-Bain and eased his machine into the rear car-park of The Black Horse Inn. He glanced at his watch, 2.30 pm. It had been a good ride out.

Unusually for the time of day there was another motorcycle parked up. He switched off the ignition listened to the crack and ping of his exhaust pipes cooling down as he swung his leg over his bike and crouched down to have a look at the machine he'd parked next to.

A brand new Honda 650 Custom. Four in-line cylinders with 4 exhaust downpipes entering a collector box under the belly and exiting as 4 beautifully polished chromed exhaust pipes at the rear. Its 30 inch seat height and swept up and back handle bars meant it would have been a bit too small for Tiger to sit on and anyway, it was Japanese, not his type of motorcycle at all.

Tiger pocketed his keys, removed his goggles and helmet, stuffing his gloves inside it as he strolled towards the back door of the public house, stooping slightly as he passed through the open doorway and into the public bar.

It took him five strides to reach the bar and in that time he noticed that there were five people in the place. Himself, Derek the barman, a couple sat drinking from tea cups in the far corner, perhaps in their early fifties, wearing hiking gear poring over a map and a blonde lass wearing black leather motorcycle leathers.

Interesting.

'Afternoon Tiger, What can I get you? Usual?'

'Hi Derek, that'll be fine thank you.'

Derek started pouring a pint of Double Diamond bitter into a glass.

12

Tiger swept the fingers of his right hand through his hair, an utterly pointless exercise in obtaining anything close to tonsorial neatness.

'What's the story then Derek? Anything interesting happened since my last visit?'

'Nope, same old same old, you know what it's like around here, quiet as a church unless it's a coach of hikers ready to walk the Viking Trail or a race meeting at Cadwell Park.'

'I hear what you're saying old boy,' then dropping his voice a notch, 'who's the blonde lass?'

Derek had finished pouring Tigers beer and leaned over conspiratorially as he passed it to him. 'Ah, that'll be the girl that's staying here. She arrived about 30 minutes ago and has booked a room for a couple of days.'

'Married? With somebody?'

'I wouldn't know Tiger mate, she arrived on her own and booked a single room though.'

'C'mon Derek, you don't miss a trick you old fox. Wedding ring?'

'Nope.'

'Name?'

'I can't tell you that, you know she's booked in as a guest, it's confidential, what's up with you? Go and ask her, it's never stopped you before.'

Tiger took a slow sip of his cold beer and didn't take his eyes off Derek, just raising a quizzical eyebrow.

'You're a sod Tiger, look, don't you be getting me into trouble now,' Derek looked theatrically over his right shoulder, knowing full well nobody was there, 'she's called Albright, Jane Albright.'

Tiger chewed this information over for a few seconds, a small frown line popped up on his forehead.

13

'Is that right Derek? Well, well, well.'

'Do you know her?'

'Maybe.' Tiger took another sip of his beer, winked at Derek and turned to look at Jane Albright. She was sat behind a tray containing a teapot and the accoutrements to enable her to top up a fresh brew. It was difficult to gauge height when someone is sitting down, but given the seat height of the motorcycle parked outside and her compact looking figure he guessed at 5'5". So, a very attractive looking blonde who rode a brand new, large capacity motorcycle.

Interesting.

He walked across the carpeted floor towards her table and she only looked up as his shadow fell across the pages of some paperwork she was reading.

'Jane?'

Jane looked confused. How was it that somebody should know her name within thirty minutes of getting here? She looked past the tall motorcyclist that had asked the question, looking pointedly at the older man behind the bar, who, after the briefest of glances had found something that required his immediate attention down in the cellar.

'Who's asking?'

'John. John Stripes.'

'John Stripes? John Stripes from Donington-on- Bain, er, here?'

Tiger moved around the table. He placed his motorcycle helmet on the seat next to her and sat down. The helmet acted as a little barrier.

'Aye, that John Stripes, the John Stripes that answered your enquiry letter regarding your children.'

Jane Albright's eyes had been boring into Tigers from the moment he'd blatantly entered her space, a form of defiance that had made her cheeks redden but as he finished speaking her eyes dropped to her lap and she whispered.

'I'm sorry.'

Damn. She felt her eyes well up with tears. She had practiced her opening gambit over and over again, even rehearsed in front of a mirror, for the occasion when she met the disinterested Mr Stripes. He was supposed to be some sort of whiz kid investigator and all she'd received was a standard letter, 'interfering in due process' this, 'without prejudice' that, well she wasn't going to let something as insubstantial as a written refusal get in her way. Her task, her *mission* was far more important than that. She had decided that she would travel to Lincolnshire and approach Mr 'without prejudice' Stripes personally, ambush him, ask him again for help. Beg for it.

She reached across the table picked up a paper napkin and carefully wiped her eyes then looked at Mr Stripes once more, full on eye contact.

'No, no, I am not sorry at all Mr Stripes. Your letter, as polite as it may have looked to you when you wrote it, was a kick in the teeth to me Mr Stripes, an ugly great kick in the teeth, so I decided that a personal visit was in order, if nothing else for to hand you my teeth, to look you in the eye, hand you my broken teeth and dare you to refuse my request face to face.' There. She'd said it, although she had been caught on the hop, never expecting to meet him within thirty minutes of getting here, her little practiced speech was now hanging out in the open.

'Tiger.'

'What?' Jane looked utterly bewildered.

'Tiger, please, call me Tiger, everyone else does. How many times have you practiced that speech? I told you politely, firmly that I wasn't in a position to help you, you need legal advice, not mine.'

15

'Tiger?'

'Yes?'

'I'm going to my room, I need to er, freshen up, it's been a long day and you have caught me by surprise, I'm not really capable of rational thought right now. Can you give me 30 minutes? Will you at least stay here that long? Please.

'Aye lass, I'll stay. I'm here for a drink anyway and I'm not going to run away from you, embarrass you or cause a scene, you have my every sympathy with your situation it must be bloody awful and you have no reason to be worried about me.'

'Thank you.'

'And of course there's another thing...'

'Another thing?'

'I have your teeth in my pocket and I presume that you'll want them back.'

Jane couldn't help but smile, she had a terrific smile.

'Thank you.' Jane stood up, unsure whether she should shake his hand or just go before he changed his mind. Her departure therefore was a bit clumsy as her arm shot out and then just as quick returned to her side as she turned to go.

Tiger had reached out his hand for a handshake at the same time, their fingers had touched briefly.

It was electric.

Jane went directly to the bar and rang the brass service bell waiting for a sheepish looking Derek to hand over her room key. Tiger sipped his pint and watched her collect her key and head out past reception to the accommodation staircase.

'She would look back,' Tiger mused.

She didn't look back.

16

Twenty five minutes later Jane returned to the bar. The only activity in her absence was the middle aged couple in hiking gear had returned their empty cups, had thanked Derek, glared at Tiger and left the building.

Tiger was sat on a bar stool chatting to Derek. Jane had changed into black denim jeans and a white heavy wool polo neck sweater. She was smiling and looked gorgeous. Tiger eased his frame from the stool feeling a little scruffy now, his scuffed leather jacket generally suited his surroundings and his needs but next to Jane it looked a little, well, scruffy.

Tiger spoke first.

'Wow, biker chick changes into lass about town.'

She blushed slightly. 'I'll take that as a compliment.'

'It was meant as one.'

Derek butted in, 'Christ, shall I get you two booked in as a double?'

They all laughed, it was just the ice breaker required. Tiger ordered a pint for himself and a large white wine for Jane and the two of them retired back to the table where Tiger had left his helmet.

'So, who starts?' Asked Tiger once they were settled.

'That'll be me,' answered Jane, and I'll kick off with an apology. I'm sorry for ambushing you this way, without any warning, I really should have written again, or called.'

'Well, I have been involved in an ambush or two in my life Jane, real ones, where people get hurt, and if that's your idea of an ambush then I have nothing to worry about.'

'Are you laughing at me?'

'Not at all Jane, apology accepted.' Tiger raised his glass and held it out. Jane lifted hers and they 'clinked them together clumsily, but it was at least an effort at calling a truce.

17

Tiger continued the conversation. 'I'm still quite firm on my decision though Jane, you have to understand that. A legal route is the way forward.'

'Tiger, I've explained this, I have exhausted the legal channels. Solicitors, Court cases, Family hearings, the whole damn shebang, I'm at the end of my tether and I can't just let the bastard get away it, and, more importantly, I want my kids back.'

Tiger sat silently, ignoring his drink and watching Jane pour out her impassioned plea. This was a difficult case and he recalled the letter that she had sent about a month ago.

Dear Mr Stripes.

I have been given your name and address by someone I believe you once worked with. I feel nervous about contacting you, but as I am now at a total loss as to where to turn, I hope that you are the person that can bring this dreadful episode of my life to a happy ending.

I have two children, Jennifer and John aged five and two respectively. I am recently divorced from a troubled marriage, and my ex-husband, Peter, has taken the children to an unknown destination and has refused to make his, or their, whereabouts known, despite the children being Wards of the Court. I have heard rumours that he is going to abscond abroad, possibly to Spain although I have no actual proof of that.

Since the Court case I have spoken to my Solicitor numerous times and I have been advised on every occasion to seek out the services of a Private Investigator. I believe that this could prove to be expensive, so my parents are putting their West Country home up for re-mortgage and thereby releasing funds for a search campaign by a professional.

The friend who advised me to contact you is called Sheila Brown. We were at school together and meet up from time to time for a drink. She now has some sort of boring secretarial job in the Home Office and told me that you helped her out once whilst she was on holiday with a boyfriend in Scotland.

I am at my wits end and really need some help. I hope you are the man who can make my life whole again.

Signed, Jane Albright.

Jane had stopped talking and was looking expectantly at Tiger who responded.

'Okay, I hear what you're saying and it is obviously a distressing situation for you, I am unsure who your friend Sheila is, although I have some idea, and if it's the same lass, the help I gave her was a completely different situation to the one you are asking me to undertake, in fact it was nothing what-so-ever to with investigative work. Finding people is not my specialist skill, it never has been and in truth, any skills I used to have are now so rusty as to be bloody worthless, but I will tell you what I will do for you, I'll sleep on the matter and see if I can come up with a name that may be able to help you. That, pretty much is all I can do.'

The tears were welling up again in Jane's eyes and she made no effort to wipe them away.

'Well I suppose that is better than nothing Tiger and I appreciate your candour, if you can do that, it would be great.'

Tiger couldn't help but be moved by the strength of purpose radiating from a woman obviously in anguish and battling the type of demons that he would never encounter.

'What are your plans for this evening Jane?'

'This evening? I haven't thought about it. Early night I suppose with an early start heading back home in the morning.'

'I need to get home and sort some stuff out, then I'd like to take you out to dinner, nothing fancy, just some good old fashioned Lincolnshire hospitality and great food.'

Jane looked at him though moistened eyes and nodded.

'That would be nice Tiger, what sort of time?'

'I'll get back here at 7.30 and we'll take it from there.

They both stood and walked back to the bar. Jane picked up her room keys and left whilst Tiger had a quick chat with Derek before heading out to the car-park.

~THREE~

Back home in his study Tiger had made a call on his phone to a bleeper number leaving an alpha numeric message with the operator. He finished the call, replaced the hand set and stared at it for a couple of minutes as if he expected it to ring immediately.

He idly glanced up at the wall above his desk and smiled at the hockey stick that he had mounted a few months previously. Miss Polly Richardson, his neighbour had sadly passed away and in a surprise move she had left her property, a little cottage, to Tiger in her will. Her funeral was well attended by her friends, mostly old ladies from her knitting circle, followed by soup and sandwiches in the village hall paid for by Tiger. On receipt of the keys from her Solicitor, Tiger had walked across his drive and entered her property. It smelled of musty old crotchet magazines and stale chocolate biscuits, he had a brief look around and decided that he'd get the builders in and gut the place, modernise it with a view to getting tenants in. On a whim as he was leaving, he picked up Miss Polly's hockey stick from the hallway and taken it home.

He was on his second cup of tea when the phone rang.

'Hello.'

'Tiger mate, it's Gruff, what's up?'

'Can you talk?'

'I'm talking.'

'Aye, thanks for getting back to me so quickly mate. I'm thinking of taking on a job but I'll need a hand.'

'When?'

'Next week, or the week after.'

'Sorry mate, my current engagement will definitely not be over for at least ten days.'

'What are your plans after this job?'

'Rest mate, plenty of rest, I'm taking two or three weeks off. I'm knackered.'

'I can get the groundwork sorted in ten days, so I'm booking you now.'

'What's the job?'

'Kidnap.'

'Well that sounds restful…Pencil me in.'

'Nice one, stay quick, stay quiet and keep low.'

'Yeah, roger that, I'll be seeing 'ya.'

The connection went dead. There was never any need for niceties and platitudes at the end of one his calls with his best friend. He finished his brew and walked into the kitchen, placed his mug in the sink and went upstairs to shower and change.

'Gruff' Wetherspoon and Tiger went back ten years or so. They'd served as cooks in the Army Catering Corps. At least that was what they told strangers who asked about their military history. It kind of killed any conversation stone dead, which was pretty much the whole point.

In reality they had both been members of 'G' Squadron, the elite inner unit of the Special Air Service reserved for Guardsmen who had left their respective Battalions, passed the gruelling marathon known as 'selection' and entered a place where their lives would be for ever challenged.

In all that time, Tiger had never known his mate's real first name. Gruff was never actually gruff - it wasn't in his nature - he was a very quietly spoken man, so why he was so called had been lost in the mists of time. What was known about Gruff was that he was an expert in hand-to-hand combat. Under a pseudonym, he'd represented Great Britain with his mastery of Judo and Karate. He could speak four languages fluently, and had declined a commission with the Grenadier Guards opting instead to join the proud Regiment as a Guardsman, a basic soldier.

He'd sailed around the world single handed. Twice. He'd saved Tiger's life. Twice. But he couldn't ride a motorcycle, much to Tiger's everlasting amusement. He just couldn't get to grips with it and had long since given up trying.

~FOUR~

It was 7.25 in evening when Tiger parked his motorcycle once more in the car-park of The Black Horse Inn. He removed his helmet and goggles and using the mirror on the handlebar he ran his fingers through his hair and straightened his skinny tie. Blue denim jeans, fresh white shirt and his best black leather jacket, it'd been a while since he'd been on a date yet he felt strangely comfortable. He ducked his head under the threshold of the back door and stepped into the pub. Reaching down to his left he placed his helmet on the floor under the clothes rack.

It was a bit busier than earlier, maybe a dozen patrons. Derek was behind the ramp with a massive grin on his face chatting to Jane at the bar. He glanced up as Tiger entered obliging Jane to twist slightly in her seat and look at who'd just come in.

'Good evening Jane, evening Derek, usual for me and one for the lady please.'

Jane looked confused.

'I thought we were going out to dinner Tiger?'

'Just a quick aperitif before we set off Jane.'

He winked at Derek then turned to get a proper look at Jane. She looked stunning. She'd pulled her hair back into a ponytail applied the minimum of make-up, blushed pink nail varnish on nails that were never meant to be stuffed into a pair of leather motorcycle gauntlets, a knee length figure hugging black dress, a pair of black pumps with killer heels finished off the ensemble.

'Are you inspecting me Tiger? And what do mean aperitif? You've come on your bike haven't you? There is no way I am going anywhere near a motorcycle wearing this.'

26

Tiger grinned. He was in a great mood and wanted this to last for as long as he could.

'So many questions! I'm not inspecting you Jane, I'm admiring and you look terrific.' He reached for the pint that Derek was holding out for him, thanks Derek on the slate please, are we good to go?'

Derek nodded, 'whenever you're ready Tiger.'

Jane looked quickly at both men. 'You're teasing me again Tiger, please don't do that, I'm on an emotional roller coaster at the moment. Very fragile.'

'I'm sorry Jane I can be thoughtless, especially when I'm hungry.'

Tiger crooked his arm and offered it to Jane, a gentleman's suggestion that she take his arm. She obliged as she slid off her stool.

'If you'd like to follow me Madam.'

'What are you up to Tiger? Really!'

'This way if you please.'

Tiger stopped at the door to the restaurant, a sign pinned to the door apologised to customers that the restaurant was closed for refurbishment for a week. Tiger opened the door and stepped to one side letting Jane slip past.

'Oh my word!'

The room had been cleared except for one table. The cutlery glistened under a lone subtle spotlight, an ice bucket containing a bottle of wine dripped beads of condensation onto the starched white tablecloth.

Tiger escorted a stunned Jane to one of the high backed chairs and pushed it in gently as she sat down, before stepping around her and taking his place opposite her.

'Tiger. This is…This is…'

'Cool?'

'Gosh yes, cool, how on earth did you pull this off?'

27

'Everybody loves a Tiger.'

'Crikey, they must do, this is 'fabbo,' a look of concern crossed her face, 'is this you still teasing me or are we actually going to eat here?'

'I'm not teasing Jane, the menu is in front of you, slightly less fare on show than would normally be on offer, granted, here, let me pour you a glass of wine.'

On cue Derek appeared through the kitchen door and plonked Tigers beer on the table and turned to Jane.

'Everything to your satisfaction Madam?'

Jane laughed and joined in the game.

'So far Derek yes, I'll give you a full report after our meal if that's in order?'

'That'll be fine madam, I'll give you a couple of minutes to choose from this evenings special menu and François will pop out and take your order,' he turned back to Tiger, 'there's a couple of quid in the jukebox Tiger, feel free to spend it, it's on a separate sound system to the bar.

Tiger thanked him and he disappeared back into the kitchen.

'Derek isn't cooking as well is he Tiger?'

'Crikey no, he's got a bar to run, the head chef has come in for the evening.'

'You're joking.'

'Nope, here he comes now.'

A tall thin man, with jet black hair swept back and jelled to within an inch of its life, wearing Chefs whites and black and white chequered trousers so fancied by European kitchen staff walked towards their table.

'Bonsoir Monsieur Tiger. Bonsoir Mademoiselle Albright.'

The northern, Paris Picardy accent leaked from François's thin Gallic lips.

28

'You are ready to order je crois? I can recommend the Loup de Mer.'

Jane was slightly flustered.

'Loop dee what?'

'Loup de Mer, it is Sea Bass Mademoiselle, very crispy with a grapefruit hollandaise.'

'Well that sounds different so in for a penny in for a pound, I'll have that please.'

'Certainement, and Monsieur?'

'I'll have the same François.'

'Bon choix.'

François scooped up the menus and practically raced back to the kitchen.

'Is he really French Tiger?'

'He's actually from Bedford,' he winked, 'but don't say anything.'

'I'll never believe another word you say Mr Stripes.' She sounded deadly serious but could only hold that tone for a micro second before bursting into laughter. 'This is wonderful, put some music on Tiger.'

'Yes ma'am, anything in particular?'

'No, you choose.'

Tiger excused himself and stood up, the old juke box was a few paces away and he knew exactly what he was going to play.

'Louie Louie' by The Kingsmen was his easy first choice followed by 'The Ballad of Easy Rider' by Roger McGuinn, well, he thought, she is a biker, and lastly, the last one was more difficult, his finger hovered over the enter button, 'make or break' he whispered to himself and punched in a really soft ballad by Roberta Flack.

He made it back to the table as the first track reached the speaker system.

29

'I love this Tiger,' Jane beamed, 'the Jack Ely version is the best one by far.'

'No arguments from me on that score Jane, I could listen to his voice for hours, and sometimes…' He laughed, 'I do!'

They enjoyed their drinks and listened to the smoky tones of Jack Ely for the whole song before Tiger spoke again.

'Jane, I have had a rethink on your problem, I have spoken to a friend who can help but not immediately, so I'm prepared to do the groundwork on my own starting next week.'

Jane put her wine glass down, her hand was shaking.

'Really? Would you really? Oh Tiger that would be fantastic, thank you so much…'

Tiger interrupted.

'Don't thank me yet Jane, there are no guarantees that I can deliver what you want, trust me, this is a huge undertaking and could be heart-breaking for you…'

'I'm already heart-broken Tiger, it needs mending that's all.'

'I'm trying to be truthful here Jane, I do not want you to think that it's walk in the park and it's going to expensive, not that I'd be earning anything but people who will have information will not give it freely, that's for sure and there will be a load of travelling, hire car, hotels…'

'I've told you Tiger, money isn't an issue, Mum and Dad are just as desperate as me and they've got the house re-mortgage to prove it…'

'I appreciate that Jane and I will do all I can to help and keep the costs down but I do not want to give you false hope.'

They had been chatting all the way through Tigers second choice. The subtle voice of Roberta Flack started. 'The first time ever I saw your face'

'Roberta Flack! I love this Tiger, let's dance.' She jumped to her feet and rounded on Tiger, who was desperately trying to hide a sense of self-satisfaction as he stood up. He grabbed a quick swig of his beer, for luck, and followed Jane as she marched to the centre of the room. She stopped abruptly and turned causing Tiger to bump into her. Whether this was accidental or contrived became irrelevant as he scooped her into in arms, locking onto each other they swayed gently to the music.

A whole three minutes and a few seconds passed before Jane spoke, whispering in Tigers ear.

'Thank you, thank you so much that was wonderful.'

Tiger started the disentanglement process and cleared his throat…

'Er yes, er…that was lovely, er…shall we sit down now?'

'Mr Stripes, I do believe I have embarrassed you, well fancy that!'

Tiger was regaining his composure after what was most certainly the best three minutes of his life in a long time.

'Er, no, not at all, there isn't any more music and the… er, food, the food will be here shortly.'

They both took their seats at the table. Jane took a sip of wine and picked up a fork waving it at Tiger…

'You're not the only one that can tease Tiger.'

They both laughed as the kitchen door opened and François entered with two trays expertly balanced on one arm, he tutt-tutted and frowned at Tiger as a cue to for him to move his pint of beer and make some space at the table.

'Tada! Mademoiselle et Monsieur, Loup de Mer, bon appétit.'

François made a small bow and retreated towards the kitchen.

'Right Jane…'

'Right what Tiger?'

31

Tiger picked up his knife and fork and took a mouthful of delicious Sea Bass. It melted in his mouth. He made direct eye contact with Jane who was patiently waiting.

'Last one to finish pays the bill...'

Forty minutes later they were back in the bar, fully sated and both drinking fresh coffee.

'Jane, we still have some details to thrash out before you leave, but I do have one question that really needs answering now.'

'Sure Tiger, what is it?'

'Your school chum, the one who gave you my name, Sheila Brown.'

'Yes, what about her?'

'Are you sure her name is Sheila?'

'Of course I am Tiger, I've known her for years.'

'She works for the Home Office?'

'Yes, she has been there simply ages she's a secretary for some big wig.'

'Is she away a lot?'

'I suppose so, I'm not sure, we're not that close really, we live in the same town we went to school together, we have mutual friends and we go for a drink every now and then.'

'What does she look like?'

'Is this important Tiger?'

'Aye Jane, it could be, can you describe her?'

Jane scratched her head and tried to describe her friend. As she spoke it sounded like a fairly generic description but Tiger was nodding as she went along and seemed satisfied.

'Thanks Jane, I was thinking of another lass with the surname Brown, I was getting mixed up.'

'She said you helped her out in Scotland.'

'Aye, maybe I did, it wasn't that important to be honest, I'd forgotten all about it.'

'Okay, next question.'

Tiger glanced at his watch, it's getting late, are you still thinking of leaving in the morning? We really should dot some i's and cross some t's before you go.'

'Well if I can stay here and help in any way then of course I'll stay, I really want to get the ball rolling Tiger, so what do you suggest?'

'Come over to mine in the morning, its only two miles from here, you have the address and we'll have a chat over tea in my office.'

'What sort of time?'

'Any time after nine would be great, I'll have some calls to make before that so aye, let's say nine thirty.'

'Okay, I'm good with that.'

'Have you ever ridden round a race track?'

'Pardon?'

'Race track. On a motorcycle, have you ever done it?'

'Not a question I was expecting... But no, no I haven't.'

'Do you fancy a blast around Cadwell Park once we've concluded business?'

'Is it safe?'

'No.'

'Absolutely yes then.'

~FIVE~

Tiger had one of the best nights sleeps he'd had for ages and was up at the crack of dawn feeling good. Really good. He was never one for a big breakfast so he just wolfed down four slices of toast and was on his third brew before it was late enough in the morning to make some calls.

Once these were out the way he settled down with his note pad and started scribbling some notes. The kit that would be required, telephone numbers of people he would need to be in contact with, some more questions he had for Jane. This was obviously going to be a fluid, dynamic case, especially in the early days. He hadn't yet got a start point, although Peter Albright's family home would be an obvious start.

Hearing the sound of a 4 cylinder Japanese bike pulling up outside, he tucked his pencil behind his ear and went to the kitchen, opened the door and leaned casually on the jamb.

Jane Albright kicked out her side stand with her left heel and dismounted her machine. She removed her gloves and helmet and turned off the ignition. It wasn't a loud motorcycle by any measure, but a still quiet settled once more over Tigers property.

'Morning Jane!'

'Morning Tiger, its lovely isn't it I reckon it's going to be a cracking day.'

Tiger glanced up at a cloudless sky and nodded. To be fair, and despite the thousands of motorcycle miles under his belt, his weather eye was bloody awful, he was for ever getting caught out in showers that his riding companions had somehow managed to correctly predict.

'Aye, I think it's going to be a cracking day lass, come in, come in, the kettles on, I'll give you the guided tour then we've got work to do.'

Jane plonked her helmet on a counter in the kitchen next to Tigers and sat down at a stool at the breakfast bar whilst Tiger sorted out two mugs of fresh tea.

'Is this all yours Tiger?'

'Aye it is I own this place, the converted stables next door that I use as a garage and the little cottage across the way.'

'It's lovely.'

'Aye it is, but it needs bringing it up to scratch, not a project I had planned but such is life and the builders start on Monday.'

'Are there any animals out in the fields?'

'Nope.'

'Any animals in the house?'

'Nope.'

'Not even a dog? I had you down for a dog man.'

'I'd love a dog, proper little loyal companion, but I sometimes I get to work away for indefinite periods, and there isn't really anybody I could leave it with.' He paused, 'maybe, when I retire, perhaps.'

Jane took a sip of her tea and tried to hide a smile behind her mug as she asked coyly.

'So you haven't got a little loyal companion then?'

'Are you fishing Jane?'

'Innocent question.'

'Yes, err, no, I don't have a little loyal companion but that's good. It works for me. Right bring your brew I'll give you a quick tour so you know where the loos are and such.'

Jane was quickly beginning to realise that answering personal questions was not Tigers strong point.

They traipsed upstairs.

35

'Right, here on the left is the guest room,' Tiger pushed the door open and Jane took that as an invitation poke her head in, it was fully furnished, double bed, small dresser with some type of flower arrangement in a bowl and it looked clean and fresh. 'My room on the right,' Tiger continued, marching past a closed pine door, so no invitation there she thought. 'Bathroom.' He pushed the door open and Jane squeezed past, this was also clean and smelled fresh, he must have had a cleaner or house maid coming in every day, her own home was nowhere near as clean as this and she spent an inordinate amount of time keeping it tidy. 'Back downstairs then.' Tiger was off again, down the staircase through the kitchen and into a room at the front of the property, 'living room come lounge,' again Jane had a quick look. A large, leather three piece suite, television set and a stack of electrical boxes that could have been a stereo sound system, it was a comfortable looking room, clean, tidy. 'Last room, is the study, nothing to see really.' She had a quick look anyway, it was just a little box room turned over to an office, utilitarian, chair, desk with a telephone, couple of phone directories, and a hockey stick mounted on a wall as if it was a ceremonial sword or antique musket. Tiger entered his office and picked up the notes he'd been making earlier and they both went back to the kitchen and sat down.

'Well that's the whirlwind tour Jane, not much to see.'

'Whirlwind indeed Tiger my head is spinning, and it's all so clean and fresh, it's very nice, how often do the cleaners come round?'

'Cleaners? Haha.' Tiger continued chuckling, 'there are no cleaners, what do you think I am? Made of money? How's your brew? Need a top up?'

The next hour was taken up with questions and answers. Tiger was a prolific note taker and was asking questions that Julie hadn't even thought about but he seemed satisfied at last. She wrote out a cheque for the agreed advance and slid it towards him but he never even glanced at it.

'Great, that's all I need for now Jane I'll make sure the builders are sorted on Monday and crack on from there. I'll be giving you an update on how things are going each evening at six o'clock. I won't call during the day unless it's urgent and you are not to call me at all, it may compromise what I am doing at the time, are we agreed?'

'It all sounds like a military operation Tiger.'

'That's because it is, military beats civilian for efficiency every time, that's why I have a clean house, come on grab your helmet lets go and have some fun at Cadwell Park!'

Tiger wheeled his Triumph out of the garage whilst Jane turned her Honda around, both engines fired up within a second or two of each other smashing the silence of the morning. Tiger pulled his goggles on and gave Jane the thumbs up sign and she nodded in reply.

Out on the main road, Tiger took the lead and after the first mile of twisting roads Jane could not help but admire his riding style from behind, every movement of his lean body was minimal, effortless, every corner was line perfect, she could never imagine that he could ever make a mistake. She felt so safe being carried along in his wake, and she had to admit the growling bark of his twin exhausts were a thing of beauty compared to her quiet sounding Honda. Perhaps she'd get some aftermarket exhaust pipes and beef up the noise.

The journey only lasted ten minutes, hardly time to get their tyres warm before Tiger turned onto the small road that headed to the entrance of the Cadwell race track. They followed the road past the box office and down into a wide open, grass filled valley, it was here that the first sounds of racing motorcycles could be heard. The thump thump of the big V twins and the screaming banshee wails of the smaller two stroke machines. The

37

hairs on the back of Jane's neck stood up as the adrenaline slowly started kicking in.

Around a sharp left hand bend and another right, engineered to stop speeding off the track, led them to the edge of the course and to a few low buildings that made up the circuit administrative units and the club house. Tiger parked up, switched off his ignition and waited for Jane to do the same.

'Can you smell it Jane?'

'What?'

'The burnt two stroke oil, it's Castrol R, some people reckon that they are addicted to it, wonderful isn't it?'

'I could get used to it. Tiger I'm a bit nervous to be honest and I haven't even seen a race bike yet, only heard them, and er, smelt them.'

'You'll be fine lass, trust me, c'mon we'll go and find Willy and if you don't want to do this nobody is going to force you, okay?'

'Thanks Tiger but I've got this.'

They set off towards the loudest part of the course, the pit area. About twenty motorcycles of different colours, shapes and sizes, some with engines running, the riders blipping the throttles causing the pit walls to vibrate with the noise, other motorcycles sitting quietly without fairings with men in coveralls tinkering with them, it was a very noisy hive of activity.

'There he is over there, c'mon Jane.'

Jane followed Tiger through a throng of motorcycles and mechanics, nobody giving her a second glance so involved were they with the machines under their care.

'Jane Albright, Willie Phillips, Willie Phillips, Jane Albright.'

38

The introductions were made as Willie slipped off a pair of bright yellow ear defenders and stuck out a big hand. Jane sort of grabbed it and gave it a bit of a shake before letting go.

'So Tiger, this is the lady you were telling me about this morning. You said she could handle a motorcycle, you never said anything about her being a bloody catwalk model mate.'

Tiger laughed and slapped his friend on the back whilst Jane grinned politely.

'So Willie, what are you putting on the track today?'

'I've got three here today, Spud, my lad is out on the track on his Suzuki T500 and I have my two favourites right here, race tuned Yamaha DS7's, they might be ten year old machines but by 'eck they fly.'

"They are nice looking machines mate, 250cc aren't they?'

'That's right mate, twin cylinder 30 brake horsepower and good for 90 miles per hour.'

Tiger turned to Jane.

'What do reckon Jane? Fancy a blast on of these?'

'Well I don't know, I haven't a clue about the course, I'd probably get lost. Does it come with a map?'

Willie was laughing hard.

'Look, here comes my lad, I'll get him topped with fuel and you can go out with him. Just follow him around for a couple of laps, nice and gentle like, there's no rush today it's an open practice meeting.'

A blue and white motorcycle came to a sudden stop at Willie's feet the engine cut out immediately as the rider squeezed the front brake and dumped the clutch lever causing the machine to stall. There were no electric starters on these race bikes, the T500 was usually kick started into life but that had ripped out as well, there was no engine kill switches either, too much weight for a decent race time, so they were stripped out along with the lights, number plates, stands and anything else that the rider thought would save a couple of ounces.

The rider on the Suzuki nodded at Tiger and Jane then flipped up his black visor.

'Now then Tiger, how's it going?'

'I'm sound as a pound Spud, is the bike going okay?'

'Sweet as a nut mate, c'mon Dad, sort the fuel out, my tyres are getting cold.'

'Listen son, you're going to take this young lady out on a couple of sighting laps okay? Same as you did last month for your cousin Mark, nice and steady now son, we know she can ride but doesn't know the track.'

'Okay Dad. What? Two slow laps for the pretty lady?' He looked directly at Jane, challenging.

Jane responded.

'Two laps will be fine to get me started Stud, thanks.'

'It's Spud, not Stud.'

'Ah, sorry my mistake,' she glanced over at Tiger and winked, 'let's get this show on the road.'

Willie had finished filling up the big Suzuki with petrol and watched as Jane secured her helmet and pulled her gloves on. She threw a leg over one of the 250cc machines and held the handlebars waiting for Tiger to release the rear paddock stand that held the bike up.

Willie shouted over to Jane.

'Once you get going girl, keep the revs up, she redlines at 9,500 so keep her up there, It'll sound like she's going to blow up but she won't, trust me. Two steady laps because you're on cold tyres, keep behind the boy and if you're up for it give her a head of steam on the third. Right, I'm pushing Spud.'

Tiger leaned in close to Jane's helmet, 'when you start rolling hook it up into 2nd gear Jane and bump her, she'll fire first time, then pull the clutch back in quick, you can find 1st gear when you're ready, okay?'

Jane nodded her head and slammed her visor down pulled the clutch in and waited. Tiger looked at her through her visor, she winked she was ready. He moved behind her, unclamped the paddock stand, checked there wasn't another bike cruising in behind them and started pushing. He felt Jane shift the bike into gear, watched her lift her bottom off the saddle and bounce it down hard to get maximum weight over the rear wheel as she let the clutch go. The engine screamed into life and Jane released a bit of throttle pulled the clutch back in and selected 1st gear. Two seconds later the blue and white Suzuki slipped past her and they were heading for the track. A marshal waved them onto the racing tarmac with a wave of his yellow flag and they were off.

Up through the gears and into 5th, the highest gear heading for the first gentle left hander she had no idea how fast she was going, the speedometer had been thrown away in the weight saving exercise, but it appeared, to her anyway, to be fast.

Extremely fast.

The Suzuki moved over the right side of the track and Spud leaned it into the bend with Jane five yards behind.

The first lap went in a bit of a blur some of the bends were very tight but most were big open sweeping bends but there was a hair-raising climb up a short and impossibly steep hill as well. Spud, she realised was definitely being gentle with her, she could feel the power from her little engine that wasn't being used. So, she was happy with the bike on the first lap, she could now concentrate on the course for the second.

41

The two machines howled past Tiger and Willie who were hanging over the fence watching, Tiger even waved but got nothing in recognition back.

Into the left hand and right hand turns known as Hall bends again, down though the gearbox and into 2nd for the right hand hairpin, short straight back up the gears and setting up for a nice right hander called Barn and onto the long start finish straight, plenty of throttle left to go and keeping the distance to about five yards, Spud had taken a couple of rear observations and seen that she was still there and picked the pace up a bit. She felt that she was screaming through the big left hander called Coppice a bit faster this second time round and watched as Spud started pulling away slightly. That was okay, Jane was still in her comfort zone and she dialled in a few more revs.

Charlie's was the next right hand bend, huge corner, open plan so she could see the start of the straight, called Park, well before she got there, this had to be the fastest part of the track, it was wonderfully smooth and on the exit from Charlie's she had to ease off the throttle slightly as she was a bit close to Spud. Ripping down Park Straight at about ¾ throttle she pulled in the front brake lever slightly for the right hander at Park corner then realised halfway round that there was no real need for that, she could have been quicker, then on the brakes again for Mansfield then a very short burst of speed to a tricky little right left jink and power on again for the next ¼ mile before the tight left had 3rd gear corner and the tight right up the steep hill, known as the mountain, where she could feel the whole bike lift on its suspension, any faster she thought and she'd probably be flying, which was an exciting worry.

She flashed past Tiger as she had spotted him this time, but had no chance what-so-ever of acknowledging his wave. Spud and his Suzuki were pulling away now, he'd obeyed his Father and sorted her out with two sighting laps and he was now going to do his own thing and was lost to her in the trees in Hall bends.

Round Barn for the third time she heaved on the bars to set herself up for the start finish straight and was surprised to see Spud only 15 yards ahead, she pulled back hard on the throttle and the little bike just changed attitude completely. She flew into Coppice at full chat, gently counter steering into Charlie's making slight throttle adjustments that would adjust her track position and onto Park straight at full throttle. The Suzuki was still just ahead of her as Spud moved over to the right to overtake a slower machine that had recently joined the track. Jane flashed past it as well, as if it was stationary and looked up as far as she could see. Park corner, she was too slow last time round touching the brakes unnecessarily. The Suzuki seemed to be drifting over to the left as they both pitched into the right hander and Jane nailed it. The little Yamaha screamed up the inside of the bigger Suzuki and she concentrated on the awkward little right left jink. The machine was perfectly behaved, it'd go precisely where she aimed it and stay there until she altered course with the handlebars or throttle. She went round the left hander and immediately into the right then up the mountain, now convinced that her front wheel had left the track for a moment tempting her into pushing the throttle forward and slow down, this would have been a disastrous move. But she didn't falter, she cracked open the throttle and settled down again for one more lap.

She was thoroughly enjoying herself and negotiated the course for a fourth and final time pulling off the course at the bottom of the mountain under the direction of another marshal with a yellow flag. Down though the gears and into 1st and going nice and slow past the array of bikes being worked on. She saw Tiger and Willie by the spare 250cc Yamaha, there was no sign of Spud and the Suzuki and she stopped, letting the bike stall as Spud had done earlier.

43

She sat astride the bike for a couple of seconds monitoring her pounding heart rate, before removing her gloves and helmet. Tiger was beaming from ear to ear.

'Bloody hell Jane you turned into a mini Barry Sheene out there! It was terrific! Willie reckons you're a shark, you've done this before.'

She said nothing as Tiger went behind her machine and set up the paddock stand that would secure the bike. She stepped off the little bike and could feel the jelly in her legs. God she needed a cup of tea.

'Thanks Willy that was terrific, where's Spud?'

'Oh, he's still on the track, I think he's got a problem he's going fairly slowly,' he peered at her closely, 'are you sure that you haven't done this before Jane?'

'Swear on my Mothers....'

'Fair play Jane, you're a natural then, I enjoyed watching that.'

'Thanks for the opportunity Willie, you are most kind, Tiger can we get a 'cuppa somewhere and I need the loo.'

'Of course Jane, thanks Willie mate, cracking morning I might catch you in the clubhouse.'

Jane followed Tiger up the steep path to the clubhouse, and whilst she visited the ladies room he purchased a couple of mugs of tea. Jane was sat back down within five minutes, her heart rate was approaching normal and her legs were working fine.

'Tiger that was fantastic, I've never felt anything like that before, it's such a buzz!'

'You looked great out there Jane, you really did I couldn't believe it and I don't think Willie did either, he had his stopwatch out for your third lap but I have no idea what the time he recorded, here drink your tea, your hands are shaking.'

44

Jane sipped her hot brew and watched Tiger from the corner of her eye. He was too good to be true surely? Handsome and laid back, everybody loved him and he was so cool to be seen with, so what was wrong? Why was he single? Was he *really* single? She'd looked into his eyes, at dinner the previous evening, deep blue with a glint of excitement but there was something else as well, a sadness perhaps, but there was no way she was going to ask him, he just didn't do personal stuff, and then it struck her. His home. Regardless of how clean and tidy it was, there was nothing personal there, no pictures on the walls, no photographs it wasn't a home, it was a house. Underneath his fun surface there was a brooding darkness, maybe not sadness then, but anger. She was sure though that she could help if he let her in.

Tiger disturbed her reverie.

'Here comes Willy.'

Willy sat himself down at their table and got straight to the point.

'Jane, I've just been up to the time keepers office and checked some stats with her and as incredible as it sounds, your third lap was only two seconds slower than the 250cc amateur club record. I can't believe you haven't been on this track before, it's one of the most technical circuits in the country.'

'I promise you Willy, until yesterday I had never even visited this County, sure I have been riding a few years off and on but never on a race track.'

'Well that's outstanding natural talent right there, Tiger we have to do something about that. Two seconds is nothing at that standard, some proper training and a decent set of one piece racing leathers and that's two seconds right there...'

Tiger took a sip of tea and said nothing. Jane looked at Tiger, shrugged and turned back to Willy.

45

'Willy you are lovely, a really generous man who certainly knows how to tune a motorcycle, your bike felt so smooth out there despite the fact I thought it was going to explode at any minute, but I'm a housewife,' she felt the tears welling up, 'and a mother to two wonderful children, I really haven't got the time,' she stood up, 'I'm sorry I need to go the ladies,' and she rushed to the ladies restroom.

'Christ Tiger, what did I say?'

'Nothing mate, she is going through a rough patch at the moment and I'm trying to help her out, you know, cheer her up, she's a friend of a friend.'

'Well I need to get back to my bikes but here's another thing Tiger, there is nothing wrong with Spuds bike, she took him fair and square on Park corner and held him off for another lap. An experienced club rider on a 500cc bike, it's incredible.'

'I appreciate you doing what you've done today Willie and I know I speak for Jane as well. I'll catch you later mate.'

Willy made his way out of the clubhouse and down the hill to his beloved motorcycles as Tiger went to the kitchen hatch and ordered two more mugs of tea. He knew Jane wasn't ready to go out on the public roads just yet, her heart would still be pounding.

Back at his seat waiting for Jane he made his mind up. He'd get this job out the way, with a happy ending if at all possible, he'd certainly give it his all and then he'd ask Jane out. Ask her out properly, try and get a girlfriend-boyfriend thing going, he hadn't really missed female company since Miss Kelly, but Jane had brought that matter back into focus.

A very sharp focus.

'Sorry Tiger.' Jane was back.

'You really should stop saying sorry to me Jane, you haven't done anything wrong since I met you, quite the opposite in fact,'

'Really?'

'Yes really,' he winked at her, 'now finish your bloody tea and enjoy your Cadwell moment.'

'It has been fun hasn't it? I could do that again.'

'I'm sure you could but one of the reasons we are sitting up here drinking tea is to allow some of that adrenaline to seep out, it's always a massive mistake to get straight out on the road on a motorcycle after spectating a race, let alone actually riding one around the track.

'Are you always this sensible?'

'No.'

'Good.' Jane nodded.

'There's a nice little cafeteria I know in Louth, it's about 8 miles from here, lovely little twisty roads and I'll treat you to lunch.'

They both stood up to go and Jane said.

'No.'

'No? No what?'

'No you're not going to buy me lunch, if we go to Louth than I'll buy you lunch otherwise no deal.'

'Okay, how about this, last one there pays for lunch.'

'Are you leading?'

'Aye.'

'That's a deal then.'

They reached the café in Louth that Tiger had in mind, he was first there, but it was closed for refurbishment. Rather than hang about or try and find another one he suggested to Jane that they go back to his place, where he could knock up some bacon and egg sandwiches and make a couple of telephone calls, get the ball rolling as he had a loose plan he wanted to try out. Jane readily agreed, the roads around Louth were very pleasant roads to ride and she had no complaints about following an expert rider in tight jeans either.

~SIX~

Back in Tigers kitchen, feeling full, they both sat in front of empty plates and a fresh brew when Tiger decided that he could start work right away on his plan. Jane wrote down her ex Mother in Law's telephone number but didn't seem confident that Tiger would get any useful information from her if he phoned her.

'Jane, can you recall the name of Peter's solicitor?'

'Hang on...'

Jane reached for her handbag and after a few moments of rummaging around produced a white envelope that contained the information Tiger was asking for.

'It's all here Tiger' she said as she passed him the envelope.

Tiger thanked her and went into his office, sat at his desk and had a brief look at the contents of the envelope before picking up the phone. Jane stood in the doorway and watched him as he made a call.

'Good afternoon, is that Mrs Albright?'

'Marvellous, I'm so sorry to trouble you. This is John Sanderson from Pretty Sanderson and Belton, Peter's solicitors... I need to send some urgent paperwork to your son, he is not answering the phone number that I have on file...'

Jane could only hear one side of this conversation and having no idea what Tigers plan was, was slightly worried and Tigers insistence of not looking at her during the pauses as Wendy Albright replied to his questions, didn't help her unease.

'Yes, I understand that, yes, but this is rather urgent...'

'Of course, of course, but if he is abroad and we sent the papers to you when would we get them back...?'

50

'The problem we have Mrs Albright...sorry, thank you, Wendy, is that if the respondent's solicitors realise that they have made a mistake, and they most certainly will and it'll be sooner rather than later, they review cases the same as we do, then it will cost your son a substantial percentage of his pension, we have to get this in front of a judge before they do. And fast ...'

'I understand your anger towards the respondent Wendy but that isn't going to help us here...'

'Of course Wendy, I do apologise. Future earnings and pensions should have been at the forefront of our minds when contesting this case but it slipped through the net and we are trying to make good now, the error has been noted, it's all part of every case review, that is why I am calling and that is why speed is of the essence and we cannot wait until Peter is back from holiday...'

'Okay, I understand... That's not an issue Wendy so if you could dig out his address, and oh, an updated telephone number would help as well...'

'Of course I'll hang on...'

Tiger looked up at Jane for the first time and grinned before grabbing a pen.

'Yes, yes, could you spell that? Yes, yes, got it, and the phone number...?

'Lovely, thank you Wendy...In writing? Of course, I'll dictate the apology personally as soon as I am off the phone to you...'

'Yes, yes of course, thank you again and we'll be in touch.'

Tiger gently replaced the receiver, took a deep breath and exhaled slowly.

'We've got him! He's in Spain and he's living there, not on holiday and he has your children.'

51

'Tiger, is that legal?'

'Is what legal?'

'Impersonating a Solicitor.'

'I don't know Jane and frankly I don't care. I am fairly sure that Wendy didn't make a recording of that call, and by the way, she doesn't like you very much.'

'Well the feelings mutual, what's next?'

'I'm going to make a few calls, hire a couple of cars, book a flight and hotel, contact an old friend in Spain then sit down and have a beer, what's your plan?

'I'll stick around until you're done and have that beer with you if that's okay?'

'Of course it is Jane, you go and make yourself at home because I'll be busy for about an hour I reckon.'

'Tiger?'

'Aye?'

'I knew you were the man for the job, thank you.'

'Don't thank me yet Jane.'

'I know, but it's better than me saying sorry all the time,' she blew him a kiss, turned around, went through the kitchen and stepped out of the house into the cool Lincolnshire afternoon.

~SEVEN~

After a relaxing weekend, some of it chatting to Jane on the phone, Tiger had a busy day ahead of him, Jane was back home in Slough and he had promised to update her every evening that he was in Spain, his hire car was arriving before noon and his flight from Heathrow was at 18.00 hrs that evening, he was packed and ready to go and the builders had started arriving.

'Morning Mr Stripes.'

'Morning, are you the chap in charge?'

'I am that, the rest of the lads will be here in the next 20 minutes or so.'

'How many are you?'

'Me and four.'

'Right, I'll grab the keys to the cottage and I'll leave you the drawings so that you can give me a quote for phase two, I'm away for a bit and you won't be able to contact me, I hope that won't be a problem.'

'No sir, not at all.'

Tiger retrieved the cottage keys and a copy of the architect's drawings from his office desk and returned to the front door.

'Mr McBride isn't it?'

'Yes sir, although everybody calls me Paddy.'

'Okay Paddy,' said Tiger tossing him the keys, 'this way.'

They walked across the wide driveway to the cottage and past a white Transit van with a decrepit looking generator hitched to the rear, in which a couple of burly looking young men were sat reading the morning papers. Paddy banged on the side and shouted.

'Look lively lads!' and turning to Tiger in a quieter tone, 'they're a good crew Mr Stripes, but I need to keep on top of them.'

'Well I'll leave that up to you as I won't be here to supervise you and I don't want to be paying for blokes sitting around on their arses, there is plenty to be getting on with here.'

They reached the front of the cottage and Paddy tried a couple of keys before coming up with the correct one, opened the door and they both entered. It was gloomy despite the early morning sunshine outside as Tiger led the way to the kitchen, opened a window and spread the plans out on the kitchen table.

'Right Paddy, Derek Jacoby from The Black Horse Inn tells me that you are first class, I trust him completely so please don't let me down on this project. I understand that you are happy to work at a day rate for the first phase which is pretty much gutting the place and cutting back the jungle out back that is supposed to be a garden, is this price okay?' Tiger pointed to a sheet of A4 paper stapled to the plans.

Paddy pulled out a battered and scratched pair of reading glasses from the top pocket of his shirt and peered at the paper before replying. Tiger fully expected him to start sucking through his teeth and stroking his chin, but he didn't.

'Yes Mr Stripes, that's fine if you're happy to pay in cash?'

'Cash is king Paddy, that won't be a problem and I'll be back before Friday to pay you. Do you need anything up front?'

'Nope, we are good to go but I've got a couple of questions though.'

'Fire away.'

'Is there any power here?'

'I'm afraid not.'

'Okay, then I'll have to add something on at the end of the week to cover fuel for my generator.'

'Fair enough, there is running water and the loo works, so it's not all doom and gloom.'

'All this stuff here, the furniture, stuff in drawers what happens to that?'

'It all has to go Paddy. This cottage needs to be completely empty and the garden has to be completely cleared before work starts for real. I don't care if you burn it, skip it or sell it but it must go. Anything you find of value in here is yours, call it a windfall.'

'Thank you Mr Stripes, I'll be having a good look at those drawings as well so your quote for the phase two refurbishment will be ready on your return.

'Excellent. If there is nothing else Paddy, I'll let you crack on, and if you finish by Thursday there will be a bonus in it for you.'

Both men returned to sunshine outside, Tiger shook Paddy's hand and headed for his house, behind him he could hear Paddy calling.

'Look bloody lively now, Baz get your arse around the back and see what you need, Gary, get this generator hooked up and get the kettle on.'

The hire car arrived at 11.30. Tiger signed the paperwork threw his travel bag into the rear, locked his front door and got behind the wheel giving a cheery wave to Paddy the builder who returned the compliment by holding up a large mug of tea. Tiger sighed, started the vehicle, found radio 4 and set off on the 4 hour journey to Heathrow airport.

~EIGHT~

Tiger had allowed plenty of time for his 18.00 hrs flight to Malaga, arriving at the busy departure lounge at terminal one, forty five minutes earlier. He had already booked in for his flight with the bored looking check-in clerk at British Airways. She would have been attractive without the ton of make up on her face, very attractive if she had smiled whilst asking him the obligatory questions.

'No,' he did not have any cases to check in.

'Yes,' he would be carrying one item of hand luggage.

'No,' he did not want a window seat.

'No,' he was not a smoker. Although having recently given up, she was seriously driving him in the right direction to take it up again.

'Yes,' he did know the way to gate fourteen.

She then had thanked him for flying British Airways, which he thought was odd, he hadn't even seen a plane yet, let alone flown in one.

He sat himself down in the departure lounge, on the same row of plastic seats as a Spanish woman who was having a bit of a hard time from one of her two children. The eldest, a boy, could not have been much older than four years old was sobbing, he was not happy about something, that much was obvious. Tiger could not understand the language but he guessed that the child was bored and tired. Under any other circumstances, he would have found a seat as far away from the whining kid as possible.

This late afternoon however he found himself smiling at the lad. Was this a deep-rooted psychological yearning for children perhaps? Or a previously unknown soft spot he had for kids? More than likely, it was the task that lay before him, the realisation that children are not objects, possessions, or pawns.

He was halfway through his second cup of strong tea, when glancing up from his notes, he noticed a smartly dressed woman walking towards him.

It was Jane.

She stopped and stood in front of him, not defiant, but determined, she had been in the office when Tiger had booked his flight and she therefore knew the flight number and departure time.

He was unable to comprehend what she was doing at the airport. The plan was for her to be at home, near a phone, in case things in Spain developed at a faster rate than he had anticipated.

It soon became clear.

Tiger stood up.

'Jane? What the devil do you think you're doing?'

'I've been thinking about this all weekend Tiger and I have decided that it would be better if I were on the scene in Spain, I'd be able to recognise my children, even at a distance, even if they were somehow disguised.'

'I understand that Jane, we spoke about this, at length, this is just a reconnaissance, it's doubtful that I'll get close enough to see the children, let alone have to recognise them when they're wearing beards and false noses.'

Jane couldn't work out if Tiger was being flippant or using humour to disguise his anger.

'What if the possibility of us getting to them presents itself? Jennifer and little John would be a lot more responsive to leaving with me, than a stranger, surely that made sense?'

'Aye lass, I know, I know what you're saying, honestly I do, but that possibility isn't going to arise, I don't want it to arise, we're not ready for it to arise, I have arranged for a professional team to make that happen next week if this week goes to plan, which at the moment, before I even get there, has ceased to be a plan.'

Jane dropped her bag, sat next to Tiger, smiled at the little Spanish boy, who stopped crying and smiled back, she then turned to look Tiger in the eye.

'I'm the paymaster and I have decided that this is the new plan.'

Tiger hated it when his plans changed, especially when he wasn't the one changing them, but he resigned himself to the fact that a very determined mother had foiled his operational plans and he had a feeling that this would not be the last time either.

'We'll work round it,' muttered Tiger

'We'll make it work,' smiled Jane.

The tannoy system crackled into life and announced their imminent departure and the flight to Malaga just sort of, well, flew by.

The Hotel sur Malaga, had the advantage of being located close to the many tourist attractions in the area, it is close to the port the Plaza de la Marina and only a short walk to the museums and fantastic buildings in the old town. The main advantage though, apart from being cheap was its anonymity.

Tiger and Jane were knelt on the floor of Tiger's room. Jane's room, two doors down, was bigger with an en-suite bath but with no wardrobes so her luggage was taking up much of Tigers room. On the way from the airport Tiger had purchased a large-scale map of southern Spain, this now covered the entire bed. Using a red marker pen Tiger very carefully marked the location that he knew Peter had a rented villa. This was going to be the starting point of the mission. He was reluctant to mark the villa, marking maps was bad trade-craft, and he had first-hand knowledge of a military mission that had gone very wrong when the enemy had captured a map, and although this was akin to a military mission he didn't want to scare Jane.

'Jane, I have enlisted the help of an acquaintance, we haven't seen each other in years though. His name is Tommy.'

'Is he good at this sort of thing?'

'He's good at everything… well he was when he was teaching us.'

'He's a teacher?'

'Not now, he's retired.'

'So, let me get this straight Tiger, you have recruited a retired teacher? Is this a joke? What's he going to do, give the kids a geography lesson on the way home?'

'He wasn't a geography teacher Jane.'

'Okay, what subject did he teach then?'

'Hostage negotiation, lock picking, anti-kidnap drills, how to move about in the dark quickly and quietly, how to kill somebody with a spoon…'

Jane looked directly at Tiger.

'Tiger, this is serious, when are you going to stop teasing me?'

'I'm not teasing you Jane, it's what he did.' Tiger shrugged.

'Where was this? Where did he do this? Round the back of the bike sheds telling tall tales whilst the young boys got off on it? C'mon, a spoon? That's disgusting Tiger.'

'It wasn't at a school Jane. He started off as a Royal Marine Commando, joined the Special Boat Service and was eventually seconded to become a Special Forces Instructor in the British Army.'

Jane, ashen faced, had stood up and was pacing the room as he spoke, she looked down at her shoes, unsure whether to be embarrassed at her naivety, or truly shocked.

'Really Tiger…With a spoon?'

Tiger laughed and Jane started grinning before joining in at the improbability of it all.

'Aye, with a spoon,' said Tiger, and continued laughing.

'Tommy is travelling from Marbella and will be meeting us in the Cosmopolita café on Larios street in an hour so we'd better get ourselves sorted Jane.

'Okay, I'll meet you in reception in 30 minutes Tiger', she left the room still unsure if Tiger had been teasing her.

Tommy, predictably, had found a seat at an outside table. The Cosmopolita café was loud and busy. White shirted waiters waltzed through the seated coffee drinkers as effortlessly as ice skaters. The continuous drone of voices and clinking glasses competed with the motors and car horns across the pavement few yards away.

With the introductions over, Tommy caught the eye of a passing waiter and in effortless Spanish ordered a strong tea for Tiger, a fresh coffee for himself and still water for Jane. It was now time for business. The plan did not take long to formulate, the only fly in the ointment was the addition of Jane, however it was decided that she was a welcome fly. Tommy even commented on the fact that it actually made good sense to have a woman on the team, as it would attract less attention than two men snooping around would. Tommy would carry out the initial reconnaissance and report back later that evening, he would make no direct approach to the property and if by chance he came across Peter and the kids he would take no action.

'Can I come with you?' Jane asked hopefully.

'No, sorry, stay with Tiger that would be best,' he pointed to the far side of the table, 'Jane, would you pass me that teaspoon please?'

Jane looked alarmed.

'What? She glanced at Tiger, who was stony faced, 'why? Why do you need a spoon? I'll stay here with Tiger, it's not a problem surely you can leave the spoon there.'

'This is true Jane I could leave the spoon there,' he stood and leaned across the table and retrieved the spoon, 'but I need the spoon.'

Jane didn't know where to look. Was Tommy going to give her a graphic demonstration of what he was capable of with simple cutlery? If she wasn't so scared she would have bolted.

'How do I stir my coffee without a spoon? What's wrong with her Tiger?'

Tiger laughed, I have no idea Tommy old friend, I suppose it could be jet lag,' he stood up, we'll speak later mate, c'mon then Jane are you coming for a stroll and some food and a proper drink?'

Jane stood up thanked Tommy and followed Tiger onto the street.

'That was not funny Tiger.'

'It was, your face, it was so funny Jane,'

'It wasn't funny I had no idea what he was going to do. You military types are bloody weird.'

'It was funny,' Tiger insisted.

'I suppose it was, a bit,' Jane conceded looking up at Tiger and smiling as they went in search of a tapas bar.

Tommy called the Hotel sur Malaga reception a little after 11pm, there was nothing to report, he'd seen nothing, he'd meet them both after breakfast and they'd all go up the coast to Peters place together. Tiger passed this information onto Jane at the hotel bar where she was chatting to a young barkeep and toying with her drink.

'Bed time for me then Jane, do you want a shout in the morning?'

'What sort of time?'

'Breakfast starts at 08.00 so I'm thinking about then, Tommy will be around at about 09.00.'

'I'll see you at breakfast then, Goodnight Tiger,'

Tiger nodded his understanding, turned to go and took a couple of paces when Jane called out, probably rather louder than she intended.

'Tiger!'

Tiger's heart skipped a beat, it been a while since that had last happened. He smiled as he turned around a cheeky scenario playing in his mind, Jane was holding up a table spoon and pointing it at him.

'No spooning tonight Tiger!'

Tiger laughed out loud, he loved her playful sense of humour.

'G'night Miss Jane.'

'Night Tiger.'

~NINE~

Peter's villa was on Calle Miramar, a side street leading off the coast road in the bustling little town of Torre Del Mar about thirty-five kilometres east of Malaga. Tiger's guidebook claimed that Torre del Mar once formed part of an ancient Greek settlement prior to the arrival of the Romans. These days the town is better known for its endless sandy beaches lined with restaurants and bars. It all made for an interesting read but the little group of investigators would not have the time to partake in such activities.

The journey was uneventful, taking a little over half an hour, the time taken up with Jane bringing Tommy up to speed on her background and as the paymaster, she had given him the choice to back out, but Tommy was a family man and although his children were now adults and had long flown the nest, his values were still firmly in place.

Jane was reassured, although she never said so at the time, by the fact that she had brought together a special team. She knew, just knew, that these were the men she could trust to get the job done.

Tiger left Jane and Tommy in the car whilst he went for a walk past the villa. He looked up the steep driveway that led to the property, it was a two storey, but split-level, the whitewashed walls, and a red tile roof were much in keeping with the traditional style. Tiger noticed the edge of an upper balcony and two large terracotta pots holding small palms.

Very nice.

There was no sign of activity and no cars in view but there was a double garage at the end of the drive. He decided to check with the immediate neighbour before committing himself to a direct approach to the front door of Peter's property.

The front door to the villa next door was accessible via a scruffy pathway, obviously not used regularly. Dogs barked from somewhere behind the large single storey dwelling, Tiger could not be sure if they belonged to the owners or a neighbouring property.

The door was answered fairly quickly by a woman aged about fifty, well presented wearing white cotton blouse and skirt, surprisingly, she was English. A short conversation ensued during which time the woman, who introduced herself as Ruth, stated that, 'there was an Englishman called Peter that lived next door, and yes, he had two little children but it wasn't a noisy area.'

'No,' she did not know if he was in or not, but he drove an English registered 4x4, a red one, possibly a Jeep. He spent a lot of time in the bars and clubs around the town, but she did not know if the children went with him.

It was a very friendly neighbourhood, she often attended his afternoon barbecues and although she liked to think it was because he found her good company, she rather suspected it was for her cooking skills. Tiger had thanked her and let her know that he would continue his search for a nice property in the area.

Tiger made his way down to the main street and climbed into the rear of Tommy's car. He updated Jane and Tommy on the new information and it was decided that he'd risk a direct approach, alone, to Peter's villa. Jane was desperate to get out of the car but the two men were adamant that she stay put.

'What pretext did you use on the neighbour Tiger? Asked Tommy.

'Looking to rent a villa in the area, there are rental signs all over the place so it's fairly simple, Ruth was just a bit chattier than I'd expected, and she was English, so it'd be a natural thing visiting Peter's place next.'

'You didn't get any bad vibes?'

'Nope, it's all good.'

Once more Tiger walked past the villa, taking stock of the surroundings. There was no way he could get to the rear. There was a small scrub of bushes on a hill behind the property but it offered little in the way of cover. It would probably give a commanding view into the grounds of the villa, but he had no reason to be there should he be challenged, and there was the problem of the dog he had heard earlier.

He had spoken to Ruth next door, so he could use her as a cover if Peter challenged him. Back home in the UK he quite often carried a dog lead, as this ruse could gain entry into lots of places. The 'missing dog sketch,' he called it. Dog owners were very friendly especially to other owners who had a missing hound. This of course was fine in Taplow or Burnham Beeches in leafy Buckinghamshire, but not in Terra del Mar in Spain. This part of town was full of ex pats and they would be sure to know each other and why would he be going house hunting with a dog? He needed answers, not questions.

Tiger had decided on the 'lost house hunter' approach, there were a number of properties in the area with 'For Sale' and 'For Rent' signs written in English, another clue as to the type of people who lived in the neighbourhood, and the myriad of side streets and dwellings on different levels meant that this excuse was as good as any. Tiger would have bet a couple of pesetas that the locals got confused.

The steep driveway levelled out as it approached the garage that appeared to be locked. He walked another dozen paces to the right and up eight concrete steps, he found himself on a terracotta terrace. Two large sliding glass doors at the front of the villa opened out onto that terrace. A wrought iron dining table and six matching chairs stood between him and a small swimming pool. The water was still and the blue tile surround was dry. It looked as if it hadn't been used that day. Tiger was taking in all the detail he could, in case he had to come back at night. The last thing he wanted was an unintended midnight swim.

He hadn't packed his trunks.

He tapped on the window and after getting no reply, he walked to the rear of the property. A neatly coiled hosepipe and pool cleaning brush were the only items he could see.

No children's toys.

Tiger peered through the glass of the only entrance. It was set into the whitewashed wall and led into what looked like a small utility room. He gently tested the handle but the door was locked.

That was enough for now.

Back at Tommy's car, it was decided that the rest of the day should be taken up with an area search of the coffee and tapas bars. Tommy would cruise the streets and car-parks looking for an English registered red coloured 4x4. Tiger and Jane would set off on foot and ask for Peter in every bar they went into. This was obviously a high risk strategy as Peter probably had a few friends scattered about the place and word would surely get to him, however, Jane was getting furiously impatient and she impressed upon the two investigators that Peter, if he was seen, would be curious and not suspicious.

They would all rendezvous in the bar at the hotel Torremar on Avenue Saladero Viejo in four hours then head back to Malaga, where, Tommy stated, he personally knew the hotel security manager, a retired senior Police Officer and he would definitely be on-side.

To say that the first six bars had been a challenge would be an understatement to say the least. 'Customers', thought each of the delighted proprietors, as the two 'Inglés' had entered their respective bars. Out of season money was not so good. so having two customers, any two customers, was very good.

Once it became obvious that the Inglés were not spending money, just asking questions, the answers were predictable after the first request for information.

'Es usted Policía?' Are you Police?

'Negocio oficial quizás?' Official business perhaps?

'Puede usted pagar?' Have you any money to pay for the information that you seek?

'No, sorry Inglés. we cannot help you, goodbye.'

Ah well, only another three hundred or so bars to go.

Jane was flagging and asked why the locals were so aggressive so Tiger reminded Jane that they were off the beaten track here, out on a limb. They were not tourists, they were not spending any money and the locals had no need to be friendly. However, word would be spreading, of that, Tiger was very sure.

It was in the seventh bar that they struck lucky.

'Si, we know Mr Peter, he comes here to watch the football, every week, nice man, spends lot of money'.

'Do you know where Mr Peter is today?'

'Yes, he is probably in the mountain bar. He spends lots of money in the mountain bar'

'Where is the Mountain bar?'

'Up in the mountains Señor, twisty road, many kilometers from here, no tourist, very dangerous'

Neither Tiger nor Jane understood if the skinny barman in the off white vest was referring to the twisty road, the Mountain bar or the fact there were no tourists, when he mentioned the word, 'dangerous'.

Back at the Hotel sur Malaga sipping from an ice cold bottle of Cruzcampo beer, Tiger surveyed the comprehensive notes he had thus far compiled, he glanced occasionally over at Jane who was on her third glass of gin and tonic, her blonde hair, once neat and tidy in a ponytail had come loose, giving her an air of loose abandonment. 'She's a very sexy lady,' Tiger had thought.

If Jane could have read his mind, she would have been horrified, 'loose abandonment would have been the last thing on her mind. She had been living on her nerves as she trawled the Tapas bars at the cheap end of town with Tiger. She was tired and frustrated and feeling attractive was the last thing on her mind. Her plan A was to drink half a dozen G & T's then head upstairs for twelve hours sleep.

Alone.

An hour later, Tommy introduced them to Señor Gonzalez Garcia. A retired Spanish Police Detective. He was smartly dressed in a blue suit over a crisp white shirt and some sort of club tie. Tiger thought he recognised it and asked if it was a GEO tie?

'Si Tiger, very well remembered,' stated Señor Garcia and he patiently explained.

The former plainclothes service, known as the Higher Police Corps, but often referred to as the 'Secret Police', consisted of some 9,000 Officers. In a way it was very similar to the British Criminal Investigation Department. The C.I.D.

The uniformed service was a completely separate organization with about 50,000 Officers, all men. The Director General of the Police Corps, a senior official of the Ministry of Interior, commanded 13 regional headquarters, 50 provincial offices, and about 190 municipal police stations. In the nine largest cities, several district police stations served separate sections of the city. The Chief of Police of each station was in command of both the uniformed and the plainclothes officers attached to the station. A centrally controlled Special Operations Group (Grupo

Especial de Operaciones or G.E.O.) was an elite fighting unit trained to deal with terrorist and hostage situations.

Señor Gonzalez Garcia, was a Sergeant Major in this elite Corps until he had retired a year ago, taking up the relatively stress free position of head of security at a number of hotels in the Costa del Sol. He had established his credentials quietly, and in impeccable English.

After this lengthy explanation, Tommy and Señor Garcia had said goodnight and graciously departed for home. Jane had sat back, listening intently and was now convinced that this would work. She began to nod off and within minutes was asleep, sat upright on the sofa.

The following morning at breakfast, Jane had apologised for the third time to Tiger before he told her there was nothing to be sorry about. She was tired and emotional. Yesterday had been a hard day for everyone and she had some questions.

'How did I get up to my room last night Tiger? I really cannot remember.

'I carried you.'

'Did you put me to bed?'

'Yes.'

'Who took my clothes off and replaced them with a nightgown?'

'You must have woken in the night and changed yourself, perhaps.'

'Why then was my nightgown on back to front?'

'Maybe you were still tired when you woke up and got changed, anyway shut up lass, and finish your breakfast.'

Tiger thought he saw a twinkle in Jane's eye, but he could not be sure.

It was going to be another busy day. There was to be no movement from their hotel until they were in receipt of a fax from Señor

Gonzalez Garcia, concerning the movement on Spanish soil of a certain red coloured, English plated 4x4. Tommy was unavailable until the middle of the week because of prior commitments but he had left them a pager number where he could be contacted if needed in an emergency.

With breakfast over, Tiger mentioned that a walk to the beach might be in order and Jane readily agreed.

They walked along the Calle Canales and turned right down Calle Alfonso Reyes. A left turn against the light traffic on Pasillo Del Matadero and then a right, four hundred metres later saw them crossing the Puenta Del Carmen Bridge.

They walked slowly. It was still early morning for the Spanish so there was little in the way of tourists or locals, it was the sort of walk that could have, and should have, been hand in hand. It would have been the most natural thing in the world.

However they walked a yard apart.

An investigator and his client.

Business partners.

Tiger informed Jane that the beaches are actually man made. Millions of tons of sand from local rivers are dumped on the beach, replacing that lost by storms, the whole of Malaga is a never-ending beach, stretching from Misericordia, which goes as far as the Port area, to the beaches of Peñón Del Cuervo near the hamlet of Cala Del Moral. This is a total stretch of around fourteen kilometers. Jane was impressed with his local knowledge and said so. Tiger grinned and removed a battered tourist guide from his back pocket.

She punched him on the arm and laughed.

Back at the Hotel sur Malaga, the desk clerk handed Tiger a fax.

He read the fax header. '¡Importante! Grupo Especial De las Operaciones. Mensaje especial'. This information, in Spanish was in a large block font.

A special message from the G.E.O. Tiger was getting excited. Old Señor Garcia still had his contacts. They both rushed upstairs to Tiger's room and sat on the bed together. 'Never mess with the old club tie Jane,' Tiger had said.

Jane looked blank.

'Never mind lass, how's your Spanish?' He asked. The fax read:

A Tiger en el sur Málaga del hotel.

1. Se ha localizado el vehículo que usted busca.

2. Barra Andalucia en Canillas de Aceituno.

3. El tema y dos niños presentan.

4. El policía local no se acercó. Respeto. Capitán Lopez. Vía Garcia.

They pored over the Spanish print but to Tiger it might as well have been hieroglyphics, he didn't have a clue and his cheating guide book could not translate anything more complicated than. 'I have a headache,' and 'I need a Taxi please.'

'Look,' said Jane, pointing a manicured fingernail at the flimsy document.

A Tiger en el sur Málaga del hotel.

'The heading is obviously the address line to you at our hotel and what's that on line one about localized el vehicle?'

1. Se ha localizado el vehículo que usted busca.

'Could that mean they have found Peters vehicle? The Jeep? And line two…'

2. Barra Andalucia en Canillas de Aceituno.

'Isn't a 'Barra' a bar?' Tiger was getting in the swing of it now, 'I think you are right Jane, Bar Andalucia. Canillas de Aceituno must be the town or village… and isn't Andalucia a mountain range.'

They both said it together. 'Mountain!'

Jane added, 'the guy in that awful Tapas bar yesterday, he mentioned mountain.'

She continued translating then her hand started shaking, 'look Tiger, line three, 'niños, that's children! Dos children, two children,' Jane wiped an excited tear from her eye, 'It's my babies.'

Tiger had a go at line four. *El policía local no se acercó*. 'The local police have not done something, but what? What haven't they done Jane?'

'I don't know Tiger.'

The last line was obviously a signing off from a Captain Lopez via their friend Señor Garcia.

Tiger scooped up the map from the night table opened it up and smoothed it over the bed. Where was Canillas de Aceituno? They both scoured the map. Was it actually a place? They were struggling to find it.

'Look in your tourist book,' suggested Jane.

'Brilliant.'

There it was. Page forty seven.

Canillas de Aceituno extends over the sides of the Sierra Tejeda, to the north of the Axarquía region. It was about a thirty five minute drive to the north of where they were the previous day, Torre del Mar. It was a steep climb to the Maroma peak (2065 m.) through a landscape of pines and rocky places which cover almost all the northern half of the municipality.

'Bingo!' Tiger whispered.

'Thank God,' whispered Jane and kissed Tiger on the cheek.

Tiger's little Fiat hire car was down to second gear on the approach to the pretty little village. The guy in the tapas bar had been right when he said it was dangerous, the road behind them snaked its way down to the sea with perilous drops into the valley to the side. There were no tourists because it was out of season, the barman they had spoken to was not being threatening at all, it was his way of saying, drive bloody carefully.

Bar Andalucia was in the middle of the village, tucked into the shade of the Church Nuestra Señora del Rosario. Parked outside on the road was a red jeep with English number plates. It was so peaceful there that Tiger could not believe this was possibly the end of the journey, it was too easy, too safe yet his nerve endings were on full alert, they needed to stop and think this through.

But that wasn't going to happen.

Jane was out of the Fiat and in through the door to the bar, before Tiger had set the handbrake on the tired Fiat and as a result he was ten seconds behind her. On entering the humble looking bar it took another ten seconds for his eyes became accustomed to the gloomy interior.

Half a dozen sun-bleached old Spaniards were at the bar, with jugs of frothy beer in front of them. More interestingly though, was the young white girl sat at a corner table sipping Cola through a straw, and a little boy in a car safety seat, propped up on a wooden chair.

If it was possible to get more interesting than that, it was the look of amazement on the face of the only other white guy in the place. A six foot tall, tanned, and well-built man who, when his jaw had returned from the floor, looked as if he would be handy in a fight.

Peter.

Jane was trying to lift little John out of his seat, Jennifer had looked completely baffled. Peter made the first move and it looked as if polite chitchat was not on the agenda today.

'Whoa, you bitch, what the fuck are you doing? He spat out aggressively grabbing Jane's arm, 'there is no way this is happening.'

Tiger stepped up to Peter, body at a slight angle, knees slightly bent left foot forward and hands open palmed at his side. To an untrained eye the posture looked harmless, docile even, but to a fighters eye it was an extremely dangerous poise, a tiger about to pounce.

'Dial it down a bit lad, you're out of order,' Tiger offered some quietly spoken advice. He noted four empty bottles of local beer at the table were Peter had been sitting.

'I'm out of order? What the fuck? Who are you?' Peter continued his tirade, 'the bitch's body guard are you eh, the big hard man eh, well if you don't back off and leave now I'm going to fucking hurt you.'

'That's not going to happen Peter.'

Peter looked carefully at what he was going up against, there wasn't the slightest look of fear in the man's eyes, he even looked a bit relaxed and he was actually smiling. Fucking smiling? He kept his distance for now but kept a grip on Jane's arm.

'Listen pal, this bitch is not just going to walk out of the bar with my kids, you had better get that though your thick skull, now fuck off before you regret it.'

Tiger had learnt a long time ago that if you start a confrontation with aggression, then you had no place else to go, so keep it quiet at first and then escalate as required. Tiger stepped closer, speaking quietly.

'Let go of Jane's arm and back off Peter, I'm not going to ask you again.'

Aggressive confrontation was not the way to do it, the children were frightened, a couple of locals had stood up and the bar Manager was talking ten to the dozen on the wall phone. The words 'Apuro ingles' were getting used.

A lot.

Peter made the first move. He turned his back on Tiger and slapped Jane hard across the face causing her to yelp in pain.

In hindsight, Tiger was not sure who had thrown the first punch, or who had punched who, although he was sure some locals suddenly turned up and joined in the affray. He was unsure who was friend or foe, so he treated everybody in a white vest as a threat, it was just a massive, ungainly bundle of bodies piling into a fight and all Tiger could do was protect Jane and the kids, defensive, not offensive and he knew there wasn't a snowball in hells chance of getting Jane and the children to the car.

It was all irrelevant now anyway. Within five minutes of the fight breaking out, the local Police had all three English foreigners in custody... and the children.

Tiger reckoned he had been in his cell for about two hours, he could not be sure because the Police had removed his watch before inviting him into their place of work.

He yelled out for attention and was surprised when a gaoler appeared immediately.

'Telephone?' Tiger asked, 'telefon, telefonio,' this pathetic attempt at Spanish was accompanied with the international hand signal, little finger of the right hand to mouth and thumb to ear.

'Ah, teléfono.'

'Yeah, that's what I said.' The smug looking Spaniard had understood the first time.

The gaoler walked with Tiger to the front office, where a smartly dressed police officer with swept back greased hair and a circa 1935 Clarke Gable moustache sat behind a desk at modern electric typewriter.

The local Sheriff.

'Forget the Spanish lesson Señor,' he said. 'My name is Captain Juan Diablo. I speak English, went to school in the town of Pinner, North of London. Do you know it?'

Before a stunned Tiger could reply however, the officer continued.

'You wish to make a phone call, yes? You are not in England now so this is only possible if I permit it as a favour. You understand, yes?'

Tiger nodded that he understood.

'Who is it you wish to call? I cannot permit an international call, and it would appear that your fellow English companions are already here, no?'

Tiger idly wondered why foreigners end every sentence with a question, but he didn't want any more aggravation so he simply asked for his wallet. The North London educated Spanish cop opened a drawer, and slid his wallet across the desktop. Tiger removed the fax he had received earlier that morning, unfolded it added the business card of a certain Señor Gonzalez Garcia and slid it across the table to Captain Juan Diablo.

It was as if the Head of the Spanish Civil Guardia had just entered the building. The change in attitude was incredible. Juan Diablo sat up, put his hat on and said something in rapid Spanish to the gaoler who saluted and disappeared back into the cellblock.

The end result was, that Tiger was free to go and Peter and Jane were also free to go on the proviso that they sort out their differences in private.

'Not in a bar brawl.'

Peter was under the strictest orders that Jane would go in the Jeep back to Peter's villa with the children. Tiger would follow in his little Fiat.

79

The Captain would not listen to reason and he was not interested in international treaties despite a possible intervention with Señor Gonzalez Garcia.

It was only a two minute walk back to their respective vehicles. Tiger told Jane he would wait at the hotel in Torre del Mar, for as long as it took. She was holding little John to her chest as tight as she could with one arm, whilst the other gripped the tiny hand of Jennifer who looked so sad behind her puffy tear stained eyes.

Peter just growled his dissent, but with the Captain of Police watching the proceedings from the doorway of the local lock up, he would have been foolish to try anything.

For Tiger, the trip downhill into Torre del Mar, did not seem as treacherous, maybe because he had other things on his mind. Peter obviously knew the road so much better because despite Tiger's attempts to keep up, he never got closer than four hundred yards.

As Tiger rounded the last bend into the town, he was amazed to see Jane, stood at the side of the road, brushing dust and dirt from her jeans.

He brought his vehicle to a halt in a cloud of dust and small stones.

'Christ Jane, are you okay? What the hell happened?'

'I'm okay Tiger, the bastard kicked me out,' she explained as clambered into the passenger side of the hire car. The tears running down her cheeks were tears of anger, and bitter disappointment.

Not pain.

Jane was swearing like a trooper, understandably under the circumstances. Her twenty-minute journey was a nightmare. Peter had exploded with rage, and driven like a maniac down the mountainside, the kids were terrified, screaming the whole way, she'd been kicked forcibly from the jeep and the only redeeming factor was that she knew Tiger was not far behind to pick her up. So once again, Peter had the children.

'We are back to square one again, I am so sorry Tiger.'

'Not exactly Jane.'

'What do you mean?' asked a confused Jane.

'Peter now knows what the game is Jane, he can defend his position so much easier, I'm afraid this is a step backwards from square one.'

'Oh Tiger I'm so sorry I have screwed the whole thing up, we had a plan, you had a plan.'

'Jane lass, we're good, every plan is worthless as soon as there is contact with the enemy.'

Tiger knew it was a pointless exercise going to Peter's villa, but he drove there nonetheless. There was no sign of Peter or his Jeep.

Or the children.

Once again they found themselves back at the Hotel sur Malaga. After a hot shower, Jane joined Tiger at the bar. He was on his third bottle of Cruzcampo beer, he would have preferred a pint of his favourite British beer, Double Diamond bitter, but the ice cold Spanish stuff was doing the trick, calming him down and clearing his mind. He had made two telephone calls. The first to Tommy's paging system, and the other to Señor Gonzalez Garcia, telling him of the day's fiasco. The Spaniard was not happy with his countryman, Captain Juan Diablo.

Jane picked up her large gin & tonic quaffed it in one go, then placed it slowly and deliberately back on the bar.

She looked Tiger in the eye and said quietly.

'I hope that you have another carefully laid plan, or at least a half decent backup one because if you haven't Tiger, I swear to God that I'll be going to prison for a long time'

Tiger raised an eyebrow in question.

'For murder,' she answered defiantly, 'with a bloody spoon.'

Tiger did have a plan, he had decided that they would both fly back to England the following morning, there should be plenty of flights and they would then regroup, lick their wounds and attack this problem from another angle.

Relieved that Tiger wanted to stay on the case, Jane thanked him, and surprisingly, given the pressure Jane felt under, the rest of the evening passed easily.

Or it could have been the sheer quantity of cold Cruzcampo and gin that was taken.

~TEN~

It had been five days since the Spanish debacle and Tiger had made and received dozens of calls, international money orders had been written up, signed and dispatched to Tommy and Señor Garcia and now he had a plan in place that might work. There was an element of deception attached though. Jane Albright would not be included in the information loop, she was, obviously, far too emotionally attached and Tiger reckoned that although he would love to work with her, there was only going to be one more chance at this.

A lot of his time had been taken up with the builders. Paddy McBride was a good as his word and had carried out a cracking job at the cottage, he'd been paid as agreed and Tiger hit him with a bonus as promised so phase one was complete and the real work could now start.

Tiger had been through the architect's drawings with Paddy, who could read a set of blueprints a lot better than Tiger could, and had never stopped reminding him. Tiger just smiled, made the tea paid the bills and omitted to tell Paddy that they had different skill sets. Paddy for example couldn't field strip an L42A1 British Army sniper rifle in total darkness and reassemble it in less than forty seconds, nor could he call in a fast jet airstrike on a Mullah's meeting in a desert wadi, one hundred miles from the nearest building and it was highly doubtful that Paddy the builder had ever killed a man. Boring someone to death about the intricacies of a set of drawing plans didn't count.

The driveway was filling up with concrete lintels, bags of sand, lengths of lumber and the hundred other things that were going to be required to drag the old cottage into the 20th century. Men in scruffy shirts and cement caked boots wandered about in a seemingly random fashion and there was the tea drinking, there was lots of that. In one way it was all quite exiting only tempered by the niggling doubts at the back of Tiger's mind, that he tried to ignore, about the upcoming operation in Spain.

On the morning of the sixth day Gruff rang. He was free and ready to go.

'Pack a bag for a week mate.'

'Where are we going Tiger?'

'Spain.'

'I love Spain, whereabouts?'

'Have you got a pen? We are meeting at the Hotel sur Malaga in Malaga tomorrow evening, get yourself an afternoon flight tomorrow afternoon and you better give me a name now that I can use to get you booked in mate.'

'Hang on,' there was a twenty second pause, 'Richard Wells, I'll give him a sun tan. Poor bloke hasn't been out in ages.'

Tiger chuckled, he'd lost count of the amount of aliases that his friend used, or the occupations that went with them.

'And who is Mr Wells?'

'Well it states on his passport that he's a journalist.'

'That's good, you'll be bringing a camera and some decent optics, hang on...I can't ever recall you being able to write anything, your spelling is bloody atrocious.'

'I've been to night school.'

'Really?'

'No, can you tell me what this is about Tiger?

'Tomorrow night, it'll all become clear, remember Tommy Bracebridge?'

'Bracebridge...Damn, what's he been up to? He's on our side with this Tiger?'

'You'll be working with him.'

'Bloody hell, Tiger you are scraping the barrel, He retired after the Crimean War didn't he?'

'You're a funny man Gruff, he's still got it, he knows the area, he speaks the lingo like a native and he's already up to speed with the ground situation.'

'Okay, roger that, mate, anything else?'

'Pack your swimming trunks.'

Tiger clicked his finger on the phone prestle ending the call and immediately dialled another number.

'Hello, Jane?'

~ELEVEN~

Tiger walked into the foyer of the Hotel sur Malaga, it was like coming home. He had a bigger room this time around and took advantage of the en-suite shower before gathering up his maps and files and heading downstairs to the bar. Gruff was sat at a corner table on the far side of the room behind a couple of glasses of ice cold beer; he was in deep conversation with Tommy Bracebridge, both men sat with their backs to the wall. Neither man looked up as Tiger approached the bar and ordered a beer but he knew for a fact that both men had noted his entrance.

'Gentlemen,' Tiger had taken a seat and raised his glass, 'thank you for coming and here's to a successful mission this time.'

Gruff and Tommy raised their glasses and Gruff said.

'This time?'

'Tommy not said anything then Gruff?'

'Nope, not a damned thing, we've spent the best part of ninety minutes covering every aspect each other's lives and he hasn't mentioned anything about this job.'

'Thank you Tommy,'

'No problem Tiger it's your show, I'm just a grunt.'

'Right Gruff, listen in... ' Tiger then spent the next thirty minutes running through the events of the previous week.

'I think that about covers it don't you think Tommy?'

Tommy shrugged, 'lot of words there Tiger, you could of simplified it with just the three, 'load of bollocks' for example.'

'Aye, I agree, it was a clusterfuck and it was my fault, I let Jane Albright have too much room to manoeuvre, even knowing that she would get emotionally involved.'

Gruff added. 'It's what girls do when their kids get snatched Tiger, strange that mate.'

'Aye, thanks, well she is not on this 'op and she doesn't know we are here, I saw her this morning at her home in Slough and told her that I might have a plan in place for the end of the week and to wait for my call, and when I call, she is to move fast.'

'Does she work Tiger? Can she just scoot off when she wants?'

'Aye Gruff, she's a locum school teacher, she can pretty much pick and choose when she wants to work.'

'This is a four phase operation. Stage one, we get more intelligence on the target, the times he goes in and out of his property, places he goes and the people he meets the full surveillance package that's you Gruff. Two, Tommy is going to befriend the target with a view to getting in the property legitimately and get his face known by the kids, friendly Grandfather stuff. Three is the snatch phase, it'll be a night time job which is why we need the villa mapped inside and out, Gruff, this'll be you, the target will need pacifying and tying up with Tommy as back up. Stage four is the recovery phase, Tommy high tails it out of dodge with the kids, I will be the cut off if there is any close pursuit, but if you do a clean job Gruff that won't be necessary and you stop for nothing Tommy, that's nothing, so flat out to Malaga airport where you'll find me and hand over the kids to mum. Okay, any questions?

Both men shook their heads, they'd both been involved in much more complicated briefings that this one.

'Right let's start with photographs,' Tiger reached into his file and pulled out two 6x4 colour pictures of Jennifer and John, 'these were taken a year ago but they are a cracking likeness.'

Next, out came the plans and sketches of Peter's villa, his car details and notes that Tiger had been compiling since he had first arrived in Spain a week ago.

'Gruff,' Tiger got his mates attention and used his pencil to point at a sketch of the villa layout, 'behind the villa is some waste ground that's well above the targets place, good line of sight not much in the way of cover but there is some, have you brought your camera gear?' Gruff nodded and Tiger continued, 'It'll help to get some shots of Peter Albright if you can, oh, I heard some dogs up there I have no idea if they are in properties or prowling around, we haven't got time to check all of them out which is a pain, but once you've got the pics you can ease off, you'll then be babysitting Tommy at a distance, making sure he doesn't get into trouble. Any questions?

'What about 'comms, have we got radios? Gruff asked.

'Aye, full covert surveillance rigs in my room.'

'Anything else?' No? Great, just one more point from me Gruff, Tommy has a mate, very influential, a retired senior cop in the GEO, he will be helping us but at a distance and we will be needing his help but we don't want to be seen with him okay?'

'Cop help is always good help Tiger, do I need to know who he is?'

'Not at present mate.'

'That's fine, right, who wants another beer before I turn in for the night?

~TWELVE~

The team met again at breakfast, they all had covert radio systems in place and had gone over the plan one more time in Tigers room. There were no questions and they were ready to go.

As they were leaving the hotel lobby, the receptionist called for Tiger, a message was waiting for Tiger in reception, an envelope. He thanked the receptionist and opened it, a single piece of paper with a typed message in English.

Peter's Jeep had been located by Señor Gonzalez Garcia, he was getting personally involved, he felt he had let Jane down once and was determined that it would not happen again. He had also taken the liberty of establishing credentials for Tommy in a bar not too far from Peter's villa so if anyone from Peter's side of the fence should start asking questions around town, Tommy was covered. There were at least a dozen Spaniards who would swear that they had known Tommy as a brother for years.

This was fantastic news and Tiger conveyed this to the team as they were getting into their cars. Communications checks completed the little convoy headed out on the coast road to the picturesque town of Torre Del Mar and Peter Albright's residence.

Once the Jeep was found it was a fairly straight forward exercise in finding the owner. It just involved waiting. Tommy parked up under the shade of an obliging palm tree with the jeep in view and waited. Gruff made his way up and around the targets villa and once there settled in a slight hollow and waited as well. Tiger stayed on the edge of town as a control point and would be taking notes as any information came in over the radios.

Tigers earpiece crackled into life, 'Zero, this is Golf contact wait out,' this was Gruff letting Tiger know that he had spotted the target and was taking photographs and nobody was to interrupt the radio channel. Thirty seconds later he was back on air.

'Hello Zero this is Golf, Tango one is leaving the building and is Foxtrot towards his Victor, please acknowledge over.' This was basic radio code, the target had left his building, and was on foot towards his vehicle.

'Hello Golf this is Zero, copied, Bravo did you copy over?'

Tommy Bracebridge answered immediately. 'Thank you Zero, Bravo copied, over'

'Golf, this is Zero, you can stand down and return to my locstat.'

'Gulf copied, wilco, out.' Gruff was going to meet up with Tiger at the edge of town.

Before Gruff was halfway to Tigers car though, Tommy came up on the radio.

'Zero this is Bravo, Tango has walked passed his Victor, I am going Foxtrot, over.'

'Zero roger, Golf do you copy? Over.'

'Golf, copied shall I divert towards Bravo, over.'

'Zero, that's affirmative, thank you, Zero out.'

As the foot surveillance on Peter Albright slowly started to take shape, Tiger knew that he had a couple of minutes at least to start scribbling notes on his surveillance log, taking careful note of times.

'Zero this is Bravo, over.'

'Zero, go ahead.'

'Bravo, Tango has entered a tobacconist on the corner of Calle Infantes, over.'

'Zero copied, Golf are you close? Over.'

'Golf, I'm just passing Tango's Victor, over.'

Gruff had reached the jeep.

'Zero, roger, hold fast there, over.'

'Golf, wilco, over.'

'Bravo this is Zero, do you copy? Over.'

'Bravo, yes, over.'

'Zero, if Tango comes out and does a recip, let him go, Golf will pick him up at the Victor, and what sort of pace is he waking at? Over.'

'Bravo, roger that, he looks fit as a fiddle, fast pace, wait, he's coming out now, wait, wait, he has a newspaper and some milk and is on a 'recip, I am holding fast, over.'

Albright was on a reciprocal route back towards his jeep. Gruff would be waiting and when he spotted him he'd walk at Albrights pace but 50 yards in front of him, it was a fair bet that he'd go directly home.

'Zero this is Golf, I have the eyeball, moving now, over.'

'Zero, roger that, Bravo you can head back to Tango's Victor and stand by, over.'

'Bravo copied, wilco, over.'

'Thank you, Zero out.'

Peter Albright did indeed go directly home with his paper and milk and seemingly oblivious to the amount of work and radio chatter he had caused in the process.

Tiger had brought his notes up date, every scrap of information could be valuable, even the most innocuous observation so they needed to know everything even down to whether their target looked fit and healthy.

Gruff opened the passenger door to Tigers hire car and got in.

'This is hot work mate, and it's only mid-morning.'

'Aye, it's going to get hotter as well, but hopefully our man will be in the pub later and not going for a run around the town.'

'Christ, sod that, I didn't bring my running kit.'

'We need to track him to a pub, get Tommy involved and we can back off a bit mate, did you get any 'pics up there?'

'Yep I got half a dozen.'

'That's good, we'll get the film to Señor Garcia tonight, meanwhile we sit tight until he moves again. If he turns right Tommy will have him, if he goes left he'll pop out of the street you came out of and then you're going to get sweaty again mate.'

'You're so romantic Tiger, which reminds me, what's the paymaster like? Crumpet?'

'Crumpet? What are you now? A schoolboy?'

'I know you Tiger and you're evading my question mate.'

She's a stand-in school teacher mate it's all sensible leather shoes, tweed and pearls.'

'Well our target, Peter, needs his eyes examining then, what would a fit young bloke like him be doing married to a dour looking history teacher eh? Answer me that? You can't can you, because you're talking bollox Tiger.'

'It takes all sorts Gruff mate, but she is a very pleasant lady.'

'It's been a while now Tiger, you know, since, er, Miss Kelly and the Scotland business.'

'I know how long ago it was Gruff, what's your point?'

'Not sure really, are you seeing anybody?'

'Bit personal Gruff.'

'I'm allowed to be personal, I'm your mate remember? We both do personal.'

'Sorry Gruff, you're right, no, no I am not dating, you'll be the first to know if there is any change in my shagging status, okay?'

'That's more like it mate... So are you giving her one?'

'Giving who one?'

'The history spinster lady you twat.'

Before Tiger could reply the radios came to life, both men tensed.

95

'Zero, this is Bravo, over'

'Zero, go ahead, over.

'Bravo, Tango is at his Victor, he is with the package, wait out.'

'Gruff, go, go, get back to your motor, we're mobile.'

'On it buddy' Guff sprang from Tigers hire car and sprinted back to his own.

'Bravo, Tango is now mobile and heading for you Zero, over.'

'Zero, roger that, hold fast, we'll pick him up, wait, wait, I have the eyeball he is turning left left left away from me, Golf can you come past, pick it up? Over.'

'Golf, wilco, passing you now, I have the eyeball, over.'

'Zero roger, Golf start making, left left left at the end of the road, get up there with Golf, over.

'Bravo, copied, turning left now, over.'

'Zero out.'

Peter Albright drove within the speed limits for about twenty minutes, leading a loose three car convoy. who's drivers were busy letting each other know of every change of direction and change of speed on the radio, Gruff and Tommy changed position a couple of times with Tiger staying at the back of it all, before Albright pulled into a small restaurant car-park. All three following cars drove past and Tiger noted the name, Club Safari.

It seemed like a very long wait but it was less than an hour before Albrights car nosed out of the car-park and headed back towards his home.

Two hours later all three men were back at the Hotel sur Malaga for the daily debrief, Tiger had added three more Cruzcampo beers to his tab and his team seemed happy as they relaxed in the corner of the lounge sipping cold beer waiting for him to start proceedings.

'Great work today lads, but the gold star goes to Tommy, give us a rundown as what happened in Club Safari then mate.' Tiger asked.

'All straight forward really Tiger, Club Safari is a pleasant little restaurant bar, and as you can guess from the name has an African themed décor, I waited until Albright got settled in with the kids and snagged a table next to them. He appeared to having a bit of trouble with the menu, the font was bloody terrible, and in Spanish with no English tourist translation, so I helped out. He thought I was Spanish with good English until I put him straight, quite funny as it happens, anyway once he was sorted I ordered and we got chatting, it would appear that he had been past the place loads of times, but never been in and fancied somewhere different for lunch with the kids. They were very polite by the way.

'He didn't suspect anything then?' Asked a curious Gruff.

'Nope, I would know if he felt suspicious but he wasn't, just another Brit having lunch, he liked the fact that I'd settled here years ago and had learnt to speak the lingo fluently, that was his game plan.'

'Did he mention Jane?' Tiger wanted to know.

'Nope, not a word and obviously I never mentioned her. I told him that I'm apartment hunting, looking for a place buy and to rent out, a bit of pension top up, loads of people do that and he bought into it straight away, so, I need to quit this place Tiger and get a room at a hotel in Torre Del Mar.'

'Why's that Tommy?' Tiger asked.

'I need to be local to him as I am his new drinking buddy and as this could stretch to a couple of days at least, getting back here every day after a few drinks would be awkward, anyway we're meeting up tomorrow afternoon for a session at a place called Bar Estrella on Calle Copo.'

Tiger rummaged around his maps and placed the street map of Torre del Mar on the table.

'What's the street name again Tommy?'

'Calle Copo.'

Tiger used his pencil to track down the street names in the index.

'Cally, cally, cally, calle, copo, here it is F7.'

He found the square on the main map equating to F7 and took another 30 seconds searching for it.

'Ah, here we go,' he pointed at the street with his pencil, 'It looks to be about a five minute walk from his place,' he placed the book back down on the table and span it around for Gruff and Tommy to see.

'Could it be a trap? Asked Gruff.

'Very doubtful mate, but we can cover the initial meet, just in case can't we Tiger?'

'Aye mate, we'll have to, what time are you meeting?'

'Fourteen hundred.'

'You'll have to lose the 24 hour clock stuff mate because he's a civvie and we don't want him to get jumpy, so, 2 o'clock then, you'll get in there thirty minutes early and wait, if you feel uncomfortable then bail out, Gruff will be opposite, or at least very close until the target shows up and it becomes obvious that it's safe, okay?'

'Yep sounds good, sorry about the 24 hour clock, it's a habit.'

'Aye I know mate, but you know better than most that it's the small stuff that could catch us out, so, what do you reckon Gruff?'

'I'm happy to baby sit the old boy,' he punched Tommy's arm, 'yes Tiger it's a good plan where will you be?'

'I'll be meeting our Police contact, I'll give him your regards Tommy, oh, I'll need your film Gruff and I'll bring him up to speed then I need to go through phase four with him, the exfil.'

'You mean the bit when we leg it Tiger?'

'Aye, that bit. Right lads, if that's it then, its Tommy's round, we need to raise a glass to phase two.'

Tommy dutifully went to the bar and started ordering the beers.

'What do you reckon Gruff?'

'This can work mate, you've got a good team here, I cannot believe the old man moved in on Albright so quickly, I know he's good, he was the simply the best operator back in the day, but that was a long time ago, it's impressive and with the background help we've got from the Spanish cop, I'm feeling confident.'

'That's what I wanted to hear mate, cheers. I'll book you both into a hotel closer the plot this evening, you can check out from here in the morning.'

'Lovely, what about you Tiger?'

'I'll be staying here, this is base and I'll be kept fairly busy plus I don't want to be anywhere near Albright for the next couple of days, if he clocks me it's game over so It'll be down to you and Tommy.'

Tommy arrived back at the table with three large beers and set them on the table. He looked at Gruff then at Tiger who raised an eyebrow.

'What's up, have I missed something, you two talking about me behind my back?'

'Yep, that's right,' said Gruff, we are both agreed you are a bit of a wanker.'

All three men raised a glass in toast and started laughing.

'Phase two,' said Tiger.

'Phase two,' Gruff and Tommy chorused.

~THIRTEEN~

The following morning Gruff and Tommy checked out of the Hotel sur Malaga and headed towards Torre del Mar, they had the morning off and couldn't book into the Hotel Miraya until 12 o'clock. Tommy was going for a stroll around the target area, get his face known, he knew he had the back up of Senor Garcia but he was supposed to be local, he should know local stuff. Gruff wasn't quite as professional, he took his alias Mr Wells for a tanning session on the beach and a dip in the sea, as he had promised.

Tiger had coffee with Senor Garcia and briefed him of the events to date, he was happy with the situation and realised that he was helping professionals, but the real test of his commitment was yet to be confirmed. Spoken agreements between two veterans chatting over a hot coffee, was a far cry from men on the run after committing a pretty serious crime.

Gruff had found himself a nice little street café where the waitress was very easy on the eye, but more importantly he had a clear line of sight 30 yards down Calle Copo to the entrance to the Bar Estrella. Tommy had sat in the same café 30 minutes earlier, but on a separate table, and Gruff had watched him walk in.

Just before 2 o'clock Peter Albright came into view and entered the bar, he was casually dressed in blue shorts and matching vest top and was alone. Gruff waited ten minutes, asked the waitress for the bill and gave her his name and telephone number of the Hotel Miraya as he paid. He then wandered slowly down Calle Copo and entered the cool gloom of Bar Estrella. He noticed Tommy sat at the same table as Albright as he headed for the bar. He paid cash for a bottle of Cola and walked back out. It wasn't a trap, Tommy was fine.

Tommy was still on his first Cerveza de bosquejo, the cheap, and more importantly, weak frothy beer, when Albright entered and went straight to the bar where he spent a minute or two talking to the barman as his beer was being poured, he had made no effort in acknowledging Tommy which worried the old soldier, but his fears were soon allayed as Albright eventually strolled over to Tommy's table with a fresh foaming beer and offered his hand.

Ten minutes later Gruff had entered, purchased a soft drink in a bottle and left, they didn't appear to look at each other but they had communicated.

All good.

The afternoon passed pleasantly enough, Albright mentioned his kids quite a lot but there was no talk of Jane. On the second round of drinks Tommy stood at the bar reading the 'tapa' the long list on the chalkboard that was hanging on the wall whist he waited to be served, he noted the homemade pâtés of scorpion, fish, salmon, Cabrales cheese, asparagus, chicken skewers, oxtail, homemade croquettes, and fried fish. It made him a bit hungry.

The conversation flowed along quite amicably as did the beer, football. Margaret Thatcher and remarkably they both enjoyed the latest chart buster back in England 'London Calling by the punk band, The Clash.' After the fourth round and a delightful snack consisting of, Chickpeas and Spinach Clams in Sherry Sauce, Octopus & Paprika Meatballs in Almond Sauce and Fried Cheese, Tommy made an excuse about a bit of business he had to attend to, and left Peter in the bar, but not before Peter had invited Tommy over to his place for a barbeque the following afternoon.

Come and meet the kids!

~FOURTEEN~

Tommy made his way to the Hotel Miraya where he found Gruff at the bar reading a two day old English newspaper and drinking coffee.

'How did it go Tommy?'

'Christ the bloke can talk for England because I don't think he has many English speaking friends over here yet, and he throws strong beer down his throat and doesn't appear to wobble much, I was expecting his speech to start slurring, but it didn't.'

'So, we aren't just going to get him drunk and walk off with the kids then. Have you got another meeting with him set up?'

'Yep, tomorrow afternoon, he's hosting a barbeque and his next door neighbour and part time baby-sitter, his neighbour, Ruth will be cooking.'

'Jeez, that's ace mate, how many people going?'

'No idea Gruff, but I wouldn't think it would be that many.'

'Have you briefed Tiger yet?'

'Nope, I'll have a couple of coffees first, sober up a bit.'

'Ha! Getting paid for drinking ale, what a life, you did keep the receipts didn't you mate?'

'Bollox, I forgot.' Tommy glared at him and ordered a large black coffee.

Tiger had been briefed and was jubilant that phase two was way ahead of the time schedule he had catered for. He had to be careful now though, not events accelerate away because at some stage he needed to arrange flights for Jane and the timing was critical.

After briefing Tiger, Tommy had decided to take an early shower and retire to bed. Gruff had other plans as the hotel receptionist had routed a call to the bar for him, a pretty waitress from the café Gruff was at earlier. Was he at a loose end that night and did Mr Wells fancy a drink?

It was a late start the following morning, which was a blessing in disguise for Gruff, he was nursing a mighty hangover and he just picked at the cheese and ham on the plate in front of him.

'I could do with a proper fry up this morning Tommy old boy, soak up some of this alcohol.'

'Alcohol Gruff? Last time I saw you was at the bar drinking coffee, did you just fancy a bender?'

'My plans were changed at the last minute old boy, remember the waitress at the café on Calle Copo yesterday?'

'Maria? Yes I remember her, very pretty, what about her?'

'Maria? Shit, I spent the night calling her Mary.'

Tommy smiled and said. 'Ha! Who's the wanker now Gruff? Enjoy your hangover mate, I'm going shopping for some swimming trunks, see you later.'

'Will you need some oversight at Albright's villa this afternoon?'

'If you want to go up the hill again and keep an eye on me for half an hour mate that'd be good, then you can get your sorry backside back down to the café on Calle Copo and give your apologies to Maria.'

'Roger that old boy, I will, enjoy your day and if it all goes to plan I'll see you back here tonight at 18 hundred.'

'You mean 6 o'clock son,' he laughed and added, 'have a good day mate and try and be good.' Both men headed out of the hotel, one going shopping the other heading for a couple of hours in the sun on the beach.

Peter's villa was exactly as Tiger had sketched. Tommy felt he could have been there before. There were about a dozen people sat around the pool drinking, they appeared to be English, but as Peter made no effort to introduce him, he would have to do it himself after he had found a way to familiarise himself with the interior of the villa. Introductions could wait.

There was no sign of the children.

Following Peter through the big sliding glass doors Tommy found himself in the kitchen. The floor and walls were of local stone and tile, but that is where the traditional element stopped. This was a modern room, chrome and steel, a big walk in fridge freezer and modern electric oven. Black marble top-surfaces, on which stood yet more steel and chrome. Pots and pans, the kettle, even the bread bin was all new and shiny. Peter asked him if he liked it.

Tommy didn't, it was all too brash, but he lied and said that he loved it.

Peter grabbed a couple of bottled beers from the fridge, opened them, and passed one to Tommy, who examined it. It was not a brand he recognised. He held it up to the light looking at the colour. Peter grinned, and told him it was a cheap Belgian import, an excellent session beer for barbeques and then offered the inevitable guided tour.

This was more like it!

Peter showed off the villa in the style of an amateur estate agent. It was classic enthusiasm without the substance. The tour did not last long, and anyway, Tommy was only interested in one room, the kid's bedroom, but that was out of bounds.

Peter explained that the kids had to have a nap in the afternoons and he did not want to disturb them.

Back out on the terrace, Tommy mingled with the other guests. He had been wrong about them all being English; there was a young couple from Germany, who, apparently had met Peter just the night before in a club in the town. The others in the group however, were from the U.K. and were regular off-season holidaymakers or had retired.

Peter was the centre of attention and made a remarkably good host, regaling his guests with stories that mostly revolved around him being blind drunk in a bar in the town. He was a good storyteller, and Tommy found himself laughing along with the others.

As the afternoon wore on, Tommy had found himself a spot in the shade next to a splendid example of a Chamaedorea seifrizii, an outdoor potted palm and he hoped that it liked cheap imported Belgian beer.

The food on the gas powered barbeque-q smelled good, the lady called Ruth from the place next door was in charge of the cooking, Tommy remembered her from Tiger's notes. Steak, pork, local fish and bread appeared to be on the menu and it was making Tommy very hungry.

After three more bottles of beer and a large plate of delicious tasting food Tommy had almost given up on seeing Jenifer and John that afternoon, but whilst engaged in conversation with a retired quantity surveyor from Dulwich, he noticed Peter standing framed in the glass doors to the kitchen, he was holding little John in his arms. Jenifer was behind him peering through his legs at the gathering around the pool and then Peter loudly announced the arrival of his children.

Tommy continued his chat, appearing polite, nodding and grunting whenever the old bore stopped for breath, his attention was on the children.

After doing the rounds with the other guests, some of whom already knew Jenifer and John, Peter approached Tommy where introductions were once again made with the children. John was not the slightest bit interested in the proceedings but Jenifer took a great interest in the six-inch scar running up the outside of Tommy's left leg and little John then started looking a bit more interested. Tommy had forgotten all about the damn scar and was wearing shorts. This could have been a big mistake. It was the always the small things...

Rule one was always try and hide personal identifying marks but Peter saved the moment by explaining to his daughter that Tommy used to be a deep-sea diver. This was true, he had been, and he had been bitten by a shark, this was untrue.

He had actually been shot whilst serving in Aden in 1964 whist fighting Egyptian backed guerrillas in the Radfan hills. His spotter on the sniper team, Gruff, had removed the bullet with an Army issue clasp knife.

Jenifer was impressed anyway and asked all the usual questions. 'Did it hurt? Did he kill the shark?' Jenifer had a new hero and for the next two hours she waited on him hand and foot, made sure he had enough ketchup on his second helping of steak, opened his beers, and never questioned the fact he was on his ninth bottle and was not even slurring his voice completely unaware that he was feeding the Chamaedorea seifrizii. The afternoon turned to evening and it was time to go home. As everyone said their goodbyes, Peter asked Tommy if he had the time to join him and his family on a special beach trip in the morning.

~FIFTEEN~

Well it would have been rude to say no.

Back at the Hotel Miraya, Tommy made a call from the public phone in the lobby, Tiger needed updating and he sounded pleased with the day's work, the call was brief and to the point. On entering the lounge he was not surprised to see Gruff at the bar again although he did raise an eyebrow at his drinking partner.

'Good evening Mr Wells,' he nodded at Maria the waitress, 'young lady...'

Gruff returned the greeting, 'hello old boy, this is Maria,' he deliberately exaggerated the sound of her name, Tommy smiled, 'Maria this is Tommy, he is a guest here.'

They made out when they arrived, that for appearance sake, they had only just met and anyway it does not take long for fellow nationalities to get together over a beer in a hotel bar. Especially the English, so the staff had no idea the two men were actually lifelong friends.

'Hello Tommy, my English, is not good you understand...'

'It sounds very good to me Maria,' said Tommy ever the gentleman, 'haven't I seen you before?'

'I work in café, I am student.'

'Which café? What are you studying?'

'Is small café on Calle Copo, good coffee, I am studying English and Art, one day I'll be famous painter!'

'That's fantastic, I wish you well Maria,' Gruff slid a bottle of beer towards him and he took a large swallow, 'I was a student once, a long time ago.'

'What did you study Tommy?' Her young pretty face was full of expectation and a gentle naivety, no wonder then that Gruff was smiling like an excited puppy he thought, as he answered. 'Military History, thanks for the beer, er, Richard.' He picked up his bottle and turned to go,

'Why don't you join us Tommy? That's okay isn't it Maria?'

'Yes of course, this is fine,' answered Maria.

'Okay, thank you, but I'll not stay long, I'll have to sit down though, you know, old legs and that.'

They all moved to a seat at the back of the lounge, Maria didn't appear perturbed that both men jostled for a seat so they'd be sitting with their backs against the wall so they could keep an eye on the door. Old habits die hard.

'So, how was your day Tommy? Gruff enquired once they were all settled.

'Very good thanks, excellent in fact, bought a new pair of swimming trunks, went to a barbeque and met some new friends, very pleasant.'

'And I suppose everybody there was a lot younger than you old boy?' Gruff laughed.

'Well as it happens they were, two of them were very young indeed, and they took a shine to me, in fact we are all off for a picnic on the beach tomorrow, everybody is so friendly in this town,' he smiled at Maria who took it as a personal acknowledgment.

'Nice one old boy, I had a right lazy old day, went up into the hills and took some photographs, then down to the beach to catch some rays, you are right about this town though, there are some lovely people here,' he gave Maria a friendly kick under the table and she giggled.

Tommy took another long drink of his beer, he was thinking hard.

'Richard you know that you said you said you'd give me a hand one evening with some stuff I am writing, you being a journalist and all?'

'Of course Tommy, when did you have in mind?'

'Well if it's not too much trouble, I was thinking, er, tomorrow night, but if you have plans with Maria?'

'I am at college tomorrow night and will not finish until late and afterwards I have to go to my Mothers so don't let me stop you Richard.' Maria butted in.

'Thank you Maria, you are so kind, letting me steal your man.'

'Please don't steal him Tommy, I want him back,' she replied and kicked Gruff back.

Tommy finished his drink, stood up and went up the bar where ordered a beer for Tommy and a white wine for Maria.

'There are drinks in for you two lovebirds at the bar,' called Tommy as he made his way out of the lounge.

'He's a nice man Richard, a great big, how you say, teddy bear, everybody must love him!'

'You're right Maria I doubt he's got any enemies in the world.' So, this was to be his last night with the lovely Maria, he'd better make the most of it then. 'Do you fancy going dancing Maria? Once we've finished here?'

Tiger knew that at some stage of the operation, this point would arrive and he would have to make a call, and after listening to Tommy's concise, but heavily disguised report, this was it. He made sure he had a pocketful of coins and headed for the public call box in the lobby of the Hotel sur Malaga.

'Hello Jane?' The line was poor but the conversation, hopefully wouldn't last long.

'Hello, Tiger? Is that you? The lines horrible where are you?'

'I'm in Malaga Jane, Spain.'

'What? Did you say Spain? What are you doing there Tiger?

The line hissed and crackled for about twenty seconds, Tiger took this chance to shovel more coins into the phone box.

'Tiger? Tiger? Are you still there?

'I'm here Jane, sorry about the line Jane, I have some news for you...'

'News? Oh God this line is bloody frightful, what news Tiger? What's going on?

'You need to take tomorrow off. You're coming to Spain, to Malaga.'

'Malaga? Okay, is this the start of your new plan Tiger?'

'Not really Jane.'

'What? I don't understand.'

'It's coming to the end of an old one Jane. Tomorrow evening, same hotel, The Hotel sur Malaga, can you do it?'

'Yes, yes of course, what do I need to bring? How long am I staying?'

'Just you and your passport with the children's names on it will be all you need Jane. You're only staying for 12 hours.'

'Oh my God Tiger...'

'See you tomorrow.' Tiger hung up the phone and hoped that he'd not made a massive mistake. He had every confidence in team Tommy & Gruff, but Jane? Had she learned her lesson?

Gruff parked his hire car fifty yards from the entrance to the villa, and made his way back to the bottom of the steep drive on foot, where Tommy was waiting with the engine and lights off.

He took the eight concrete steps one at a time, and stood quietly on the familiar concrete terrace, a small black holdall in his left hand, he passed the swimming pool and headed for the patio doors, Tommy was a couple of steps behind him.

The large glass door opened with a soft hiss, Gruff stood and listened for five full minutes before signalling to Tommy that he was going in.

He stepped into the darkened kitchen and waited again, he needed to get a feel for the place. Every property has its own sounds, even when empty.

Moving slowly and stopping at the open door to the lounge Gruff could sense Tommy entering the kitchen behind him. Peter Albright was asleep on the sofa.

Gruff placed the holdall on the floor and removed a large roll of industrial ducting tape. Tommy joined him.

Using minimum effort, and with an ease that suggested that these two 'Security Consultants' had done this sort of thing before, they had their drunken target sat upright on the sofa and securely bound. Gruff took one of the seats opposite the hapless Peter, as Tommy soft footed it down the corridor. He entered the small bedroom and without speaking gently lifted little John from his cot, a little bundle in a one-piece romper suit and walked out of the room and moved silently into the adjoining room where he gave Jennifer a gentle shake before scooping her into his arms with some of the bedding. She stirred and put her arms around Tommy's neck, she was obviously still dreaming.

Tommy paused at the door to the lounge. Gruff was sat down looking calm and relaxed. Thumbs up, and he was through the kitchen and onto the terrace, down the eight concrete steps heading for the comfort and relative safety of his car.

Malaga airport was only twenty minutes away.

Tiger knocked on Jane's door, she opened it immediately and it was obvious that she had not bothered going to bed. 'Come in Tiger, what time is it? Any news?'

'It's time to go Jane, phase 4 has started.'

'Phase what? What's happening?'

'It's all going to plan, chuck some water on your face and let's skedaddle.'

Tiger walked with Jane across the moonlit car-park and opened the passenger door of his hire car. Jane stood for a moment and was about to say something before sliding into the front passenger seat. Tiger walked around the vehicle and entered the driver's side and looked straight at Jane who turned her head and looked straight back at him.

'What were you going to say Jane?'

'When?'

'Just before you got in the car.'

'Nothing.' She paused and continued, 'please tell me this is going to work Tiger.'

Tiger looked at her, the desperation pouring from her face, her tear filled eyes full of hope and expectation. It was at this exact moment in time, that Tiger fell in love.

'We are not high and dry just yet Jane, but we are close, very close. You wouldn't be sat in this car if I wasn't very happy with the plan so far.'

Jane reached across the small gap and squeezed Tigers arm. 'I...I...trust you Tiger.'

Tiger was convinced that she had just changed the word 'trust' at the last second.

'Belt up Jane, we're off,' and he started the car and headed out into the night and Malaga airport to meet Tommy and the children.

Back at the villa, Peter was awake. He looked across the space between him and a stranger. A hard looking stranger.

A hard looking stranger in his lounge.

He could not quite grasp the situation he was in. That was until he tried to move his arms. Realisation dawned on him in small waves. The first wave was accompanied with bleating little noises. The second with panicked movements, and the third and final wave less than a minute later was an attempt to release himself from his bondage, with roars of fury.

Gruff was relaxed but on his guard, Peter looked like a fit man but there was no way he was going to break loose.

No one ever had.

Malaga airport. Tommy met up with Tiger and Jane. Jane was overjoyed at the sight of her babies, hugging little John and Jennifer to her chest, tears streaming down her cheeks, but there was much to do. As moving as the little reunion was, there was remained an element of danger.

The check in desk was about to close as Tiger and Jane entered the airport, the check in clerk had politely, but firmly told them that although there were no seats available on the flight that was next to depart, it was an academic exercise anyway, because the tickets that Jane produced were not valid on that flight. She would have to wait until the next one.

The next flight was not until 0730hrs. Four and a half hours later and they'd have to pay a surcharge to get on that one. Jenifer was beside herself.

Who had booked the bloody tickets?

There was nothing else to do except wait. Even the coffee shop was closed. The only movement around them was a member of the cleaning staff. An old man in green dungarees was pushing rubbish in front of a broom from one side of the terminal to the other. It was really stretching a point by calling it cleaning.

Back at Peter's villa, Gruff glanced at his watch. He had no idea if Tiger, Jane and the children were in the air or Tommy was stuck on the side of the road with a puncture. He could not call any one as Tommy had disabled the villa land-line.

Peter was strong. The duct tape was strong too. It was becoming an interesting fight.

In the blue corner was the manufactured composition of industrial strength fabric coated with adhesive. In the red corner was a very angry man. Gruff would have bet on the blue corner.

Every time.

But this time he would have lost his bet. Peter ripped the tape apart, and in his current mood, he was not going to be a pleasant man to be around, he certainly wasn't about to make his house guest coffee. Sure Gruff could have handled him physically, but that would have meant hurting him.

Badly.

That was not in the plan and therefore not an option.

Gruff made a command decision. His brief had been to keep Peter away from vehicles, telephones and airports for as long as possible. This was as long as it was going to be.

He ran.

Safely out of town, Gruff was in no hurry, he had bags to pack, two hotels to check out of, and two hire cars to return. He may spend a couple more days in the Country, he liked it here.

Peter's first instinct was to chase the stranger, a second later he altered his priorities and checked in the two small bedrooms, noting immediately that his children were missing. He let out a raging howl of anger before running down the steps to his vehicle. He was raging, thumping the steering when the engine failed to start on the first attempt and positively apoplectic when it failed to start on the fifth attempt. It was twenty minutes before he realised that the high tension leads to the spark plugs had been disconnected.

If Peter thought he was going to get any one stopped at an airport now, he was very much mistaken. Somewhere between Peters villa and the airport would be a Police vehicle waiting. Waiting for a certain type of vehicle and a certain registration number which would be stopped for speeding, whether it was actually speeding, or not.

There would be the paperwork and the language barrier. That was just for starters. The well-oiled wheels of a machine operated by a certain Señor Gonzalez Garcia would just start slowly turning.

Jane was worried sick, Tiger was seated next to her looking calm and relaxed, the children were asleep, Tommy was sat in his car observing the carpark entrance, but she knew that Peter, or the Police could overpower him eventually and enter the airport at any time and it would all be over.

But there were no Police. There were no Airport Security Officers. There was no drama, just the ordinary sight of a tired mum, holding her two children with a fit looking man sitting next to a suitcase. The flight was called and Tiger and Jane were first in the small queue. Unbelievably, Jenifer and John were still fast asleep. The check in girl accepted Tigers credit card and loaded the surcharge.

Thankfully, there were no questions asked as to why Jane had entered the country alone but was returning with two children. Jenifer and John were both properly registered in her passport, but the last thing she needed was another stay in a Police station.

116

Tommy moved his car closer to the departure entrance and got out of his vehicle, he knew it was safe now. He saw them walk safely through the security barriers into the departures lounge. Jane turned and blew him a kiss and mouthed a 'thank-you.' It was going to be okay.

Tommy blushed.

~SIXTEEN~

Tiger had arranged for Jane and the children to stay in Social Services accommodation in Lincoln City. It wasn't an ideal situation but when Tiger had spoken to the Judge that sat at the original Family hearing during the planning stage, it was a recommendation that he strongly advised. Pre-school would have to be booked for Jennifer and Jane would have to let the teaching agency know that she would be away for a bit. There was a lot to cover and it was desperately important that every one of these agencies respected the temporary anonymity of Jane and the children. Tiger had also arranged for a hire car for Jane.

A couple of days later, Jane had phoned and asked if she could pop over whilst the kids were at playschool, they appeared to be very happy there and showing no signs of distress at all.

The building work on the cottage was coming along nicely, and although Paddy and his team had tea mugs seemingly welded to their hands, they were getting the job done. Tiger had taken Jane over to the cottage and had a look around, Tiger was impressed but Jane appeared to be disappointed.

Back in Tigers lounge, Tiger asked her directly.

'Are you okay Jane? I understand that your whole life has been a whirlwind since coming back from Spain, and you're still dazed by it all, but I just want to help, I really do.'

'Oh Tiger, you are lovely, a kind and generous man, but I am not unhappy, I am out of sorts, I am here, intruding upon you, I have none of my personal belongings, I'm in a kind of limbo.

Tiger interrupted, 'What sort of limbo?

'I am out of sorts Tiger and embarrassed, because I can probably never go back to my home again. If you could help me with my personal things, clothes, the kids toys, you know, my stuff.'

'Oh Jane, I am so selfish, I never gave that a thought, of course you want your belongings, please forgive me. Tell you what sweetheart we'll sort that out tomorrow, first thing, now, what about the embarrassment thing?'

'I am living here at your expense, you haven't asked for a penny in keep, it's obvious that you haven't got a full time job and you are spending Lord knows how much on the cottage, I feel like I am sponging, and another thing, Mother tells me that you haven't cashed the cheque she gave you.'

'Right Jane, can I clear a few things up? I do work, but not full time, I am a consultant and paid a retainer, when I do go out to work it is for a couple of weeks at most and I get paid handsomely for it. As for the cheque, there isn't any need for it...'

'No need? That operation or whatever you call it, must of cost a fortune Tiger...'

'Aye, it would have under normal conditions. However, we all waived our fees and split the cost of the flights, cars and hotels. We had a meeting, it was unanimous.'

Jane sat back in her armchair, her look of astonishment made Tiger smile. 'We are all mates, good mates, brothers in arms at one time, looking after each other in hellish conditions, this was more of a holiday for them, a reunion of sorts and I'll hear no more of it if that's okay by you, and another thing when you make the necessary calls to your landlord and utility services tomorrow, I'll arrange collection of everything in your house and have it delivered to here...'

'But Tiger hang on a...'

'I haven't finished yet Jane, I want to take you back over to the cottage, take a pen and paper with you, because I want you to choose, the paint, the wallpaper, the fittings the sink and the light switches.'

'But why Tiger?'

'Because if you would like to and it would make me so happy if you did, you can move in, it'll be yours, now it's just a thought, if you'd rather do something else then I'll support you in that as well. What do you think?'

Jane stood up and paced the room. If I do this Tiger, I would want to pay the market rate for rent, I'm not having you keep me for free, that's not who I am or what I do.'

'I wouldn't have it any other way,' said a delighted Tiger. 'This will give me time to get to know the kids as well, they've only ever seen me scrapping with their dad, not the best of starts to be honest and having you and them around will make me so proud.'

'What about the mess Tiger? The toys scattered around the place?'

'I don't mind mess Jane...'

Jane looked around his immaculate living room and they both laughed so hard that the tears started flowing. Jane launched herself across the living room and grabbed Tiger around the neck and cuddled him. Between tears of joy she just whispered, 'thank you, thank you, thank you.'

~SEVENTEEN~

Early the next morning Tiger was on the phone.

'Gruff, Tiger.'

'What's up mate? Any fall out from Spain?'

'Nope, it's all good, very good in fact…'

'Aye aye, what's this I am hearing? My spider senses are kicking in and I can sense…Schoolteachers, tweed…'

'Leave it out Gruff, I have told you that you'll be that first to know okay? Now, listen, can you get a removal van sorted for today or tomorrow? It'll be a house clearing at Jane's pad in Slough and an uplift to mine. If you can get a self-drive and hire a couple of heavies for the lifting I'll square you up when you get here. Then it's me and you, the pool table and beers for a few days, how about it mate?

'Okay, that sounds like a plan, is the lovely Jane up at yours at the moment then?'

'Well, not yet, I'm making the wee cottage available.'

'That's definitely a plan then, I'll give you a bell when it's confirmed, which means you have to stay near the phone, in your office…Not the bedroom, haha! Cheers mate.'

Tiger replaced the receiver and laughed. This could all work out.

Jane had packed up her children and driven over to Tigers and had arrived for breakfast, she needed to see the interaction between them and Tiger, no matter how much she adored the man, her children would always come first and she was under no illusion that Tiger was a single man and didn't seem to have had much contact with children.

Tiger had set to in the kitchen, boiled a dozen fresh eggs and made soldiers out of buttered toast and milkshakes for Jennifer and John..

They were going to have breakfast together for the first time. It all went well although the children were very quiet they did started giggling at one point when Tiger made a funny face at them. Tiger was actually enjoying himself. Once he had finished he started clearing up the plates and taking them to the sink. He looked at Jane and said.

'I'm not saying this is a one off Jane, but I am not going to make a habit of it.'

'Spoilsport!'

'Not at all lass, it's your turn tomorrow!'

Jane picked up a half-eaten egg and playfully threw it at him, he caught it one handed, and returned it her. She laughed.

'Go on get out so I can dressed and sort the kids, go and tinker with your motorcycles or something. Tiger walked towards the door, turned around and waited, filling the doorway and looking directly at Jane.

'What? Jane enquired, in a playful tone.

'Nothing sweetheart.' He closed the door softly behind him. Jane heard him whistling a tune as he made his way along the path to the cottage. She smiled and sipped her tea.

Later on that morning, brew in his hand, Tiger was passing his office when the phone rang.

'Hello?'

'It's Gruff mate, did I get you out of bed?'

'If it makes you happy and it'll shut you up, then yes. Not only in bed, but in the lounge, in the kitchen, in the garden and swinging from a tree, okay?'

'I knew it, I bloody knew it...'

'You are Madam Mystic and I claim my crystal ball, what's up mate?'

'Removals sorted, the lads are on it, the landlords letting us in, I can make it to yours this evening mate.'

'That's cracking work Gruff, nice one and thanks, I'll see you later.'

Tiger wandered out towards his garage, he hadn't been this happy for a long time. He unlocked the big padlock and pulled open the door. It took a full twenty seconds before he realised that his T140 Bonneville motorcycle was missing.

Feeling numb and holding down a small knot in his stomach he entered the garage, a pointless exercise because he knew exactly where it should be, and it wasn't. Jane's Honda was where she had parked it and it hadn't been moved.

His first course of action was to see if anything else was missing, it all looked to be in place, he then went around to the rear. Nothing. No obvious place where anybody could have broken in. He went back into the garage and checked the skylight. It had cobwebs in one corner and looked although it hadn't been opened in years and anyway nobody could have fitted through such a small gap.

He then walked across the courtyard and called out for Paddy the builder, who appeared in the cottage door way with the omnipresent mug of tea.

'Paddy, have you seen anybody lurking around my garage in the last couple of days?'

'Er... No Sir, we keep a close eye on that sort of thing.'

'Are you sure man, this is important, have a think.'

'Nope, I can honestly say that I haven't seen any strangers hanging about Sir.'

'What about the rest of the lads?'

'I'll ask them Sir.'

'Okay Paddy, thanks, you're doing a grand job.'

'Thank you Sir.'

Paddy turned around and shouted into the cottage door.

'Meeting! Out here now, all of you.'

Paddy and his team went into a small huddle and after a minute the meeting broke off, Paddy turned to Tiger and shrugged and opened his palms to the sky.

~EIGHTEEN~

Back in his office Tiger was sat at his desk, the tilt mechanism of the chair was back on its limiter, his boots were up on the desk and he was thinking.

'Penny for your thoughts?' Jane was stood in the doorway looking at him with a smile that could stop a man in his tracks.

'Sorry Jane, I didn't hear you, I was away with the fairies wasn't I?'

'You were indeed, is everything alright?'

'Not really no, but I can deal with it.'

'Okay, you did remember that Mum is coming up today?'

Tiger looked confused. 'Today?'

'She's picking up the kids and having them for a week, have you forgotten?'

'Christ, sorry Jane, it had slipped my mind, what time is she getting here?'

'Should be around lunchtime, I can't believe the incredible Tiger has memory loss?' She laughed, a soft sound that started deep in her throat and poured out like honey.

'I'm sorry Jane I am all over the place, oh, your removal lorry will be here this evening. Gruff and a couple of his mates are sorting it.'

'Oh wow! That's fantastic news Tiger, have you got somewhere to keep it all, I don't want to fill your home with all my stuff.'

Tiger wouldn't have minded at all, in fact he'd love to have all her 'stuff' in his house, but he didn't say that. 'Aye lass, it's all sorted, of course you can make yourself comfy in the spare room with anything you need and anything you won't need immediately can be stored in the garage.'

'Thanks Tiger, that's brilliant. Now come over here, I want to kiss that frown away!'

Tiger, of course, needed no second bidding. He stood up and pulled Jane into his arms and kissed her on her forehead, before slowly pushing her back and looking deep into her eyes. 'Jane…You are a wonderful woman and you are making me a better man.'

'Wow. Tiger. That's a bit heavy! It's not even 10 o'clock yet.' She laughed again. Tiger loved her laugh, well to honest he loved every single atom in her body, now that *is* heavy, but he refrained. As Jane had pointed out, it was a bit early.

'Jane?' Tiger looked serious.

'Yes honey.'

'The kids going away with your mother…'

'What about that?'

'Well, I really do not want to interfere, but so soon after getting them back, they're off with Grandma. I would have thought you'd want to keep them both in your sight forever!'

'I've thought long and hard about this Tiger, I have discussed it with Mother and although she was reluctant at first, she has come around to my way of thinking.'

'And what is that way of thinking?'

'The kids, especially Jennifer seem to miss their father, I find it incredible but that's how it is. She is constantly asking when can she see him again, she is obviously too young for the truth, but she appears to having difficulty in bonding with me. She absolutely dotes on Granny, so we've decided it is best all round if we start the bonding process all over again, but slowly. Mum will start the process, letting Jennifer know that her mum loves her and that she won't be seeing her father anytime soon. I hate doing it this way Tiger, I really do, in one way it appears appalling behaviour, however, Mother and I really believe this is the best way.'

'Wow! Jane, I never thought about it like that, but you obviously know best, I'll support you in any decision you make and make this journey you're going through, as painless as possible.

'Thank you Tiger, it's a decision that I haven't taken lightly, please understand that and thank you for your support.

Five minutes later, Tiger was holding another brew and watching through the kitchen widow as Jane and the children larked about in the garden. John was just starting to walk and Jane and Jennifer were encouraging him. Jennifer was holding John upright and Jane was knelt down with her arms out, urging John to take more than five steps. He took three and plonked his bottom on the lawn, they were all laughing. Tiger moved away from the window, a sudden pang of guilt spread through him, it was if he was spying on them. He would have loved to have joined in however awkward he would have been, as he'd never played with a child in his life. He could of course teach him how to disarm a Soviet land-mine, or how to kill a bear with a stick, but Mum would disapprove, he imagined that most Mums would, and anyway, he really wasn't in the mood for a bit of fun.

Lunch time came around all too quickly and Jane's Mum, the indefatigable Mrs Angleton rolled across the courtyard in a spotless blue Rover 75. This was supposed to be the 'poor mans' Jaguar, but Tiger knew that if Mrs Angleton wanted a Jag, she'd be in one.

Tiger opened the driver's door for her. 'Thank you er, Tiger, you are such a gentleman. Jane Darling, would you mind opening the boot, I've taken the liberty of buying you a few things and I need a proper sit down, and a 'cuppa.' She winked at Tiger, who fought off the urge to wink back.

Jane removed a couple of bags from the boot with Jennifer trying to help but struggling, whilst Tiger put the kettle on. 'How do you take it Mrs A?'

'I do hope you are referring to the tea young man?' She said, with a twinkle in her eye before adding, 'Jane dear, where are the children?'

'John is upstairs having a nap, Jennifer has disappeared. She is probably hiding under Tiger's desk in his office, it's her little den. Jennifer! Jennifer darling come and say hello to Grandma. '

Jennifer came traipsing out of Tigers office holding a large stuffed rabbit by one ear and stood behind Tiger, clutching his leg.

'Hello my gorgeous, aren't you beautiful, come here and give Grandma a hug.'

Jennifer reluctantly left Tiger, who was now looking slightly embarrassed, and sheepishly approached her Grandmother who deftly swept her up in her arms and sat her on her knee.

'Jane, why don't you take a pew and have a family catch up, whilst I finish making the tea?' Asked Tiger in a way that made it pretty much an order. It was difficult doing the 'happy families' thing, although he knew that if he wanted to make a go of it with Jane, he'd have to buck his ideas up, and quickly.

Tiger took his time in the kitchen and even bothered to spread a couple of biscuits on a plate before returning with a tray of drinks.

'I'll be Mum,' he smiled and sat down with his tea spoon at the ready. He caught Jane's eye and waggled the spoon at her and she giggled, 'stop it Tiger, you're impossible.'

Mrs Angleton raised an eyebrow but didn't say anything, discretion being the better part of valour. She'd get to the bottom of all these little actions between Tiger and her daughter later, it's what she did.

Tea over, it was time to round up the kids, get them suitably strapped in Grandma's car and wave them all off, with a 'a safe journey.' Mrs Angleton had explained that she and the children would be staying with one of her old school friends. Peter was not aware of the address, or the school friend' so it wouldn't be a problem if he came back to the UK looking for them.

Back in the kitchen, Jane came over and started drying the plates as Tiger washed up. You are acting a bit oddly today Tiger, well not oddly that's the wrong word, different, cooler. Are you going to talk to me?'

Tiger continued to absently wash the dishes, he had to tell her sometime, but he would prefer it if he had a plan first, some good news to follow the bad, but at the moment he had nothing.

'C'mon Jane we've finished here, let's go into the lounge and have a chat.'

They both sat on the sofa, bodies slightly turned to face each other. Jane started first.

'Is it me Tiger? Have I somehow upset you? I know it must be a huge burden for you having me and the kids here, that wasn't in the original plan I know, but…'

Tiger interrupted before she could get into full flow.

'No Jane, it's not you, or the kids…Come here, I need a cuddle.'

Jane raised her eyebrows, she wasn't expecting this and she slid along the sofa into Tigers arms.

'Jane, I'll get to the point. I got up this morning and found out that my motorcycle has been stolen…'

'What! Jane exclaimed. Who?...When?'

'I don't know Jane. I haven't been on her since I got back from Spain, I haven't bothered to look in the garage, so I have no idea, your bike is fine, it hasn't been touched.'

'Oh Tiger,' Jane was close to tears, she was really feeling his loss. 'You have to tell the Police, have you told the Police?'

'No Jane, I've done nothing, I feel paralysed, I don't know when it happened and the place is next to the cottage, which is in effect a building site, there is dust and crap all over the garage. I don't even how it was stolen, the place is secure, no damage and it's still got my big padlock on the front door, the Police are bloody useless, they'll take a cursory glance, if they bother to turn up and even then all I will get is a crime number. Then the insurance company will try and run me ragged and get me to jump through hoops. No. The only way I can sort this is my way Jane.'

'Your way? What's that Tiger? Jane was slowly massaging Tigers neck as she spoke.

'I haven't got a *way* at the moment, but Gruff will be here this evening, we are a good team, we'll sort it Jane. Oh, by the way, I'm going to give you ten minutes to stop doing that to my neck.'

Jane smiled and she felt good that she was making Tiger smile and especially pleased that she and her children were not the problem, although she was now worried on a different level.

'Can I tell you something Tiger?'

'Of course you can Jane,'

She looked straight into his eyes. 'I am really fond of you Tiger, but you really are rubbish at this, so, if you can't be bothered I can. Can we start dating? Proper dating, boyfriend girlfriend dating?'

'Proper dating? Asked Tiger?

'Yes proper dating.'

Tiger pulled Jane closer and they kissed, softly at first and then with a sense of urgency that left Jane breathless.

'Wow! Kissed by a Tiger!' Exclaimed Jane when they eventually broke off for air.

'Kissed by a gorgeous girl who is going to make me a better man,' replied Tiger and they kissed again. Tiger gently pushed her away, looking into her eyes; she nodded and followed him up the stairs to his bedroom. They made love, twice. The first time slowly and gently, Janes orgasms rolling into one massive explosion of joy. The second was wild, a tangle of arms and legs and heaving bodies. Twenty minutes later, Jane sat astride Tiger and leaned forward, her breasts just touching Tigers chest, her hair stuck to her blissful face reddened with sweat and she kissed him, deeply, and shuddered as he came inside her.

It was only later, much later, that she realised that Tiger hadn't actually answered her question.

~NINETEEN~

The furniture truck arrived that evening and it was all hands to the pumps. Jane oversaw the whole thing and made sure nothing was broken and the right box went to the right place. Stuff she'd need fairly soon went in Tigers house, stuff that could wait went in the garage.

Tiger thanked and paid off the two removal men, who were more than happy at the generous remuneration, as they jumped into the truck and prepared to head south.

All three settled into the lounge, Tiger and Gruff drinking beer from cans, Jane sipping wine from a glass.

'So.' Gruff started the conversation. "What are we going to do about your stolen bike?"

'Go to the Police,' chimed in Jane.

'I'm not so sure,' countered Tiger. 'I have already told you Jane that nothing will come of that, other than a flimsy crime report number for an Insurance claim.'

'Tiger will want *his* bike back Jane, not another one.' Gruff added.

'Well go to the Police first, please, for me and if you get no joy there, then, and only then will I listen to any other plan that you have Tiger, because at the moment you don't seem to have one.'

Tiger remained quiet for a moment, conscious of the fact that two people were watching him, waiting for him to speak. 'Okay then, I'll call the Police now, it'll be an exercise in futility I'm telling you.' He got up from the sofa, leaned over and kissed Jane on her forehead and made his way to his study.

'Is he always this stubborn Gruff? Surely it's the sensible thing to do?'

'Yep, he's stubborn, but the annoying thing is, he's nearly always bloody right!'

They sat in silence for a minute, enjoying their drinks, Tigers voice was an indistinct mumble in the background.

"You've known him a long time haven't you Gruff?'

'Yes Jane, yes I have and I can see the way you're looking at me, that your next question is going to be personal.'

'Not really. Why is Tiger still single? He's obviously a great catch.'

'I knew it. That's personal Jane.'

'It's not really.'

'It is really, and if you want to catch a Tiger, you have to tread carefully, be patient and don't be surprised if it gets away. Tigers are very fast runners. That's all I'm saying on the matter Jane.'

'Okay, fair enough, I respect your friendship and your unwillingness to disclose Tigers personal situation, but can you answer me this, I really like Tiger, does he like me? He must have mentioned something?'

Gruff drained the last of his beer, crushed the can in one hand and tossed it neatly into a waste bin on the other side of the room. 'Trust me, if he didn't like you, you wouldn't be here.'

Before Jane could answer, Tiger came back into the room.

'All the Police would tell me, before they issued a useless crime number, was that a white van had been captured on camera, speeding through a local village the last day we were in Spain.' Tiger was looking at Gruff as he spoke. 'This van may, or may not be associated with the theft of my bike.'

Gruff spoke. 'Did they give you the registration number mate?'

'No.'

Gruff stood up. 'Can I use your phone mate?'

'Aye, it's in my study, fill your boots.'

Tiger went into the kitchen and returned with an open bottle of wine and a fresh can of beer. He topped up Janes glass sat down heavily beside her and popped the can open with a hiss.

'Tiger?'

Tiger looked at Jane. She leaned over.

'Kiss me.'

Tiger willingly obliged, tasting the sweet white wine on her gentle lips.

'Thank you.' She whispered as they broke off.

'Thank me? For what?'

'Does there have to be a reason Tiger?'

Tiger leaned back in to the sofa and stretched. 'No I guess not Jane.' He turned to look at her again. 'I am so glad you are here.'

Jane smiled contentedly.

Gruff strolled back into the lounge clutching another can of beer and a notepad. He sat down opposite Tiger and said matter of factly. 'It's a white transit, registered in Cork city in the Irish republic. I have the keepers address.'

Tiger smiled, Jane lurched forward, nearly spilling her drink. 'What?' She exclaimed. 'How do you know this? You've only been gone two minutes? Did you call the Police back?'

'Not quite. Gruff replied.

'Nina?' Tiger asked. Gruff nodded.

'Nina? Who's Nina? Jane was mystified.

'A friend of ours Jane.' Tiger replied with a grin on his face, adding. 'Bloody hell Gruff, Nina! How's she keeping?'

'She's sound as a pound mate, and she wants to help.' Gruff replied.'

Jane looked bemused. 'You two and your secrets, does it never end?'

'I hope not.' Came the chorused answer.

~TWENTY~

The following morning Tiger slipped out of bed without waking the sleeping Jane. He leaned over to her and gently kissed her cheek causing her to stir slightly. "You're beautiful,' he whispered before getting dressed. He tip toed across the hall and lightly tapped on the spare bedroom door before opening it. The bed was empty and neatly dressed down to air.

He was in the kitchen waiting for the kettle to boil when Gruff knocked on the front door and immediately entered the house. He was wearing black jeans and windcheater with a black woollen cap comforter on his head, the sort of thing that can be pulled down into a ski mask.

Tiger raised an inquisitive eyebrow; Gruff ignored it with a smile and said. 'NATO Standard please Tiger.' It was army slang for two sugars,' He then made his way into the lounge. Tiger sat next to him on the sofa, after handing him a mug of hot tea.

'What's the story Gruff?'

'Story?'

'Don't be coy. You're dressed for sneaking about in the night.

'Your builder, Paddy.'

'What about him?'

'He's involved.'

'Involved? In what?'

'The theft of your bike. He managed to get into the house when you were away; he simply took the garage key, popped the padlock and placed it back in the kitchen where it normally hangs.'

'And you know this how?'

'I visited him in the early hours of the morning.'

'Christ Gruff, what did you do?'

'Put it this way, his bedroom is soaking wet and he's not doing any more work for you mate. He's a tough old bastard and his arm sort of broke'

'Wait. What? You water-boarded my builder and broke his arm?'

'Well, it was the other way round, his arm was broken first, but yeah, that's the gist of it.'

'Fuck me Gruff, why didn't you tell me this was on your mind last night?'

'Would you have agreed?'

'No,'

'Then I'm asking for forgiveness, not permission, I think it was you that taught me that.'

'Did you get a name?'

'Yep, I got two names and the name of a motorcycle club.'

'A motorcycle club?'

'Yeah, the two thieving scroats in the van had a bike in the back of that white van, well two really including yours. They were at a weekend bikers party up near Hull, guests of the North East Lincs Wanderers MC.'

'Christ Gruff. They're a heavy mob; they kicked the Hells Angels out of their own clubhouse a couple of years ago.'

'That may be, however, these two arseholes belong to a motorcycle club in County Cork. They call themselves The Celtic Fist MC. They were kicked out of the party for some undisclosed firearm incident, apparently they're bad news, and even their own club finds them a massive embarrassment.'

'Okay, so what's Paddy the builder got to do with this motorcycle gang?'

'He's an uncle to one of them.'

'Fuck me.'

Tiger leaned back on the sofa and took his first sip of his tea. It was lukewarm. "So, what's next mate? I presume you have a plan?'

'Of course.'

'Does it involve me this time?'

'Only if you want in?'

'I want in.

~TWENTY ONE~

Jane walked into the lounge in a dressing gown. 'Morning Tiger morning, Gruff, anybody fancy a brew and a bacon sandwich?'

Both men looked up at her and stated that would be great, Gruff went upstairs to shower and freshen up whilst Tiger followed Jane into the kitchen.

Jane was looking out of the window, the Lincolnshire Wolds rolled all the way to the far horizon. Tiger softly kissed Jane on the nape of her neck giving her goose bumps.

'What was that for Tiger?'

'Do I need a reason?'

They both laughed and Janes hand slipped down to gently squeeze Tigers crotch.

'Whoa there sweetheart, we've got a guest.'

Jane slowly turned; not releasing her grip and feeling him harden.

'Did you just call me sweetheart Tiger?'

'Mmm, not sure, did I?'

'I think you did, have you showered this morning?'

'No not yet, I didn't want to wake you.'

'How sweet, let's have a shower, now.'

'What about the bacon rolls?'

'Gruff's a big boy,' she murmured softly, nuzzling into Tigers shoulder, 'he can make his own breakfast.'

They sneaked upstairs like naughty school children and entered Tigers bedroom, he closed the door softly behind him.

'Get the shower on, I'll get undressed,' whispered Tiger.

Jane let her dressing gown drop from her shoulders and walked naked into the en-suite bathroom. Tiger watched her every step before striping off in double quick time and joined her in the shower.

Jane was against the shower wall with her head back, warm water cascading down her face as Tiger entered her. She was soaking wet and ready for him. She moaned softly and used her vaginal muscles to clamp around his erection. She wrapped her arms around his neck and said. 'Don't move Tiger.' She moved her pelvis slowly back and forth, savouring the excitement that was building deep inside her. Tiger kissed her neck and turned her face to his, kissing her, his tongue going deep into her mouth as she orgasmed.

'Bloody hell Tiger. What are you doing to me? Quizzed Jane, as she pulled on a tight pair of Levi jeans.

'Me? I'm not doing anything Jane, you seem to be doing all the work.'

Jane laughed. 'That's true, I'm training you up!'

'Really? Training me up for what?'

'That's a secret. You've got yours so I can have mine.'

Tiger grabbed her around the waist and pulled her onto the bed. Keeping his arms around her he looked her in the eyes, thinking, he could do that for ever.

'Jane, can we be serious for a minute?'

Jane looked puzzled and a little worried. 'Sure Tiger, what's on your mind?'

'This thing about boyfriend and girlfriend, I didn't answer your question yesterday.'

'I noticed that.'

'Well it's difficult…' He couldn't finish the sentence, not when Jane looked so worried and fragile. 'It's difficult for me. When I fall in love with a girl, its total, I immerse myself in her…'

'You don't have to worry about me…' Tiger placed his forefinger on her lips to gently silence her and smiled for reassurance. He continued. 'Its total, I go all in, I don't know if that's a good thing or a bad thing but it's what I do. What is a bad thing though is when I lose a girl, it's unbearable and I do lose them. I have the most exciting feeling about you Jane, we are great together and I don't just mean in bed…'

Jane interrupted and whispered, 'or in the shower.'

'Shhh baby, this is serious, I'm trying to be serious.'

'What's happened to your previous girlfriends then Tiger?' Asked Jane innocently, as she wriggled away from his muscled arms in order to look at his face. 'Did you leave them or did they finish with you?'

Tiger swung his legs over the bed and stood up facing her.

'Well, recently, one was blown up in a park for being a spy, one was pushed under a train and the last one was crushed by falling masonry.

'Bloody hell Tiger, I thought you were being serious? You shouldn't tease like that, it's horrible, so if you're not going to tell me that's just fine. You've got me now and I'm not going anywhere. You got that Tiger?'

Tiger smiled at her naivety. 'Yes Jane, I got that.'

Downstairs Gruff was washing up, the smell of crispy bacon lingering in the kitchen. 'Kettles on folks and Tiger I have news.'

'Fire away mate, what's happening?'

'Firstly, I have been on the phone again. Nina is on her way up here."

'Wow!' Said Tiger, 'that's quick work.'

'And secondly, Sheila Brown is with her.'

'Bloody hell, I know they're good, top in their field, but surely this is a muscle operation? Where are the tough guys?'

'We're the tough guys, me and you.'

'Okay, I'm good with that, so you obviously have a plan?'

'I do, and I'll lay it out when our team gets here.'

Jane piped up. 'All this secrecy. Is this about your motorcycle Tiger? Can I help? Am I included in any plan to help?'

'Jane, I think it will be an easy job, we think we know where the bike is so we just have to go and get it.'

'Really?' Jane stood with her hands on her hips and glared at the men. 'Really? So who is this mysterious Nina? And why is my school friend getting an invite to the party? What can she do that I can't? She's only an office clerk, why is she even coming?'

Gruff prodded Tiger in the leg with the toe of his boot. "Jane's school friend?'

'Aye,' said Tiger, 'Jane and er, Mrs Brown went to school together, they meet for coffee every now and then.'

'Well bugger me. It's a very small world,' replied an amused Gruff.

~TWENTY TWO~

Jane had raided Tigers sparsely loaded fridge and pantry and at 6 o'clock that evening, she had prepared a simple roast chicken dinner for five people. Sheila Brown was of course surprised and delighted at seeing her old friend and Nina usually very quiet, was chatting quite amiably with her dining companions. Nobody mentioned their previous meeting, their excursion to Scotland, Jane wasn't vetted for that and anyway it was a catastrophe best forgotten.

'I'm afraid there's no pudding,' explained Jane as she gathered the empty plates.

'Here, let me give you a hand with that,' offered Tiger.

'No, sit yourself down, I can manage, tell a joke or something whilst I make coffee. I presume everybody would like coffee?'

Everybody agreed that coffee was in order and Gruff said. 'What do you reckon Tiger? Shall I get my notes?'

'Aye mate, I don't think Jane is going to be a problem, she kept a proper cool head in Spain, given the circumstances.'

'Okay.' Gruff excused himself from the table and went upstairs to his room. On his return Jane was once again sat at the table and everybody had a cup of coffee in front of them.

'Right,' said Gruff, 'I will start the proceedings if I may?'

Tiger nodded.

'Ladies and gent, we are going on a short break to County Cork in the Republic of Ireland, the small village of Rosscarbery to be exact. It's on the coast and about 40 miles south of Cork city. Tiger and Jane will travel in a hire van, Sheila and Nina will be in Sheila's car. I will bounce between the two during fuel breaks, I'll keep everybody up to speed with information as it comes in. We'll be travelling in convoy from here to Wales where we are booked onto a Ferry. Nina?'

Nina leaned forward and looked around the table as she spoke.

'The ferries are booked in our own names and we need to be at Swansea docks at 15.00 hrs the day after tomorrow. The ferry sails at 16.00 and we dock four hours later. The travelling time to Rosscarbery from the docks is 90 minutes. Tiger and Jane you are booked into the Celtic Ross Hotel as Mr and Mrs Smith. No passports are required by the hotel and they don't need to know your real names. Myself, Sheila and Gruff will be staying elsewhere and again you do not need to know where. but we will be in constant communication with each other. Sheila?'

Sheila glanced at her own notes before proceeding. 'Tiger, this is not your operation, it is ours, and you are part of it, as is Jane. The whole thing will only work on a need to know. You have to be happy with this before we go. Agreed?'

Tiger nodded and said. 'Aye, I'm in agreement so far, but I do have a question.'

'What's the question Tiger?' Asked Sheila.

'Jane. Nobody has asked Jane if she wants any part of this, shouldn't she be asked?'

Jane butted in. 'I've already been asked Tiger, when you and Gruff were out in the garden reminiscing, us girls had a bit of a chat, well quite a long chat actually and I am in full agreement, I could do with a short break and so could you. We're doing this. Okay?'

Tiger raised both arms, palms upwards. 'I really am a passenger on this one aren't I? I'm not comfortable with that, but okay Sheila, I trust you so what's next?'

Sheila continued. 'Thank you Jane. Right, moving on. The hotel is booked for just two nights so we can't dick about, it's going to be a very fluid operation, plenty of tempo from our end and absolutely no room for cock ups. Tiger this is not a real holiday, just because you're lounging about in a nice hotel and visiting the many sites of historical interest in the area, you are to remain sharp, you too Jane, You need to be by the phone in your room every day at 14.00 for 30 minutes and from 19.00 onwards, all night until 08.00, you'll be on a moment's notice to move, to get that hire van at the right place at the right time, if we have any chance of getting your precious motorcycle back, and that means no alcohol, are we all clear?

Nods from around the table assured Sheila that she had been heard and understood.

'Any questions?' This from Gruff.

'The hire van,' asked Tiger, 'is it big enough for my bike and has it got a ramp and lashing down straps?'

'Sorted.' Said Gruff.

'When is the van arriving?'

'Tomorrow afternoon, the driver is one of ours, I'd like him to stay here, when we are away Tiger, I have a feeling that your builder may be a tad angry and want to visit.'

'Fair enough Gruff, that's fine, a bloody good idea actually, I hadn't thought of that. What about the sleeping arrangements for the next two nights, unfortunately I haven't got room for all of us here.'

Sheila answered. 'Gruff is away tomorrow for 24 hours, he's got things to do, Nina and myself are booked into the hotel in the village. Tonight for two nights.'

'One last question,' asked Tiger. 'Cost? Why aren't I paying for this? It's my bike were going to get.'

Nina stood up. 'You're paying nothing, the costs are covered, we are authorised to treat this as a training operation, it's not a personal matter anymore Tiger, it's part of National Security exercise, so it's fully funded. If you wish to make a donation on a successful outcome, then that is entirely up to you Tiger.'

Nina walked toward the door followed by Sheila. 'We'll let ourselves out and we'll pop over and see you tomorrow. Thanks for Dinner Jane, it was lovely.'

'Night ladies, and thanks,' said Tiger.

After Sheila and Nina had left, Tiger turned to Gruff and said. 'Well, you old bugger, we have ourselves an operation. Again.'

'Indeed we do old friend, indeed we do. I'm off to bed, I have an early start and a very long day tomorrow, thanks for dinner Jane, well, thanks for everything really, especially for looking after my mate.'

'You are welcome Gruff.' Jane approached Gruff and gave him a quick kiss on the cheek. 'Anytime.'

Gruff blushed slightly and wiped his cheek. 'Night Tiger,' and he left the room.

~TWENTY THREE~

The Cork Ferry berthed bang on time and the lorries and cars started rolling out at 8pm. Tigers van was a couple of vehicles behind Sheila's nice looking Saab 900. The plan was to continue as they had on the ferry, no recognition of the two little groups. Gruff was sitting in the rear of the Saab as it bounced along the steel exit ramp. He turned and could see Tiger and Jane some 40 yards behind. He probably wouldn't see his mate again for two more days.

Tiger drove the transit van away from the docks, at his slightly higher driving position he could see the roof of the blue Saab as it cleared customs and headed west for Cork city. He was under orders to keep away from it.

They passed through the port town of Ringaskiddy, it was drab and dreary, a blanket of silence had fallen over the streets, the shops had closed for the night and the soft smog of burning peat fires from the homes permeated the air as they continued towards Cork city.

'Have you been to Ireland before Tiger?' Asked Jane.

'Not to the south no, well, not officially, I was once based in the north, In Northern Ireland and let's just say that our map reading wasn't as good as it could be.'

'Was this when you were in the army?'

'Aye lass, it was. We were not allowed to venture into the Republic under any circumstances, even though there is no hard border. As soldiers we obviously carried weapons, and to cross uninvited into another country when under arms is tantamount to declaring war, it's very serious, all sorts of people get hot under the collar when it happens, and it did. The trick was not to get caught.' Tiger laughed at his own last statement.

'I never met a soldier before I met you Tiger.'

'I'm not a soldier Jane.'

'You know what I mean, mister pedant.' They both laughed. Tiger turned the radio up the familiar chords to an Irish Republican Army song bounced from the small speakers. 'Armoured cars and tanks and guns, came to take away our sons,' Tiger joined in, 'But every man must stand behind the men behind the wire...'

Tiger turned the radio volume down, Jane looked at him. 'What on earth is that song about?'

'It's by a band called the Wolftones, it's a drinking song about the men locked up in the Maze prison, terrorists who prefer to be called political prisoners. The song is banned in the UK, I'm quite surprised to hear it here to be honest.'

'Well we are in County Cork Tiger, it's known as the Rebel County.'

'Indeed it is Jane, have you been doing some homework?'

'You forget, I'm a history teacher Tiger, well I used to be.' She turned from Tigers look and gazed out of the window as they sped along the city ring road.

'You're still a history teacher Jane, treat this as a sabbatical.'

'I have a feeling that my teaching days are over.' She sounded sad and Tiger didn't have the words right there and then to cheer her up.

They drove in silence for twenty minutes. Passing through the small town of Bantry, Tiger broke the silence. 'I reckon it's about another twenty minutes, ten to Clonakilty and another ten to the hotel in Rosscarbery. Would you have a look at the map for me?'

Jane pulled the folded map from the glove box and rummaged in her handbag for a small torch. She searched for a couple of seconds to get her bearings then spot lit the correct portion and she agreed with Tiger. 'You're right, it's no more than fifteen miles now.'

Tiger pulled into the carpark of The Celtic Ross Hotel and killed the ignition. He stretched his arms and looked over at Jane. 'Hi honey, we're home!'

'You silly fool.' Jane was laughing, 'come on let's get checked in and see if the restaurant is still open, I'm famished.'

Checkout was a breeze, no questions asked, no raised eyebrows at the name 'Smith' just a pleasant West Cork welcome. Unfortunately the restaurant had closed, but if they'd like to choose now from the bar menu, sandwiches would be made available and brought up to their room.

Tiger and Jane entered the lift, Tiger stabbed button the marked two, the doors hissed closed and they were silently on their way to the second floor. Jane leaned over and unzipped his flies.

'What?'

'C'mon Tiger, let's have a quickie, here, now,'

Tiger stood open mouthed. He had a bag in each hand and was pretty powerless to do anything if Jane dropped to her knees and took him into her mouth.

The lift pinged as it reached the second floor. Jane skipped out laughing and without looking back said.

'Tiger, your flies are undone you naughty man.'

Tiger dropped the bags and zipped himself up.

'Bloody hell Jane I thought you were serious!'

They were both laughing as Tiger opened the door. Their room was modern and spacious. Jane took to inspecting every nook and cranny, behind the shower curtain, in the bathroom cabinet…

Tiger crashed onto the King sized bed, it was a bit soft for him but it would do for a couple of nights, he had no interest in how clean the room was. He heard Jane moving around the bathroom, you could find dirt anywhere if you looked hard enough and it looked clean enough for him.

Jane's search for faults was interrupted by a firm knock on the door. Tiger was off the bed in one fluid movement, he was wide awake. Putting a hand up to Jane who was leaving the bathroom, ordering her to stay there, he stood to the side of the door, not looking through the spyhole and asked. 'Hello?'

'Room service sir. Sandwiches.'

Tiger pressed the door handle and let it swing in, allowing the staff member to pass him. The young night staff waiter was wearing Celtic Ross Hotel corporate colours and carrying a try of sandwiches wrapped in cellophane.

Tiger relaxed and nodded when the young man asked if it was okay to leave the tray on the small table next to the television set.

After he had left, Jane said. 'That really put me on edge, you scared me.'

'Sorry sweetheart, old habits die hard, we have to be on our toes now, we have no idea what sort of hornet's nest Gruff and the girls are stirring up.'

'Did you just call me sweetheart? Again?'

'Er, no, I don't think so...'

He stood up and used the phone, the call took twenty seconds.

'That was a quick call?'

'Aye, just checking that Gruff was sorted, we don't need hours on a phone like you girls!'

Jane sidled over to him and kissed his neck. 'That's not fair, she pouted, now get in the shower, you sexy man, you stink.'

'Did you just say I stink?'

'Yes I did, now get in the shower. With me.'

They both hurriedly undressed and headed naked for the bathroom.

'Wait.' Ordered Tiger.

'What? Do you think there may be a ruffian in there, waiting to do us harm?'

'Not at all. I just wondered if it was clean enough for you?' Tiger slapped her bottom and entered the bathroom, turning on the shower.

'You cheeky so-and-so Tiger.' Jane was giggling as she joined him under the showerhead. The hot steam slowly filled the glass shower screen, obscuring the embracing couple.

~TWENTY FOUR~

Twenty minutes' drive away, to the north of the pretty fishing village known as Union Hall, Gruff and Nina had booked a room at the Lis-Ardagh B&B. There was no stirring of hornet's nest by Gruff, there was no stirring of anything, he was flat on his back on a couch, fully dressed, wide awake, his neck crooked into a pillow, with Nina in her bed opposite him, completely naked under the covers, not six feet from him.

'Christ alive that was a boring journey,' muttered Gruff, half to himself. 'You two girls could talk for England, I couldn't get a word in edgeways.'

'We were talking about you, not to you,' Nina countered.

'Ha! Very witty, if you were any sharper you'd cut yourself. Seriously I don't know how you do it.'

'Talking of serious Gruff, thanks for helping me lug these boxes up.'

Gruff moved his head to the right, four metal suitcase sized boxes had been opened revealing an array of screens and dials, electrical cable snaked between the boxes and were plugged in to their respective jack sockets. The whole thing was obviously switched on, green lights were showing and the whole ensemble emitted a low power humming noise.

'Well, it's what we gentlemen do. Help the ladies.'

'Well thanks anyway, I'll make some satellite calls on it tomorrow first thing and see if the answers tie in with the intelligence that you've got.'

'Wonders of modern bloody science.'

'It's a two day Op Gruff, we haven't got the time to do it the old fashioned way, boots on the ground knocking on doors, and you know that.'

The hotel phone rang and Gruff snatched it up, he knew who it would be. The call lasted less than twenty seconds.

'Was that Tiger? Nina asked.

'Yeah, he's fine.'

'You don't look so good.'

'I know, I know, I'm just tired, my necks got a crick in it, I'm never going to get any sleep on this damned couch.'

'Okay, you can share my bed, but if you start misbehaving, you're straight back on the couch.'

Gruff was hallway across the bedroom floor, hopping on one leg trying to get his trousers off before Nina had finished her sentence.

Thirty seconds later a red light on one of the boxes flashed and a ringtone pierced the quiet room. Somebody had called the restricted number.

'That's odd.' Nina sat up in bed and looked at her equipment.

'What's odd?'

'That phone call was from Sheila, but it wasn't to us, it was to a secure Dublin number.'

'Why's that odd? She's got an office there.'

'Because it wasn't in the plan Gruff.'

The same night.

Sheila Brown was unrecognisable. She was sat on a bar stool at a bar called O'Shaughnessy's in Skibbereen, her hair had been dyed blonde and she was dressed as a bikers moll. Tight fitting leather trousers and black leather jacket over a white, low cut blouse. She was the bait.

O'Shaughnessy's bar was a notorious hangout for the motorcycle gang known as the Celtic Fist MC. Testosterone leaked from every pore of the building, half a dozen Harley Davidson motorcycles were parked in a line outside, ignoring the double yellow lines and no parking signs, there was little fear of a passing Gardaí Police car putting tickets on them, let alone entering the bar and identifying the owners.

Rock music pumped from the jukebox, it may have been a Rolling Stones number, but the volume of shouting and laughing drowned out any recognisable lyrics. The clientele, with the exception of Sheila were bikers from the Celtic Fist MC. The clubs distinctive mailed fist logo, sewn onto the backs of leather waistcoats was evidence of this. A dozen or more men and a handful of women, wearing similar waistcoats to the men, without the logo but instead bearing the words, 'Property of the Celtic Fist MC' proclaimed brashly where their allegiances lay. Sheila, a very experienced undercover operator, felt slightly intimidated by the scene surrounding her. Wherever she looked there were big men, with tattoos, some of them grotesquely scrawled across their faces. Every man had a beard, Sheila didn't look too hard, but was fairly certain that some of the women were sporting one as well.

She was drinking Budweiser from a bottle, her usual tipple, a fruity white wine wouldn't cut it here, in fact she doubted that they had ever heard of such a thing, let alone stock it.

It started on her second bottle.

A heavily built man of indeterminate age, but probably middle aged, bearded with a large green snake tattoo, appearing from the top of a dirty grey vest, coiling up his chest and around his neck, ending somewhere under a shock of oily, curly, shoulder length hair, sat down on the vacant stool next to her. He smelled faintly of fish.

'Dia duit a stór' the man spoke, his heavy West Cork accent mingled with alcohol.

Sheila looked at him. 'If that was Irish Gaelic, then I have no idea what you're saying.' She had dropped her own Home Counties accent and replaced it with a reasonable rendition of Essex Marsh. Flat vowels and easy to remember, just pretend your common as muck, she had reminded herself as she practised, in front of a mirror, back at her B&B.

'So, you're a fucking Brit are ye?' The man had switched to a mangled form of English. 'I was saying, Ello darlin.'

'Really,' replied Sheila, 'How fucking charming.'

The man leaned forward, his nose almost touching hers. 'Yer a cheeky wee fucker, I'll give you that.' He placed his paw of a hand on her left leg and moved it slowly towards her crotch. Sheila didn't flinch. 'And yer fucking brazen with it. What's yer name?'

'Mary,' said Sheila, still matching his unblinking gaze, 'Mary Grace.'

'You've got some Catholic in yer have ya? Well how do ye fancy some more?' He had removed his hand from her leg and grabbed his own crotch as he spoke. He then rocked his head back and started laughing at his own fine joke. The snake tattoo across his Adam's apple bobbed up and down as he continued to guffaw.

'My Mother is from 'Skibb.' The local nickname for the town slid easily from Sheila's tongue, 'she died a while back, so that's why I'm here. I'm visiting her grave.' This of course was a lie, part of her researched legend, her well-practised background cover story. She had a fake surname, Malley, a driving licence to back that up, a real one, issued by the DVLA back in England. She knew where the graveyard was and where on the site her 'Mother' was buried should anybody feel the need to check her out.

'Lads, lads, we've got a Brit lass over here, says she's got a dead mother buried here in Skibb, whadda ya reckon?' The fish smelling biker had turned from Sheila and was addressing no-one in particular. A young looking girl, she couldn't have been older than 19 years old, wandered over. Her right arm was covered from wrist to shoulder in tattoos. 'So, you looking to steal one of my men are ye?' She asked.

'Not at all,' replied Sheila, 'I'm here on a mini pilgrimage, I love motorcycles and rock music so where else can I go in 'Skibb for that?'

The tattooed girl replied quickly. 'So you like bikes do yah? Do you ride one?'

'No, I wanted to, but I was on the back of an old boy-friends bike, he was riding like an idiot, he crashed and died, I broke both of my legs and I need a stick to walk now.' Sheila held up a walking cane that was leaning against the bar by her stool. She didn't need it to walk, but she knew exactly how to use it, as a defensive and offensive weapon.

'So you're a bit of a cripple then?' The young girl looked quite pleased with herself, this older girl with a cane and knackered legs was no longer a threat to her little world.

'Yep, but that doesn't stop me wanting to party does it? Retorted Sheila, with a smile on her face.

The bearded biker sat next to her chimed in. 'Party? You like to party huh?'

'Yep, I love it, beer, rock and bikes, what's not to like?'

'So, Mary girl, are you up for a party tonight? We've got something going at our clubhouse later.'

'Yeah, why not? I don't have to be anywhere else, I'll have to make a quick call though, let my landlady know that I won't be in tonight.'

'Great darling, make yer call, the phones at the back there,' he said, pointing vaguely at the back of the pub, 'and get back here, I'll keep yer seat safe.'

Sheila slipped off her barstool, and emphasising the use of her walking cane, hobbled through the throng of black leather, not making eye contact with a dozen inquisitive biker's stares, to the back of the bar where the battered looking phone booth was located. The number she called had been committed memory.

~TWENTY FIVE~

The group of bikers had moved outside. The music from within O'Brien's had reduced to a dull thud. Some of bikes had been started, the big distinctive 'V' Twin engines thumping away on tick over.

'Yer on the back of me.' The biker with the snake tattoo had obviously taken Sheila under his wing and was telling her that she was now his pillion passenger on the back of his Harley. He was making a statement to the others in the group that she was his property, for now.

'Have you got a spare crash helmet then?'

'Here, put mine on if you're worried, I'll go without.'

Sheila awkwardly threw her right leg over the saddle and sat down on the low saddle. She gripped her cane in her right hand and pointed it rearward. There was no 'sissy bar' at the back of the saddle, the upright back rest that some machines have fitted. She had no idea how she was going to stay on once they started moving.

One of the bikers revved his engine and waved his arm in the air, this was obviously the signal to move off and Sheila felt and heard first gear being engaged, a loud clunk from the lower left side of the bike and a little jerk.

'Hang on darling, we're off!' The big Harley moved smoothly away from the kerb and fell in behind another motorcycle. The noise from the exhaust pipes cascading from the bike in front was deafening, Sheila was grateful that this was going to be a short trip, she knew that the bikers clubhouse was only a ten minute ride away on the shore of Lough Abisdealy. This stretch of water had no residential houses around it, in fact Sheila's research had only found the bikers club house and no other building for 3 miles.

Although the journey was mercifully short, Sheila hated every mile, she had one arm around her rider, not through choice but through necessity, her cane got in the way, her borrowed helmet was way too large, the wind threatened to tug her off the small saddle and the noise and smell of exhaust fumes were making her giddy. It was a blessing when the bike stopped outside the clubhouse and the engine was finally turned off.

Sheila stepped off the bike with wobbly legs, and she actually needed the cane right now, although she never envisaged for a second, that this would be its prime purpose so early on in the operation.

The other bikers turned off their machines and peace was slowly restored. Sheila noticed one of the men, he was of slight build, much smaller than the others and he was clean shaven, was devilishly handsome. He walked with a purpose and confidence that was beyond his age. He had no visible tattoos and if he wasn't wearing the Celtic Fist Kutt with the appropriate regalia, there was no way he could be associated with this crowd. She was sure he must have tagged onto the rear of their little convoy during the short journey from Skibbereen, because he was definitely not in the bar earlier. He was looking right at her as he walked past and it wasn't the look of love. Sheila couldn't gauge his mood, was he angry? Suspicious? She'd definitely have to keep an eye on him.

The man that had passed her was called Callan. He had been orphaned at an early age and wandered the streets of Cork as soon as he was old enough to leave school, a place he hated. Eight years earlier, the then President of the Celtic Fist MC, Gary 'Slab' Adams had been attending one of a number of appearances with his solicitor in the City, on leaving the solicitors back door, he didn't want to be seen going in and out the front, he had heard a commotion coming from a dank looking alley on the way to his parked motorcycle. He investigated and came across a kid with his fists up and blood streaming from his nose and surrounded by three rough looking men.

The kid couldn't have been more than sixteen years old. Slab was about 10 yards away and an urge came over him to help the kid out, he couldn't say why, and he'd thought about his actions for many years afterwards, with no definitive answer.

Slab, didn't look for trouble, when there was, and there often was, trouble came to him. It took him less than five seconds to cover the distance to the back of the nearest man, he kicked him hard in the back of the knee and the man collapsed to the dirty alley floor with a yelp. He stepped over him and watched as the kid punched the second man in the face as he turned to see what had made his companion cry out. It was a beautifully placed hooked uppercut, his fist connecting with a nose, the bone and tissue cracked, the man's head whiplashed back and he too fell to the floor holding his face. The third man stood motionless, any aggression in him had faded. 'Fuck off, and do it now.' Slab uttered the words viciously and the third man needed no further instruction, he turned and fled.

'So lad. What the fuck was all that about?'

The kid didn't say anything, he just stood there, his fists still up in the defensive position, his eyes darting from the two moaning men on the floor and Slabs large presence.

'I aint going to hurt you kid, I've just fucking rescued you, why would I do that?'

Slab could see the defiance in the kids' eyes, he softened his tone.

'Look son, I'm on your side here, I'm helping you. Have you got anywhere you need to be? I can give you a lift, drop you off someplace.'

'I aint got no place to go.' The lad dropped his arms to his side.

Slab noticed the kids eyes soften slightly, behind the hard Cork accent was a troubled child, a child with nowhere to go. Slab recognised the situation instantly, because it wasn't a million miles removed from his own troubled childhood.

'Well, you have now son, what do you call yourself?'

'Name's Callan.'

'Okay Callan, let's go, c'mon and by the way, nice punch back there. I've got some friends, they'll get your nose fixed up before that break sets.' Slab turned his back and started to walk up the alley.

Callan gingerly touched his nose then wiped the blood and snot away from his mouth with the back of his hand.

'You one of them Celtic Fist bikers then?' The bike clubs logo clearly visible on the back of Slab's leather waistcoat.

Slab didn't turn around and kept walking. 'Yeah, kid I am, you're safe, c'mon now.'

Callan followed Slab out of the alley and into the bright sunshine. They turned right and Callan warily kept a couple of yards behind Slab. They reached Slabs immaculately presented Black Harley Davidson motorcycle.

'Wow man, that's some bike!' Exclaimed Callan, 'I've dreamt about owning one of those.'

Slab turned to look at Callan. 'Well, if you come with me, you're one step closer to that dream, 'Hook.'

And a nickname was born.

~TWENTY SIX~

Sheila followed the snake tattoo biker into the Celtic Fist MC clubhouse. A single storey brick built building sat among a handful of rickety looking outbuildings. The front door was solid wood, probably oak, with a sheet steel backing and its potential strength was increased by four steel bars that were lying against the wall next to the door, ready to lay horizontally on purpose built hangers.

They were either paranoid about security, she thought, or there was a very good reason for such measures.

It was gloomy inside and smelt of stale beer and bleach. Sheila walked along a short corridor with two closed doors either side, before entering a larger room, obviously the main congregating area. It had a bar top running ¾ the length of the left hand side of the room with a tall skinny man stood behind it, deep in conversation with a leather clad girl sat on a barstool. A battered looking pool table off to the left occupied four men's attention.

'I'll introduce you to the club President Mary, be polite.' Snake tattoo had spoken and she followed him to the far end of the room, where a large bearded biker was sat at a table playing cards with three other men, their leather waistcoats hung over the back of their respective chairs.

'Evening Prez, this is Mary, picked her up at O'Brian's, she wants to party.'

The big biker spoke. His voice addled with years of alcohol and hard drug abuse. 'Mary huh? Where you from Mary?'

Sheila responded. 'Essex, Ma was from Skibb.'

'Essex? A Brit huh? We don't like Brits Mary, bastards the lot of them, but if you say yer Ma was Irish, then you must be half Irish, no?'

'Yes, yes and I am and I'm proud of that.'

'She been checked out Snake?'

Sheila had wondered what his moniker was, it was now obvious really.

'Yeah, she's good Prez.' Sheila wondered why he had just lied to his president.

'Right, get her signed in with the VP and look after her.' The club president was referring to the clubs vice-president.

Sheila nodded her thanks as the President returned to his game and followed Snake over to the pool table.

'Hey VP, how's it hanging?' The snake directed himself at one of the pool players. He was lining up for a shot and said nothing until he had potted his chosen ball.

'Hey, Snake, whassup?'

'Prez says can you check this bird in, names Mary Grace.'

'Book's in the corner, sort it will ya? I'm busy trying to win this.'

'Sure thing VP.'

Sheila noted the deference to which Snake had given the hierarchy. Now she knew who was in charge, there were only two more obstacles to cross, one was known as the Serjeant-at-Arms. Every MC had such a person and they were usually the biggest maddest biker, 100% committed to running the discipline, dishing out punishment as directed by the President and enforcing the club rules. The other was the unknown quantity of the man that had eyeballed her on the way in.

Sheila walked over to bar and sat next to the girl that was already there. She was still chatting to the man behind the bar. Snake had excused himself and had headed for the lavatory. Sheila opened the conversation. "Hi there, I'm Mary.'

The girl turned to look at her, heavily made up with black mascara around the eyes, Sheila realised that she was much older than herself.

'Hi Mary, you can call me Mamma, I'm the adopted club mother, I saw that you came in with Snake, don't let him paw you, he's a fucking menace a borderline sex pest.'

'Well he's been okay so far.'

'He's not fucking drunk yet, but he will be, just be careful girl.'

The conversation was interrupted by the man behind the bar. 'What you drinking Mary?'

'I'll have a coke please, the drink, not the line.'

Both Mamma and the barman laughed.

'You won't fit in here with that attitude girl,' said Mamma, and they both laughed again.

The barman introduced himself as Dave as he handed over Sheila's drink, the girls were not allowed to pay, because the member that had invited her into the club had that privilege. Dave had no nickname yet, he explained, he was a prospect, a new guy that was going through the harsh process of being a fully patched up member of the club, a two year process, that he was halfway though, and it involved lots of fetching and carrying, being on call 24 hours a day at the Presidents whim and the biker called Sledge, that had sponsored him, who was currently in the USA on an official visit to another, unspecified bike club. Slab was the old club President, but his trips in and out of prison over the years had aged him beyond his years and slowed down his reactions. He had reluctantly admitted this and another President was duly sworn in. Slab's seniority and respect from within the club hadn't changed though and he was still a man to be reckoned with.

Dave's current duty involved keeping the bar open until the last club member had stopped drinking, or fallen unconscious, a regular occurrence apparently.

There was no opening and closing times here and no Gardaí or licencing council staff that would be checking.

Snake had joined the little group at the bar and ordered a large Jack Daniels. He never offered Sheila anything and never paid for his. Dave didn't chalk it up or seem to write it down anywhere either.

Sheila realised that with booze on tap like this, she had to be very careful, on the plus side, because she knew that people who drink at an apparently free bar didn't usually last long before they collapsed. The conversation was free flowing with plenty of foul language thrown in, whether this was to strongly undermine a point or as a matter of course Sheila didn't know. Nobody seemed to mind that she wasn't drinking alcohol and for that she was grateful, this could be a long night.

'Does anybody actually live here?' Enquired Sheila.

'Only me,' replied Dave, but there are bunk beds for members that are too pissed to get home, or they just want to retire for a bit of company with their women, their old woman.

'Old woman?'

It's what we call a members girl, she can't be touched by anybody else, she's the member's property.

Snake grinned at this and grabbed Sheila's leg. 'Yeah, that's right darling, so whenever you get the urge, let me know.'

'Pack it in Snake, Mary's your fucking guest not your old lady.' Mamma glared at Snake and he removed his hand form Sheila's leg.

'Just sayin,' muttered a chastened Snake.

Sheila was grateful, and impressed that a fully-fledged back patch member of an MC could be cowed by a woman. This part of the biker's ideology had not been mentioned in her briefing notes. She decided there and then, not to stray too far from Mamma if she could.

The club door opened, two bikers walked in, laughing and joking and slapping each other on the back.

"Jesus,' Mamma muttered, 'here come the fucking terrible twins, those bastards are trouble Mary, stay away from them.'

'What have they done Mamma?' Asked Sheila.

'What haven't they fucking done,' she replied, 'fucking animals, they've just got back from a party in England, fucking disgraced themselves over there. Getting kicked out of another clubs party is a fucking no-no. Brought our clubs name into disrepute they have. The wankers.'

Sheila didn't push for more information; she knew exactly who these men were. These were men that had stolen Tigers bike, the Kennedy brothers, nephews to Paddy, the builder that Tiger had taken on. The brothers were drunk. The bigger one, Patrick, was clean shaven and had a rat face complete with red eyes that never sat still, always looking for a chance, always looking for danger or a way out of it. Unwashed, greasy, shoulder length hair hung to his shoulders and from time to time he swatted it from his eyes. The smaller brother, Liam, was similar looking, but was completely bald. He had a big bushy beard that had never been groomed and was a jungle. His eyes were hooded and glazed and he obviously had trouble focussing on anything.

Both men were wearing the familiar leather waistcoats, both covered in grime making the various badges and patches very difficult to read. They were not a pretty sight. They reached the bar and Liam shouted at Dave. 'Drinks over here and put some music on prospect. Dave flinched, but never moved, the Serjeant-at-Arms was walking across the space from the pool table to the bar, heading purposefully towards the brothers as they stood, totally unaware, as they stood swaying at the bar.

'You two cunts come with me.' The Serjeant-at-Arms barked his order, the brothers turned around ready to fight but relaxed as soon as they saw who they were facing. The Serjeant-at-Arms turned on his heel and headed for the Presidents card table, the brothers meekly followed.

'Uh oh,' Mamma whispered, they're in the shit now.

Sheila asked in a low voice, 'what's going to happen?'

Dave leaned over, 'pretty sure that the Prez is going to centre punch em.'

'Centre punch?'

'It means they're 'gonna lose their patches.'

The worldwide MC community had three patches on their backs, the name of the club at the top and where they came from at the bottom, in this case it was CELTIC FIST MC at the top and WEST CORK at the bottom. The centre patch was the revered club logo, a mailed fist.

For a club member to be centre punched involved the Club President ordering the centre patch to be removed and handed back to the club. It was a humiliating experience, effectively demoting the biker from a fully-fledged member, to that of a probationer. It could take years to get re-patched.

The clubhouse had gone very quiet. The blokes playing pool had stopped and were smoking their cigarettes nervously, Dave the barman was actually shaking, the last thing he needed was those two horrible bastards dropped to his probationary level, because he would be in direct competition with them if they got busted.

The club President stood up. 'Kutts.' He was referring to the bikers name for a patched leather waistcoat.

The Kennedy brothers didn't argue, they both removed their waistcoats and handed them to the Sergeant at Arms who stood with his arm out.

'Cut em off Serjeant-at-Arms.'

The Serjeant-at-Arms reached for his belt and removed a wicked looking blade from the sheath at his waist. He carefully, almost reverently, picked at the stitches and sliced the club logo from both Kutts. He handed the Mailed fist logos to his President and turned to the brothers.

'You've been centre punched, disgraced, It'll be up to a unanimous club vote as to whether, or even if, you get your patches back.' He dropped the centre punched waistcoats at the feet of the brothers, they flinched when he tapped his knife a couple of times on its sheath before tucking it safely away.

Liam was high on cocaine, pissed on alcohol, or both, because he questioned the decision. 'Was that absolutely necessary Prez?'

The President roared. 'Get out of my fucking sight you pair of cunts, you've brought my club into disrepute more than once, your fucking behaviour in England was a disgrace and was the final fucking straw, Serjeant-at-Arms escort these cunts away and make sure that they are billed for tonight's drinks.'

The Club President had spoken, his word was law

Mamma broke the chilled silence at the bar 'Fuck me Snake, what do you reckon to that?'

Snake was impassive, he was giving nothing away, the snake at his Adams apple was dancing up and down.' That shouldn't have happened now, that was club business and should have stayed in the club, no offence Mary girl, but you shouldn't have witnessed that.'

Mary quietly replied. 'Don't worry Snake, I have no idea what just happened and it's none of my business.'

'All the same,' muttered Snake, 'that was out of order in my book.'

'So what can you do about it Snake?' Asked Mamma.

'Fuck all.' Snake replied, adding, 'Probationer, get some drinks over here, and Mary, you're not drinking fucking coke all night, you said you wanted to party, well, let's fucking party!'

'Bud for me then Snake.'

And the party started.

~TWENTY SEVEN~

It took about an hour before the biker known as Hook approached Sheila. He'd obviously been busying himself somewhere else and wasn't present when the Kennedy brothers were centre punched. He stood between Snake and Sheila effectively blocking him out of any conversation.

'So girl, what's the craic?'

'The craic?' Sheila responded to his softly worded question.

Yeah, the craic. What's your story?'

'I haven't got a story, have you?'

'My story is none of your business, what you doing here girl?'

'I'm a guest of Snake, I'm enjoying a drink, that's what I'm doing here.'

'Okay, what's your name? Where you from?'

'It's Mary, I'm from Essex.' She added unnecessarily, 'that's in England.'

'Essex, huh. A brit eh? I'm not sure about you, I've had my eye on you and I've done a bit of checking.'

Sheila's heart missed a beat, she was sure that her legend was in place and she knew at some time she may be questioned, but all the same, it was unnerving. 'And the result of your enquiries showed what exactly?'

'That you check out, you seem to be who you say you are and there is an old lady with the name Grace, buried in Skibb.'

Inwardly Sheila breathed a sigh of relief, she'd passed some sort of test with one of the men she was most worried about.

'You have nothing to worry about from me. What's your name?'

'Hook.'

'I can see that, it's printed on your waistcoat. What's your real name?'

'It's Hook, that's all you need to know girl.'

'Fair enough, Hook.'

The jukebox behind the bar had started another rock number, 'Milk and Alcohol' by the band Doctor Feelgood. It wasn't the sort of music that one would dance to. Sheila would have loved to stand with her thumbs in her belt and shake her head to the music, but her legend came with knackered legs and a walking cane.

The night progressed, Mamma and another biker were smooching in the middle of the club, dancing slowly, going round and round in a little circle while Sheila and Hook were chatting away like old friends, Snake had earlier decided that three was a crowd and had wandered outside, where someone had started a barbeque. Hook told Sheila all about the reasons he joined the club, how slab had rescued him from the streets and given him some purpose in life, how the club was now his life. Sheila thought that joining an MC that edged around the law at every opportunity, was not really classed as having purpose, but she kept her thoughts to herself.

'So, where is Slab now Hook?'

'He's in prison. Dublin.'

'Wow! What did he do?'

'He's innocent.'

Of course he is thought, Sheila, aren't they all? 'Okay then, I won't pry.'

'That's for the best, prying is dangerous around here.' Hook looked sharply at Sheila when he spoke.

'I have no intention of prying Hook.' This of course, was the polar opposite of what she actually wanted to do. 'C'mon Hook, show me your bike.' She knew that bikers love showing off their machines, and it was a good excuse to get out of the clubhouse, she really wanted to get a look in the small sheds if she possibly could.

'Sure, c'mon then. Do you know anything about Harley's?'

'Not really, but listen, have you got a phone here? I need to phone my landlady and let her know that I will be back very late. She worries and of course it's a courtesy thing.

Hook walked her to the phone at the end of the bar and stood real close. Sheila dialled a Dublin number from memory, it was answered immediately and Sheila smoothly went into coded language. 'Hi there, it's Mary, I'm in Skibbereen and I'm hooked up with some pals and will be out late, see you later.'

The fact she mentioned Skibbereen meant that the call would be fixed as soon as she put the phone down, that way anybody dialling a call back would get a Skibbereen number, the actual number of her B&B and not a Dublin one. Hooking up is the clue that she was with a guy named Hook and checks would be made on that moniker, she used the word pals, if she was with friendlies she would have used the word friends. All so simple and innocent sounding.

'Right Hook, I'm all yours,' said Sheila after replacing the handset. 'Where was I? Oh yes, an ex-boyfriend rode a Kawasaki, he died whilst we were on it and, well, this cane is my perpetual reminder of that dreadful night.'

'Kawasaki huh?' Sheila thought he was going to spit, he certainly didn't look happy about having the name of a Japanese motorcycle manufacturer in his mouth. He didn't seem bothered about the dead boyfriend either.

'Each to their own Hook and anyway, it was a long time ago.'

They both walked out of the club house into the front yard. The aroma of meat of some description infiltrated the night air. A small group of club members were standing around the barbeque, drinking from beer cans and laughing at a dirty joke. Two girls were topless and dancing to nothing in particular, some shared tune in their heads perhaps, stopping for a deep kissing session when the mood took them. Three bikers and Snake stood next to them occasionally spraying beer on them. The girls seemed oblivious to the bawdy degradation. There were considerably more motorcycles here now. Sheila guessed at twenty, there were a couple of beaten up looking cars as well. It was certainly a party atmosphere.

'Here we are Mary.' They'd reached Hooks motorcycle. 'It's a 1970 FLH Shovelhead.'

'Shovelhead?' Asked Sheila, genuinely intrigued.

'Look at the side of the engine, those chrome bars going up to the cylinder head are part of the rockers, if you imagine it upside down, it looks like an old coal shovel.'

'Oh I see it that now, it looks beautiful Hook.' And it did.

The conversation was interrupted as a motorcycle started up, It appeared to be coming from one of the sheds, a moment later Liam Kennedy rode out of the shed and into the yard, he was laughing like a maniac, revving the engine, the rear wheel spinning so hard, white smoke from the tyre enveloped the rear of the machine. As the bike inched forward, the smell of burning rubber enveloped the yard.

'For fucks sake,' muttered Hook, 'where did Liam get that bike, it looks like a Triumph, he doesn't own a Triumph, none of our members do.' He strolled over to the noisy scene and pulled the ignition key from the barrel, killing the motor dead. Silence reigned.

'What the fuck do you think you're doing?' Raged an angry Liam.

'What the fuck do you think you're doing, probationer,' Hook countered.

'It's a fuckin party man, give me those keys back.'

'You aint getting shit man, and whose fucking bike is this?' Hook walked to the back of the motorcycle, 'It's got fucking Brit plates on! Where the fuck did this come from? You idiot.'

'None of your damned business Hooky boy, it's mine now and that's all you fucking need to know.' Liam was defiant in his tone, but Hook could see that he was scared and he was already in deep shit with the club, it wouldn't take much for the club President to banish him completely.

Liam kicked the Triumph's side stand down and stepped off the bike. A small crowd had gathered. Big bikers holding beer cans and they didn't look amused. The club's Serjeant-at-Arms had stepped out of the club house and the other men made way for him as he approached the bike. 'What the fuck have we got here then?' He didn't direct his question at anybody in particular, so Hook spoke up. 'Liam's nicked this Triumph from somewhere, it's on Brit plates.'

The Serjeant-at-Arms was furious. 'Liam? Well? What have you got to say for yourself?'

'It's mine bro, fuck all to do with anybody else.'

'Really?' The Serjeant-at-Arms pulled a revolver from the rear waistband of jeans, pointed it at Liam's face as the small crowd stepped back a couple of paces.

'Really? He repeated.

'No need for that bro, put the gun away, it's only a bike man. We were in England last week, I found it and we put it in the back of Patricks van.

'You were a guest at one of our brothers' party last week, In England, you shamed yourself and you shamed the club, you've been punished for that, quite lightly in my opinion.' The Serjeant-at-Arms paused for a moment as another thought came to his head. 'Did this bike come from that club in Lincolnshire? Have you stolen from a brother?' His arm was rock steady, the gun never wavered in his hand.

'No man no, it belonged to a citizen not a brother, I wouldn't do that bro, you know me, I aint a thief man.'

'You are a fucking thief Liam and this bike tells me that you're a thief.'

Liam was now visibly shaking, he knew that the Serjeant-at-Arms would have no compunction of shooting him in the face, he'd seen the man in action before he got promoted into his current position in the club hierarchy and the reason he got that promotion, apart from his 100%, proven, loyalty to the club was his complete fairness in the interpretation of the club rules and an utterly ruthless trigger finger.

'It's yours, bruv.' Liam spat on the floor as he walked away from the stolen motorcycle and the gun that was still aimed at him.

Hook stuck the key back in the ignition.

In the events that happened next, Sheila had trouble recalling the sequence on a time line, they happened so quickly.

The Serjeant-at-Arms dropped to his knees with a small red hole in the centre of his forehead, immediately followed by the retort of a rifle from the treeline one hundred yards away.

~TWENTY EIGHT~

Nina rolled over in her sleep, her arm flopped onto an empty space where Gruff had been lying, she didn't register that he was missing. At the same time in room twenty two of the Celtic Ross Hotel, Tiger had slipped away without waking Jane.

He started up the van and headed for Union Hall where he knew Gruff would be waiting for him. Sure enough, as he passed the small Bed & Breakfast, Gruff was sitting on a wall by the car-park, looking like he didn't have a care in the world. Tiger stopped the van and Gruff slipped into the front passenger seat.

'Nina asleep?' Enquired Tiger.

'Yep, what about Jane?'

'I've left her a note.'

'You old romantic.' Both men laughed as Tiger manoeuvred the van and they set off for the far side of Skibbereen.

'Did Sheila manage to get the tool bag?' Asked Tiger.

'Yes mate, it's in the SAAB.' Gruff held up a key on a leather fob. 'Stop worrying old boy, whilst you've been getting some er, sexy history lessons, some of us have been working.'

'Sexy history lessons? How old are you? Twelve?' They both laughed again. 'Jane's thinking of jacking in the teaching game.'

'Why's that mate? Is it because of you? She really likes you Tiger, she has been bending my ear about you.'

'Trying to find out if I really am single?'

'Yep.'

'I suppose you told her that I have a lot of previous bad luck with girlfriends.'

'Yep, I told her your whole life story.'

I know that you didn't and anyway I've have already told her.'

'Told her what?'

'I told her about my recent bad luck with women.'

'Bollocks you did.' Gruff paused for a second, 'really? You did? Christ mate, what did she say?'

'She didn't believe me and laughed it off. Told me to stop teasing.'

'For fucks sake! She should know Tiger, if your relationship is going to take off.'

'I know mate, but I don't know how to handle it. I'll wait until after this op and take it from there. Here we are, Sheila's lodgings. Tiger drove into the carpark of the Glencora Bed and Breakfast and killed the vehicles lights. Sheila's SAAB was parked in darkness in the furthest corner from the accommodation building. Tiger stopped the van and Gruff got out, he moved to the trunk of Sheila's car and opened it. He returned to the van a minute later with a canvas holdall and placed it in the foot-well between his feet.

'What have we got Gruff?'

Gruff leaned forward and unzipped the heavy duty zip on top of the bag. 'For you sir'. He handed Tiger a black automatic pistol.

'Nine milly, very cute, I haven't used one of these in a while.' Tiger was referring to the barrel size of the weapon, so called because it used a nine millimetre bullet. It was the standard issue British Army side arm, the Hi-Power made by Browning. 'How many mags are there? Tiger weighed the weapon in his hand as he spoke. He knew it weighed exactly 2.2 lbs or for those of a metric persuasion 2.2 kg, it had a barrel length of 4.7 inches and packed a punch in the right hands. Tiger had the right hands. The army had taught him that the maximum effective range was around 30 yards, this was for an average trained soldier, Tiger knew from experience that he was deadly accurate at 40 yards, but much preferred to be closer to his target and he always aimed for a definite kill shot. Wounding a hostile enemy was for the movies. And bad shots.

'Five mate, twelve hollow points in each.' The box magazine could accommodate thirteen rounds, but the spring inside was notoriously weak, so good owners and users of the Hi-Power never loaded to full capacity.

'Sixy rounds huh? Well if that's not enough, we won't be going home in one piece. What have you got?

Gruff produced a hand grenade and tossed it lightly from one hand to another. It was bottle green with a thick yellow band around the middle. 'The good old L2A2 mate, four for me and two for you.'

'Not like you to be greedy Gruff. No side arm then?

'Nine milly, same as you, five mags as well. Plus of course the PE4 if things go horribly wrong, or I get bored. PE4 was the plastic explosive of choice for those that couldn't get hold of the American C4 designation.

'You got any tie wraps in there?' Tiger was referring to the plastic strips that worked were used in households and mechanic's workshops for strapping stuff up. They also made fantastic handcuffs.

'Of course mate. Half a dozen each.'

'Right then, we have ourselves an army, let's go.'

Tiger reversed slowly out of the car-park and didn't turn on the headlights until he was fifty yards from the guest house. The two men kept the chatter to a minimum, Gruff was checking over the two deadly Browning Hi-Powers whilst Tiger concentrated on his driving.

'Here we go mate, this roundabout, we're going right on the R595 Cork Road, heading south. They drove in silence for ten minutes.

Tiger spoke first. 'Start looking for a small road on the left leading to Russagh Mill mate, I don't want to miss it, If we go past it we'll be too close to the target and I don't want to be fucking about doing U turns anywhere near it.'

'Roger that Tiger.'

Another couple of minutes passed, the dull yellow glow of Skibbereen was behind them now, all that lay ahead was darkness and the Lissard forest road. Tiger slowed the van down to less than 20mph.

'There old boy, slow it down.' Gruff had spotted the little sign depicting the mill, as soon as it hit the vehicles headlights.

'Nice one mate, steady as we go.' Tiger had turned onto a small metalled single track and drove very slowly until the deserted mill hove into view. He drove around the dilapidated building, checking for other vehicles. There were none. He killed the lights and the ignition.

Gruff slid out of the passenger door and opened the sliding side door of the van. It moved freely and quietly on its runners. Tiger joined him and Gruff handed him a black rucksack. 'Hold this Tiger,' he whispered, 'I'll load it up with the PE and detonators. He transferred his equipment from the canvas holdall. Tiger strapped on a holster and slotted his Hi-Power into it, Gruff had already preloaded the first magazine. He pocketed the remaining four magazines and donned a black cap comforter, the sort of head-gear the commandos preferred during WW2. It had stood the test of time.

Tiger sat in the doorway of the van and checked and tightened the laces on his black tactical boots. He whispered. 'Right mate, jump test.'

Both men jumped up and down a couple of times, they were checking for rattles of equipment, coins in a pocket, anything that could make a noise.

'Check watches.' Both men had identical chronometers, the Omega Seamaster, specifically designed for and issued to members of 22 SAS. The premier fighting Regiment of the British Army.

'Zero two thirty...Mark' Gruff pushed the small winder to the side of his watch, they would both have exactly the same time, to the second, for the rest of the night.

'It's shank's pony now Gruff, from the end of this mill road it's about five kilometres to the club house, are we good to go?'

Gruff silently closed the van door. Tiger made sure the vehicle was locked and buried the keys, one pace from the driver's door.

'Let's do this Tiger.'

Both men melted into the night.

Ten minutes later Gruff raised his hand. Both men stopped and listened. The sound of vehicle tyres hissing along on the tarmac road, coming from behind them and moving slowly. There was no light, just the sound of the tyres. Tiger and Gruff jumped into the undergrowth beside the road, twenty seconds later, the dark shapes of two vehicles slowly crawled past them and disappeared up the road.

'Tiger,' whispered Gruff, 'what the fuck was that?'

'Fuck knows mate, but we've only been on the go ten minutes and were on plan B already, and mate, that was a bloody good call, I never heard a thing man.'

'That's because you're deaf, a deaf old man, c'mon we're following those guys.'

Tiger and Gruff kept up a steady pace, following the vehicles that had just passed them. Both men now on high alert. They passed a lane to their right, which they knew led to the Celtic Fist clubhouse, five hundred yards away. They turned onto a small track to the right that ran parallel to the lane and once again Gruff raised his hand and they stopped. He dropped to one knee, Tiger did the same. Gruff shrugged off his rucksack, opened it and pulled out a set of NVG's. Night Vison Goggles. Tiger placed them over his head and turned them on. A soft whining noise indicated that they were starting up. Five seconds later he lowered the eye pieces and could now see the world through a green haze. Gruff adjusted his set, chucked on the rucksack and they were off again.

After 3 minutes of steady walking along the track, Tigers eyes had fully adjusted to the green world around him, he saw Gruff, only one yard ahead of him, turn, put his finger to his lips, point in the direction of the lane to their right and put his thumb down. Keep quiet the enemy are over there on the lane.

Tiger followed Gruff as he turned right and moved cautiously through the trees towards what he had heard or seen. He stopped again and both men dropped to one knee. It was deadly quiet. Tiger could see the vague outline of a vehicle, a Range Rover, possibly one of the vehicles that had been sneaking down the road. Tiger's goggles flared with white light for a second and he could see a man sitting in the driver's seat. The flare meant he must be smoking, a sin when on active operations. Gruff worked his way to the side of the vehicle and crouched down next to the passenger door behind the driver. Tiger tapped a couple of times on the rear window.

The driver extinguished his cigarette and was twisting around to see where the noise had come from. Tiger tapped on the window again. The driver's door slowly opened, a man's foot hit the floor followed by a handgun in a right hand. Gruff moved, his knife in his right hand flying forward and making contact with the drivers throat, the speed and impetus of the move instantly rendered the driver useless, ripping his throat out, his weapon dropped to the ground and he died as Gruff pushed his leg back into the vehicle and closed the door.

Tiger kicked the handgun into the bushes as he walked past the car, not even glancing into it, he'd seen Gruff in action many times. The second vehicle, also a Range Rover was parked slightly off the track and was empty. The guy in the first vehicle must have been the rear guard. Tiger caught up with Gruff. 'Fucking hell mate, plan C now.'

'Don't hold your breath old boy, there's plenty of letters left in the alphabet.'

In the distance the sound of a heavy rock band could be heard, it was loud and couldn't have been more that 100 yards away, Tiger and Gruff walked quietly towards the sound. The sound of a rifle opening fire stopped both men instantly. They dropped to the floor as one. Under normal circumstances a soldier would not deviate from moving forward on hearing gunfire, it was *effective* enemy gunfire that forced one to take cover. Of course Tiger and Gruff could not tell how accurate the shooter was or what direction he was shooting in, the forest deadened all the usual clues. Tiger shimmied up to Gruff. 'We need to get into the forest mate, follow the treeline. This is really crap field craft being out here.'

'Agreed, let's go.' On hands and knees they crawled back into the bushes and entered the sparsely populated forest, ahead and to the right, between the trees, they had an intermittent view of the area to the front of the clubhouse. Men and women were shouting above the sound of the music, there was a large fire, but that looked like it was a controlled bonfire. They inched towards the edge of the trees, they needed to get a bigger picture as to what was occurring. Tiger had fully expected to carry out a quiet reconnaissance at this time of the morning, perhaps a couple of drunken bikers lolling about, a chance to have a quiet undisturbed search and hook up with Sheila, but this was madness. Fucking mayhem.

~TWENTY NINE~

Hook dived at Sheila, grabbing her by the waist and they started falling, Sheila's head scudded against the fuel tank of the Triumph and they crashed into the ground.

'Stay still Mary, some feckers shooting at us.' Mary had no option other than to stay still, the blow to her head had rendered her unconscious.

The group of men that had gathered around the triumph to watch the Kennedy brothers get torn a strip by the now dead Serjeant-at-Arms had scattered, most ran back to the clubhouse, some ran for their bikes, everybody was yelling, nobody had a clue what was going on. Some of the Harleys were fired up, the big engines and loud exhausts just adding to the cacophony, the two girls kissing and dancing around the bonfire continued to gyrate, they were not at this moment of this planet.

Hook picked up the limp form of Sheila, his muscular arms soaked in sweat and dirt easily carried her weight and he made his way at speed to the relative safety of the clubhouse. He had only just got through the big wooden door when Dave, the bar tender slammed it shut and started blocking the door with a large oak plank.

'Who's still out there?' Dave asked.

'The Serjeant-at-Arms and a bunch of fuckwits,' replied Hook.

'The Serjeant-at-Arms? We can't leave him out there!'

'We fucking can, lock the doors Dave and get the keys to the armoury, I'm taking Mary to the bunks and I'll see you there.' Hook headed for the bedroom area and Dave carried out his superiors orders.

Hook laid Sheila down onto a bed, rolled her into the recovery position and strolled over to the armoury, a grand name for a little storeroom behind the bar. He passed the club President who was laying on a couch, dead to the world with drink, whilst Mamma knelt beside him, the Presidents cock in her hands, unsuccessfully trying to get an erection out him. Hook quickly glanced around the club. It looked like Dave the prospect barman and himself were the only sober fuckers in the club, he was now, de facto, in charge of this situation.

'Right Dave, it's me and fecking you lad, what we got in here anyway? Hook entered the armoury behind Dave. 'Is this it? This is fecking shite, there's people out there fecking shooting at us, fecking killing us, and we've got one fecking shotgun! Is that fecking it?' Hook was raging. 'What's the fecking point of having a fecking armoury for one fecking shot gun? Where's the rest? Where's the automatic stuff you prick?

'I don't know Hook, I've never looked in here before, it's out of bounds. It's not my fault.'

'I didn't say it was your fault, but you're the cunt prick I'm blaming, go on, feck off and polish some fecking glasses or something.'

Hook looked at the shotgun, it was ancient, double barrelled, probably nicked off a shit scared farmer as protection payment. He looked around for some ammunition and spotted a bandolier on a shelf, it contained four rounds and on closer examination Hook noticed it was birdshot. It would have been like firing cocoa pops if it actually worked at all. He grabbed the shotgun anyway, pulled the four rounds of shot from the bandolier, he pulled the top lever to one side, snapped open the barrel and held it up the shade-less lightbulb that illuminated the room. The smooth bores of both barrels were filthy, it obviously hadn't been cleaned for months, if not years. Christ knows when it was last fired. He jammed a couple of cartridges in anyway and snapped the barrels back against the breech before storming back into the bar. Dave was shouting at someone on the other side of the door.

Hook yelled. 'Who the feck are you yelling at?'

Dave replied. 'It's Liam Kennedy, he wants to come in.'

'Fuck him, that fecking door stays locked and barred, if you go near it again, I'll fecking shoot you.' Dave shuffled away from the door and headed back to the bar.

Hook took a quick look out of a window, he could see the Serjeant-at-Arms lying on his front, the back of his head was missing, the two girls were still dancing, and it was at this point that Hook realised the jukebox was on full volume. 'Shut that music off. I can't hear myself fecking think.' Dave dutifully hit the kill switch and the club fell silent.

Hook took another look out the window, he saw nothing, the hairs on the back of his neck told him, that whoever had been out there, hadn't gone away. He gripped the shotgun and used the butt to smash the glass. Nothing.

He cocked the shotgun and poked the barrel out of the window, he wanted a reaction. Nothing.

With a grimace and a Hail Mary, he pulled the triggers, the shotgun boomed, the barrels bounced to the top of the window frame and back down again. Before Hook could register his surprise that the piece of shit actually worked, a volley of automatic gunfire raked the front of the clubhouse, an almighty explosion told him that a hot round had hit a Harley fuel tank, he didn't need to look but he did. A flaming motorcycle was 30' in the air, spinning with great gollops of burning fuel spouting from the fuel tank, it smashed into the ground and exploded again, rattling the glass in the remaining windows. Hook had got his reaction, but now what?

An unknown quantity of men were in the treeline opposite the club, they had a sniper rifle and at least two automatic machine guns and they were prepared to kill. Hook had one sober probate and half a dozen pissed up unconscious club members and two shotgun cartridges full of birdshot that wouldn't trouble a cow's arse. He had no idea what these people wanted and he was fecked if he was going to go outside and ask.

~THIRTY~

Tiger had flipped up his night vision goggles, it was far too bright, the bonfire and a burning motorcycle had turned the front of the clubhouse into a chaotic daylight.

'How many attackers do you reckon Gruff?'

'I've seen seven. All armed.'

'We can take seven if we can get up behind them, what do you reckon?'

A loud bang, probably a shotgun, sounded from the clubhouse, Tiger thought he saw a barrel briefly poke out of a shattered window. 'They've got a weapon in there as well mate.' Tiger was getting worried now, a quiet night out was slowly turning into a shit storm, their plan letter was at least halfway through the alphabet and he was increasingly worried for Sheila's well-being.'

'That was birdshot Tiger, now't to worry about. Let's get behind the guys with automatic weapons, make some noise and see what they're made of.'

'Roger that mate, let's go.'

Tiger and Gruff eased back into the tree line, turned right and eased their way carefully back to where the vehicles were parked.

'Crossing the road now Tiger,'

Tiger waited until his friend was safely across. Going first was safest. If the enemy had seen the first guy cross, they wouldn't have had the time to aim a weapon and fire, but they would certainly be ready for a second person...

Tiger crouched and tensed his thigh muscles and pounced. Three fast strides and he was safely across.

'They're amateurs Tiger, a dickhead on guard in a vehicle and nobody watching the road, they'll have nobody watching their rear either, let's go.'

They cautiously moved through the forest, night vision goggles now back in position. A couple of minutes later, Gruff held up his hand and dropped to the earthy floor, Tiger stopped and dropped to one knee, Gruff motioned him forward. Tiger slid onto his belly and leopard crawled, using his elbows to propel himself forward until he was next to Gruff. He could then see what had stopped Gruff. Ten yards ahead of them, a group of men silhouetted by the fires were talking excitedly making no effort at concealment.

Gruff whispered. 'No need to kill, let's make some noise, a couple of rounds each, five seconds apart, test the water,'

'Agreed mate, I reckon they'll leg it.'

Gruff turned again to look at the men ahead of him, turned to Tiger and nodded.

BLAM! BLAM! The first two bullets flew from the Browning Hi-Powers at 350 metres a second, Tiger had aimed high, he didn't want to put rounds anywhere near the club house that was easily in range.

Two rounds was all it took, the group of armed men took off like startled rabbits, one of them yelled. 'To the vehicles.' And they were gone, as easy as that. A minute later Tiger heard one of the Range Rovers start up and with engine revving was obviously trying to do a U turn and get the hell out of dodge, the second vehicle was twenty seconds behind the first, that crew obviously needed to move a dead body from the driver's seat.

'Fuck me mate. That was easy.' Said Gruff, slowly exhaling and getting his heartbeat down. It didn't matter how highly trained you were, at the start of a firefight when the potential odds of winning are stacked against you, your heartbeat went up. It was by keeping to the marksmanship principles, of which controlling your breathing was one aspect, which stopped the heartbeat from soaring, the difference between an expert and a rank amateur.

'Nah, piece of piss mate, let's see what sort of reception we get at the club, stick a detonator in a piece of that C4 and we'll take the door off, then take it from there.'

'Roger that Tiger, give me a minute.' Gruff unshouldered the rucksack and sorted out the explosives. 'I'll stick it against the door with a ten second fuse, that'll do the trick.'

Both men cautiously made their way forward and to the side of the clubhouse. Tiger covered Gruff as he crouched down and ran quietly to the big wooden door at the front of the clubhouse and set the fuse. He then made his way to the opposite side and waited. The seconds ticked by and BOOM! The plastic explosive worked its magic.

~THIRTY ONE~

Hook was still considering his next move when he heard two shots in close succession. They were not from an automatic weapon and he didn't hear, or feel any rounds hit the side of the clubhouse. Then a shout went up, he glanced out of the shattered window once more, a group of men, still hugging the treeline were running back up the track towards the main road. Had they gone for good? Who fired the two shots? He was still pondering those questions as he walked back to the bar, when an almighty explosion rocked the clubhouse, the concussion wave hit him hard, knocking him over a table scattered with beer bottles and onto the floor. The shotgun flew across the room and landed twenty feet away.

The tables nearest the door overturned, glass smashed and the air in the whole area reeked of dust and explosive. Hook was stunned senseless. As he tried to pull himself up to his knees, somebody rammed something solid into the side of his head and said. 'Get back on the floor, do not move.' An English accent, what the fuck? Another voice, also English, 'Another one, behind the bar.' That would be Dave they'd found.

'Put your hands behind your back.' Hook hesitated. 'Do it right now you fucker.'

The Englishman had the sort of voice that commanded immediate attention, Hook put his arms behind his back and felt his wrists slam together as plastic tie wraps immobilised him. 'Stay there. Do not move.'

Hook stayed there and did not move. If these English wanted him dead, he'd be dead by now. He liked living. He heard some more doors opening and slamming shut and shouts of 'clear' as the men searched the rooms.

Fifteen minutes later, Hook was sitting on a long couch together with Dave and half a dozen semi-conscious club members, all had been immobilised with plastic ties. Tiger and Gruff were happy that there would be no hassle from that front as they figured out what to do with Sheila, who they had found unconscious, but otherwise seemingly unhurt in a bed room.

'My bikes out front Gruff, it's on its side but it looks okay, I reckon I could ride it to the van, get it secured and get back here in fifteen minutes, then we'd be good to go with Sheila. Can you handle this rabble whilst I do that mate?'

'Not a problem Tiger, if you see those Range Rovers, head back here pronto though.'

Tiger exited the clubhouse, stepping over the shattered front door. Because of the absence of a shaped charge, the best way to blow a heavy door off its hinges, the explosive had been placed on the floor, where most of the blast had gone upwards and outwards. He picked up his bike, it appeared undamaged, save for a dent in the petrol tank and that was easily fixed. He turned the ignition key, the ignition light came on and he waited a moment for the fuel in the carburettor to settle, motorcycles didn't like lying on their sides, he thumbed the starter and the big motor turned over, it fired up on the second attempt and Tiger swung his leg over the saddle, clicked it into first gear with his right boot and headed up the track towards his van.

Gruff watched his friend ride off and returned to his prisoners, wait, was there one missing? The tall skinny guy who said his name was Dave, he wasn't sat on the couch with the others.

Gruff heard a tinkle of glass behind him, somebody has stood in some glass, he threw himself sideways and rolled onto the floor, just as both barrels of a shotgun let rip scattering the bar with birdshot. As Gruff quickly picked himself he grabbed a spoon that was lying on the floor amongst some debris. Dave was standing over him with a look of puzzlement on his face, how could he possibly have missed? Gruff launched himself at Dave, the handle of the spoon entered Dave's left nostril and continued upward to his brain, shutting off the start of his scream of terror, a quick twist to cause maximum damage and Dave started dropping. Gruff pulled out the snot and blood covered piece of cutlery and rammed into Dave's exposed throat, tearing it to the side, bright red arterial blood spouted out and sprayed across the room as his body slumped to the floor, thus guaranteeing that Dave wouldn't be bothering him, or anybody else again.

Hook was stunned. He'd seen Dave sneak up behind the Englishman with the shotgun, he couldn't miss. But the guy was super-fast, Hook had never seen anything like it and now, four seconds later, Dave was dead. Unbelievable.

'Right you fuckers, I don't want any more nonsense, just sit still and this will all be a dream real soon.' Gruff was really only speaking to the big biker that he'd dragged along the floor to his present position, the others were still lolling about in a drunken state.

'He added. 'Is there a kettle in this shit hole, don't know about you, but I'm parched.'

'Behind the bar.' Hook replied, adding. 'There's a coffee machine.'

Gruff made his way to the bar and made himself a brew. He sat on one of the bar stools where he could keep an eye on the captives, especially the one that had just spoken, and the gaping hole that was once a front door, and waited.

Tiger reached his van in four minutes. The vehicle keys were exactly where he'd left them, under a light coating of soil near the driver's door. He opened up the rear doors and pulled out an alloy ramp. Within two minutes his bike was securely strapped down. 'That isn't going anywhere.'

he said to himself.' Quietly closing the back doors, he eased himself into the driver's seat, started the engine and left the mill.

Five minutes later, he was driving carefully down the track to the clubhouse, there was a Range Rover parked, with no lights, close to where it was parked earlier on. Tiger placed his Hi-Power on his lap and drove slowly past the vehicle, it appeared empty. As he reached the clearing he noted that the bonfire was still going but the motorcycle fire had gone out, more importantly he saw four men, two either side of the clubhouse doorway, all four had weapons drawn. They looked as if they were ready to storm the building.

Tiger turned on the headlight switch and flicked them onto high beam, before setting the handbrake and exiting the van at speed. The four men had no time to react, eight shots, four men down, each killed with the infamous 'double tap' as taught in Herford, headquarters of the 22nd Special Air Services. From the corner of his eye he saw Gruff at the corner of the building, he'd obviously heard them coming and was going to deal with them on his own.

Gruff holstered his Hi-Power and walked towards his friend. 'Fuck me that was good timing old boy, nice shooting as well.' It wasn't natural for Gruff to dish out the compliments, but on this occasion he reckoned it warranted it.

'Cheers mate. Apart from these clowns sneaking about, any other drama's whilst I was gone?'

'Not really Tiger, some twat got a bit uppity with a shotgun, but I dealt with him.'

'Right mate, let's get Sheila and fuck off, I know the Garda are a lazy bunch, but it's been a bit noisy around here of late, one of them might get a bit nosey.'

Between them the carried Sheila out to the van. She began to stir when she breathed in fresh air and mumbled something under her breath. She was coming round. By the time she was wedged against Gruff in the front seat her breathing was returning to normal and she opened her eyes.

'What, wait, what's happening?' She looked at Tiger who had started the van and was in the process of reversing away from the clubhouse.

'Gruff will explain I need to get us out of here.'

They headed for Sheila's B&B as Gruff tried to explain to a dazed Sheila what had been happening. At the B&B Tiger asked for Sheila's keys and grabbed her overnight bag, Gruff hopped out of the van and drove Sheila's car to his bed and breakfast, where he could update Nina and help her pack away all the radio telephone equipment, that wouldn't be needed again for a couple of days.

Sheila was wide awake now. They were not far from his hotel. Tiger glanced at his watch. 07.00hrs. 'Our hotel kitchen will be open now, let's have breakfast.'

'Sounds great Tiger, for some reason I'm famished.' They both tried to laugh.

Tiger pulled into the carpark of the Celtic Ross Hotel and they made their way to the restaurant. Sheila ordered a cup of tea, Tiger popped upstairs to his room to find Jane still sleeping. He stripped off and took a shower, the memory of what had occurred there not twelve hours earlier was still fresh in his mind. At that moment he wanted nothing else, but to have and to hold Jane next to him. He couldn't leave Sheila alone downstairs though. He finished his shower, wrapped a soft white towel around his waist, entered the bedroom again, leaned over and kissed Jane's forehead.

Jane's eyes open and with a voice still husky from sleep said. 'Morning Tiger, You're up early, come back to bed.'

'I'd love to darling, but come on, we need to get downstairs, there has been, er, a development.'

'Development? What's happened?' Jane was awake now and sat up in bed.

'I'll explain over breakfast.' Tiger said, as he hurriedly dressed in blue jeans and white T shirt.

'Okay Tiger, is everything okay?'

'Aye sweetheart, it's fine, c'mon now, breakfast, I'll see you down there.'

Tiger left Jane to dress, as he went downstairs and back into the restaurant, he sat opposite Sheila and ordered strong coffee.

'Well that was quite a night Tiger.'

'That's one way of looking at it I suppose,' answered Tiger, adding, 'I don't intend to tell Jane the whole story though, it might freak her out.'

'Well that's up to you Tiger, but from what I've seen of Jane, she's a tough cookie, a lot tougher than perhaps you realise.'

'Aye, you may be right...'

'I *am* right, Tiger, but it's your choice, don't let your reluctance come back and bite you on your tight little arse.'

'Wow, Mrs Brown, a bollocking and a compliment in the one sentence. Go you!'

'Shut up and drink your coffee, here she comes now.'

Jane joined them at the table, fresh from the shower she looked radiant. The immaculately dressed waiter approached them. 'Good morning, are we ready to order breakfast?'

Jane was dying to ask Tiger about this latest development of which he had spoken, Sheila had that look about her, she obviously knew and for some unfathomable reason this irked her, she curtly ordered toast and English breakfast tea. Tiger had the full Irish fry up and Sheila opted for the porridge. The waiter scribbled in his pad and returned to the kitchen.

'You've dyed your hair Sheila and if I'm honest you're dressed as a tart and what's that smell?' Jane was on the attack.

Before anybody could answer, she turned to Tiger.

'Well? What's the story Tiger? How can you know of any 'development,' she waggled her fingers beside her head as if miming a quote as she spoke. 'You've been in bed all night, with me, and what about you Sheila? Do you know what's happened?'

'Well, not the whole story...' She stole a glance at Tiger, the subtle movement of her head wasn't missed by Jane.

'Well, I somehow feel the odd one out here Tiger, what on earth is going on?' Jane was getting angry. Tiger took a deep breath and dived straight in.

'I wasn't sleeping next to you all night Jane,' he was watching her face intently, he would change the tone of the nights events, depending on her reactions and at the moment her mouth was open in astonishment. He continued. 'Sheila started the operation by going undercover, getting access to the Celtic Bikers clubhouse, that's why she is dressed like that and the smell, well that's probably sweat and explosive residue.'

Jane's jaw dropped further, her eyes the size of plates. 'Explosives?'

'Jane, I slipped out last night and met Gruff. Sheila was tasked with keeping the bikers occupied and keep an eye out for my bike then report back to Nina when she could. Gruff and I were on what is known as a CTR, a close target reconnaissance, mapping out the outbuildings, checking on ow many bikers were there so we could formulate a proper plan later.'

Jane was utterly confused. You left me in the night? Met Gruff? Explosives?'

Tiger looked at Sheila who nodded, so he continued. 'Aye, explosives, the night was interrupted by some men with guns who had some sort of beef with the bikers, we found ourselves in the wrong place at the wrong time.' Tiger loaded up his fried bread with baked beans and took a large mouthful. Sheila continued.

'These men started shooting as us. One of the bikers grabbed my to drag me out of the line of fire and I cracked my head on Tigers motorcycle...'

'Your head hit my fuel tank, there's a big dent in it,' interrupted Tiger.

'Well yes, maybe so Tiger, it knocked me unconscious, I don't know anything else, I woke up in Tigers van with Gruff supporting me.'

'Jeezus Tiger!' Jane's look of amazement was slowly turning to anger. 'I thought you wanted my help on this, why am I even here? What was the bloody point Tiger? You have your mate Gruff, his mate Nina and this woman, the bloody mysterious Mrs Brown. Did you actually need me or was I just your bit of comfort on the side?'

'Jane, darling keep your voice down, it was nothing like that we went for a look see, we had no idea that it would turn out like this, honestly, it was a shit storm, we were worried for Sheila and acted accordingly.'

Jane still looked far from pleased and Tiger continued.

Somebody was shooting from the clubhouse, we chased the unknown men off and blew the clubhouse door off in order to find Sheila, and here she is.'

'You sneaked out without telling me.'

'I did Jane, I didn't want you to worry, I was only supposed to be gone a couple of hours...'

'You bloody sneaked out without telling me.'

'I didn't want to worry you darling.'

'I'm not bloody twelve years old Tiger, you should have told me.'

'What would you have done if I'd told you?'

'I don't know Tiger. Go with you, I don't know.'

'I'm sorry Jane, I should have told you.'

'Correct answer Tiger. Where's your bloody motorcycle?'

'In the van, in the carpark.'

'Really? Well that's alright then. Are we going home now?

Tiger and Sheila looked at each other, Tiger tried to hide his face behind his coffee cup.

'Well? Jane wanted an answer.

Sheila provided it.

'Not yet Jane, there is something I have to do and Tiger has offered to help me.'

'Okay, what is it? Find another motorcycle? Jane was very good at sarcasm.

'Not exactly Jane. We're going to kidnap somebody.'

~THIRTY TWO~

Back at the clubhouse, Hook sat quietly. He'd been doing that for ten minutes. Trying to recollect the events of the night, none of it made any sense. There was a complete silence and Hook decided whatever it was that had happened that evening, it was over now. He made efforts to release himself. He couldn't reach the knife on his belt, he needed another one. Dave had one.

He walked cautiously over the glass strewn floor towards Dave's inert body. It was a mess. He couldn't believe the speed and efficiency that the English bastard had dispatched him. He had no tears for Dave, the bloke was an idiot, he could have been a hero, he had the chance, but now he's dead, death by spoon, the fecking idiot.

Hook knelt down on the blood soaked carpet and shuffled his way around so that he could draw Dave's knife from its scabbard, he made his way back to the couch, turned around and with some difficulty wedged the knife handle, up to its hilt in a small gap between the seats, and began sawing through the plastic tie wraps. It took a couple of frustrating minutes and he'd cut himself at least three times on the sharp blade. But he was free.

He ventured carefully outside, fecking hell it was a war zone, four dead men near the door, the flies had already started buzzing in swarms around them, the dead Serjeant-at-Arms was still there, a burnt out Harley Davidson on its side, hardly recognisable as a motorcycle, let alone the beautiful machine it once was. Two girls on the far side of the bonfire were lying on the floor. Hook approached the nearest one and gave her a poke with his boot. She stirred and moaned. Sleeping. He turned and made his way back to the clubhouse and noticed the Brits Triumph was missing. No! Surely not, all this carnage to get a motorcycle back? No, one of the lads must have ridden it off as the first shots were fired. One of the Kennedy brothers probably. Those two feckers won't be welcome back. Not now.

His attention turned to the dead men by the door, he recognised one of them. Sean bloody Keally. He was the West Cork cell commander of the IRA, the Irish Republican Army. Contrary to what Army command in Belfast said, the IRA operated illegally from safe houses in the Republic. Hook knew this as fact because Sean Keally was his superior officer and the principle enforcer, the hit man.

What the actual feck was going on? The only reason the IRA would be visiting the clubhouse would be to see him. That move however, would be unprecedented. Nobody outside his cell should know anybody else in one. That is how it worked. If the IRA was infiltrated, and it often was, the intruder would only know about four or five people, nobody else. That's why it worked. Nothing was making sense.

He entered the clubhouse. He walked to the phone behind the bar, he should call this in. Let Belfast know, then call those useless cunts the Garda, the Irish Police. He made the two calls and poured himself a JD and coke. Then he waited.

~THIRTY THREE~

'Kidnap? God it never stops, who are you people? Jane was perplexed and angry. Tiger should be confiding in her, why all these secrets?

Tiger spoke up. 'Jane, Sheila works for the Government, she catches the bad guys and she's very good at it,'

'And Gruff?'

'I honestly do not know who Gruff works for, or Nina. They're in an organisation that doesn't really exist, totally deniable. I don't ask him because he wouldn't be allowed to tell me, but they're the good guys as well.'

'And you Tiger? What about you?'

'I'm a retired soldier Jane and I sometimes do some freelance work.

'Have you killed anybody?'

'I was a soldier Jane.'

'Answer the bloody question Tiger, I'm tired of being in the dark.'

'Yes, yes I have.'

'Recently?'

'Yes'

'For God's sake, what is really going on here?

'I don't know what you mean Jane, do you mean generally, or something specific?'

'I'm going to my room, to pack, to think.' Jane left the table and headed for reception and the lifts to the upper rooms. Tiger looked at Sheila for a full minute, gauging her, before he finally spoke.

'Well that went well Sheila. She's going to leave me now.'

'She needs time to think Tiger, trust me, she wasn't as angry as she is making out.'

'Well she sounded pretty pissed off to me.'

'You're a bloke Tiger, you're missing the signs. Can I use your room? I stink and I could use a shower.'

'Of course you can, I'm having another coffee, here's my room key.' He slid his key across the table and caught the waiter's eye and mimed another coffee as Sheila excused herself and also left the table.

Outside room twenty two, Sheila paused before knocking, she really needed a shower, but she also needed to speak, woman to woman with Jane, she wanted to get her story straight and not frighten the girl. She knocked firmly, Jane answered almost immediately.

'Oh, it's you.'

'Who were you expecting? That would knock?

'Come in Sheila or whatever your name is, I presume you'd like to use the shower and change?'

'That would be nice Jane.' Jane stood aside and Sheila entered her room, the door closed quietly behind her, Jane leaned back on it and eyed Sheila warily as she began to undress.

'He loves you, you must know that?' Sheila kicked off the conversation.

'I'm not sure what I know.'

'Trust me, he does.'

'Trust you Sheila? Trust you? I don't even know your name for God's sake.'

'My name is Sheila, everybody knows me as Sheila, Sheila is my name.'

Jane was still unsure, watching Sheila's every move. Sheila walked naked over to the bathroom, completely unabashed. She stopped before she went in.

'Jane, if you are waiting for me to get in the shower to check my purse, I'll save you the trouble of searching for it, it's in the side pocket of my overnight bag.' Sheila stepped into the bathroom and closed the door.

Jane sat on the edge of the bed. She was in two minds whether to look in Sheila's purse for some sort of identification. How did Sheila even know that's what she was thinking? She's a Government agent, that's why, she's trained for this sort of thing. Of course any i/d would be in the name of Sheila Brown. All these thoughts were flashing through her mind. She wanted Tiger, correct that, she needed Tiger. He was downstairs drinking coffee on his own, He'd probably had a hell of a night, he may even be physically hurt and she hadn't bothered to ask. Some girlfriend. Shit, shit, shit.

Tiger was on his third coffee and he too was talking to himself. He shouldn't have taken Sheila's advice and come completely clean, or maybe it was right to do so, bloody hell, he'd never been in this situation before. Jane was upstairs, God alone knows what Sheila is telling her, she probably thinks I'm a monster now. She's definitely up there confused and hurting. Shit, shit, shit.

Back with Gruff and Nina in Union Hall, no such complicated conversations were going on.

'So how did it work out Gruff?'

'We got Tigers bike back a day or two earlier than expected and we pulled Sheila out of a shit situation. She's with Tiger at the Celtic Ross, I've got her car.'

'Any collateral damage?

'Yep, some.'

'Anything that could blow back to us?'

'Nope.'

'Sweet. Let's get showered and packed and head out to the Celtic Ross, it's going to happy families there.'

Gruff held his tongue, he wasn't so sure. He stripped off, walked into the small shower and Nina followed, with a huge grin on her face.

They checked out of the B&B in Union Hall, jumped in the SAAB and as Gruff turned on the ignition he turned to look at Nina. 'So, what was all that about in the shower Nina?'

'What shower? Drive the bloody car big boy.' They both laughed, easy in each other's company.

~THIRTY FOUR~

Things were not going so easy for Hook at the Celtic Fist clubhouse, the Garda were swarming all over the place asking question after question, he would have to admit he had fired the poxy shotgun at some stage, the detectives were taking gunshot residue swabs. He was the only club member that was coherent, or alive, that could help sort out the mess, but he really didn't have a clue what had happened last night. He never mentioned that he recognised one of the dead men by the front door, he said that he was tied up in one of the bedrooms and knocked unconscious, but other than that, he couldn't help.

A uniformed Garda handcuffed him, and placed him in the back of a patrol car, he was told that he'd be driven to Skibbereen barracks, where he would get a shower, something to eat and face some more questions. He politely asked what the charge was and was told that the Garda detectives are still compiling the list, it was a long list and murder was at the top of it. He asked about his prized motorcycle, who was going to look after it? Where would it be taken to? The Garda didn't give a toss. 'Mind yer fingers,' as the uniform slammed the car door.

Hook was still sat in the back of the Police car, his wrists were numb from the handcuffs, not because the Garda that put them on was overzealous, it was because it was the second time that night he'd had his hands cuffed behind his back. He heard an excited shout from behind the car and a minute later, the cop that had placed him into the vehicle sat heavily in the driver's seat. 'We found another body, up the track a bit, a male, what do you know about that one?'

'I have no idea what you're talking about, what body? Who is it? A club member? How did he die?'

'We'll be asking the questions, you hear? Sit back and enjoy the ride son.'

Hook's mind was racing, he was desperately trying to sort out the jigsaw but nothing made any sense. Okay, he could understand the four IRA guys, they were probably after him, but feck knows why, and who killed them? Who was the dead guy up the track? But more importantly, who were the two Brit bastards? The quietly spoken one and the professional killer? Were they an SAS kill team? Surely not here in the Republic. Try as he might, he had no answers and even if he had, he wouldn't be spilling his guts to the Garda.

There were a couple of coincidences to ponder though, the Brit bird, Mary, with a dead mother buried in Skibb and of course the Brit Triumph motorcycle, stolen from the UK by those clowns, the Kennedy brothers. There had to be a connection. Hook didn't believe in coincidences, not when the outcome was seven dead bodies. He spent the remainder of the journey deep in thought.

~THIRTY FIVE~

Tiger tentatively opened room twenty two at the Celtic Ross Hotel, Jane was sat on the edge of the bed, Sheila was sat in the room's only chair opposite her, they'd obviously been talking and probably about him, he thought. Both women looked up at him as entered, Jane had been crying, her scarred mascara melted his heart.

He sat on the bed next to Jane and put his arm around her back, she rested her head on his shoulder. Stage one complete, thought Tiger, smiling to himself. Thirty nine stages left.

'Tiger?'

'Yes Jane.'

'We need to talk.'

'Agreed. Who starts?'

'I do. The last hour has been a rollercoaster of emotions for me, some good, some bad, but mostly bad.'

'Bad?' Enquired Tiger.

'Shut up Tiger. Just listen.' Sheila scolded Tiger into silence.

'Yes bad.' Jane continued, 'I thought I was part of this operation, not in a key role, granted, but involved all the same, yet on the first night, off you pop with Gruff, ghosts in the night, sneaking about and causing mayhem and then stroll back into out bedroom without a care in the world, quick shower and down for breakfast like it's all in a nights work. Well this isn't going to work is it? No. Don't answer that, it's a rhetorical question.' Jane paused and wiped a blob of mascara from a wounded eye, 'this, us, it's not going to work, unless,' She paused again, 'unless you involve me, trust me.'

Tiger remained silent.

'Fucks sake Tiger, it's your turn so say something.' Sheila was once again chastising him.

Tiger had spent years in the British army, he'd spent a large part of his service to his country in the 22nd Special Air Service, based in Hereford, he'd fought in hand to hand battles with Arabs in Dhofar in the Omani desert, he'd called in airstrikes, jet fighters with 500lb bombs, dropping them within 100 yards of his hidden position, a situation known as 'Danger Close', a situation that will definitely destroy an enemy and most probably kill the person ordering the airstrike.

He'd carried out dozens of covert operations for the Government of the day, his name was whispered in Whitehall, London, the real decision making headquarters of Government. He was a master military tactician, he could field strip weapons from a dozen different countries armouries, in the dark, in seconds, and here he was, sat next to the woman he loved and rendered speechless. He gave it a go anyway.

'Jane, oh Jane, how can I make you understand? I care for you, my heart bursts when I see you but the work I sometimes do is dangerous, I don't want to see you harmed. Women who stick around with me often end up dead.'

'I thought you were joking about that.' Jane turned to look at him.

'Joking about what?'

'Your ex-girlfriends dying.'

'I wasn't joking Jane, it makes me sick just thinking about it.'

Jane twisted on the bed and placed his head in her hands, holding his face and looking deep into his eyes. 'Oh Tiger, my wonderful Tiger, I had no idea, but listen, I have a plan.

'Plan? Is this your plan or Sheila's plan?'

'It's my plan baby and Sheila agrees with it.'

Tiger moved his head to one side and looked directly at Sheila, she nodded subtlety.

'Okay Jane. What's this plan?'

'You live on your own, you don't have a secretary and you don't have somebody to sort out your accounts, somebody to keep a watch on your diary, someone to watch your home when you're away. You have none of these things, so I presume that you are doing it yourself?'

'Are you offering your services as my secretary?'

'Yes I am Tiger. Your secretary, your accountant, your general dogsbody, keeping the books and looking after your back when you're away to places I am not allowed to go.'

Tiger was astonished. He was expecting a massive backlash, he expected that Jane was going to give him the old heave-ho, but no! She actually wanted to hang around. With him!

'I don't know what to say Jane, I wasn't expecting this, I really wasn't.'

'Bloody hell, what you are trying to say Tiger, is yes. Yes Jane that is a good plan.'

'Okay.' Tiger paused for a second, his mind reeling, looking for a downside and finding none he continued, 'okay, that's a plan, a good one Jane.'

'Great,' replied Jane looking relieved, 'I'm glad we got that sorted. Now, Sheila what's the story with this kidnapping?'

~THIRTY SIX~

Gruff parked Sheila's SAAB in a slot next to Tiger's van in the Celtic Ross carpark and turned off the engine. He turned to look at Nina who appeared to be sleeping.

'Are you asleep girl?'

'Yes.'

'Well we're here.'

'Define here.'

'The Celtic Ross Hotel in Rosscarbery.'

'Great and what's here?'

'Well there's Tiger and Jane and Sheila.'

'Is that it Gruff?'

'Okay, there's a shower...'

'Mmmmm.'

'And food.'

'Beautiful, I'm starving lets go.' Nina was out of the car and striding towards the hotel entrance before Gruff managed to get from behind the steering wheel.

"Hey up Nina, wait for me!'

They entered the hotel together and approached the receptionist and the young girl behind the counter informed them that Mr and Mrs Smith were in in room twenty two. They used the lift to get to the second floor and made their way to Tigers room.

Sheila had commandeered the only chair in the room, Nina joined Tiger and Jane on the bed while Gruff stood, leaning against the door frame to the bathroom. Tiger spoke first.

'Right, that didn't go as planned, but as we know, any plan is scuppered with first contact with an enemy.'

'Amen to that,' muttered Gruff with a wry smile.

Tiger continued. 'So, I have got my bike back which should mean that its mission accomplished, however, Sheila has thrown a spanner in the works and I believe that something else has cropped up that needs our attention, so I'll hand you over to Sheila.'

'Thank you Tiger, it was a hell of a night, but I am glad you got your bike back. By the way, did you notice the dent in the fuel tank?' Tiger nodded and Sheila continued, 'well I think you'll find that it's exactly the shape of my head!'

'What? What the hell happened?' Jane interrupted, looking alarmed. Tiger nudged her leg with his knee, looked at her and frowned.

'I'm just asking Tiger...' Jane whispered. Sheila continued.

'Before this op started, I had a word with a colleague in our Dublin office. You know how it works, protocols, professional courtesies, let them know that we are on their turf, that sort of thing. Anyway, I was asked to keep an eye out for a certain Mr Dermot Callan, a biker with the Celtic Fist MC and goes by the nom de guerre 'Hook.' Well, I met up with Mr Callan last night and in fact, I believe Mr Callan may have saved my life.'

'Why would your people be interested in the fellow? Asked Gruff, adding. 'What did he look like? Give us a description Sheila.'

'He's short, good looking, aged twenty eight, or thereabouts and doesn't fit the biker profile at all, in fact he looks out of place among all the beards and tattoos.'

'I met him as well,' replied Gruff, 'in fact I tied him up, he wasn't very happy about that. So who is this bloke and why are your people interested in him?'

'All I know,' answered Sheila, 'is that this character is an Irish Republican Army informant but he's gone rogue. My colleague's believe that he is now giving information to the IRA about us, not the other way around.'

'For fucks sake Sheila.' Tiger interjected, looking very angry. 'We've got ourselves mixed up with the Provo's? That's bad news because those guys are not the ones to be messing around with...'

'Unless we have guns.' Added Gruff.

'Which we have,' replied Tiger, 'but all the same, their Dad is a whole lot bigger that our Dad, and if I am correct in assuming that the trail of destruction that we left behind last night involved the IRA, then guaranteed they will not let this lie. They lost five men last night, so that was probably the complete West Cork cell. Fuck me, this is bad news.'

'We have an answer.' Said Sheila.

'It had better be the best bloody answer I've heard for a while Sheila, seriously, I had no idea those murderous bastards were involved.'

'We need to kidnap Mr Callan.'

The room fell silent whilst the rest of the group digested this. This was the second time that Sheila had mentioned kidnap that morning, but now the enormity of the undertaking was beginning to sink in.

'Do we have support from your people?' Asked Nina, who had remained quiet up to that point.

'Yes, but it's limited.'

'Deniable?' This from Gruff, who knew the answer before Sheila confirmed it.

'Of course, these things always are.'

'Where is this Mr Callan right now Sheila?' Asked Tiger.

'I'm not sure, I suspect he is in custody with the Gardaí, charged with multiple offences relating to last night's escapade at the Celtic Fist clubhouse. If he is in custody, we can spring him, the security at

Skibbereen barracks is pitiful and as they have no idea who they really have, he'll be treated as an ODC.'

'ODC?' Enquired Jane.

'Ordinary Decent Criminal, the rather affectionate name given to prisoners that are not rapists or terrorists.'

'Charming,' added Jane, who was learning very quickly the jargon of this strange and dangerous new world she had entered.

'The prison population use the term, not the authorities,' Sheila continued, 'it makes them, feel a little superior to the really bad boys.'

'I'll need to make a call, but I am pretty sure he's banged up in Skibbereen nick.'

'That's all well and good,' said Gruff, 'and if he's in there, how do you plan to get him out? I'm presuming he doesn't want to be with your people so he won't be coming quietly and the Gardaí are hardly likely to hand him over to us are they?'

'Firstly, you are correct. He doesn't want to be with our people, there are consequences for leaking our secrets, especially to the criminal fraternity. Secondly, the Gardaí will not hand him over to us, so we are going to break in and grab him. Nina, the barracks plan if you please.'

Nina reached into her handbag, had a brief rummage about, produced a folded sheet of paper and handed it to Sheila. She unfolded it and flattened it out on the table behind her.

'Thank you Nina, now gather round folks, you will need to see this and memorise it. It's the only copy.'

The small group dutifully gathered around the table. They were looking at a plan of the Gardaí barracks in Skibbereen. Basically it was just a Police Station, the Irish republic had Guards to satisfy their uniformed security, not coppers and they worked from a barracks. Sheila started the briefing.

'As you can see, there is a gated front entrance and high stone walls all the way round. Within the walls are four buildings. The armoury just inside the front gate to the left, the patrol room is opposite, that is emptied after a briefing and the Guards go to work. At the southern corner is an admin block, this is where the civilians work and the gaol house is opposite that. Unfortunately we have no plans for the gaol house because we just didn't have the time to obtain them.'

'It's the gaol house we are interested in and there is no floor plan?' Tiger was incredulous. 'The grab team is going in there blind then?'

'Sorry, said Sheila, the buildings are owned by the local council, this is an ad hoc operation, we haven't got time to fill in the forms and apply to them for a copy of a floor plan to a restricted building. That's how it is.'

'So what have we got Sheila?' Asked Gruff.

'During the working week there will be forty people in the barracks, mostly admin staff. After 18.00 hrs the civilian staff will have gone home leaving around twelve uniformed personnel. At 22.00 hrs this is reduced to six Guards. Four of them will be on vehicle patrol in and around Skibbereen. This leaves just the two, the gaoler and the custody Sergeant. It is run on pretty much the same format as the British. The custody Sergeant is responsible for booking in prisoners and their welfare before they go to court. The current Sergeant at Skibbereen is nearing retirement. He is overweight and will not put up a fight. The gaoler is taken from the shift, so could be one of the five night duty Guards. We do not know which one will be on duty tonight, it may even be one of the women, there are two of them.'

'Okay, that's good intelligence,' replied Tiger. 'So how are we going to get in?'

'Well firstly Tiger I need to know who wants to do this. The original plan was to get your bike back, we've done that, this is a new scenario. I'm doing this with or without your help but to be honest, I'd like your help.'

The room was quiet for a moment.

'I'm in,' said Jane who had said nothing since the start of Sheila's briefing.

'Me too,' seconded Tiger.

'Not gonna miss this one Sheila.' Gruff smiled and looked at Tiger. 'This will bring back some memories mate.'

'Sure will old boy, although we probably won't have to exert ourselves on this one!'

'Famous last words Tiger.' Both men laughed.

~THIRTY SEVEN~

Back at Skibbereen barracks, Hook had been hauled unceremoniously from the back of the patrol car. He still hadn't figured out what the hell had happened last night. One of the Guards held his arm and led him though the security door and into the detention building. A uniformed Sergeant sat behind a slightly raised desk. The Guard spoke to him.

'Sergeant, after reports of gunfire were heard in the vicinity of the Celtic Fist clubhouse, we attended that property and walked into mayhem. This, er, gentleman, identified himself as Hook Callan. He was the only sober person in the building and I have reason to believe that he has committed multiple offences. He was arrested on suspicion of handling a shotgun, a section four weapon under the firearms act of 1964. This weapon has been seized and is devoid of a makers name and serial number. Detectives are at the scene now and there will be confirmation of other offences within the hour. Detective Sergeant Bradley wants to interview him about his role at the clubhouse last night.'

Right then Callan, you heard what the Officer said, I believe that the arrest is lawful and I am detaining you for further questioning, do you have anything to say?'

Hook remained silent and glared at the custody Sergeant.

'I'll put down no comment on the arrest sheet then, empty your pockets lad, don't be clever because you will be searched.'

The arresting Guard watched as his prisoner emptied his pockets onto the counter, where the custody Sergeant placed them in a clear plastic evidence bag and made a note of each item in the arrest ledger. Cigarette packet with six cigarettes, blue disposable lighter, three boiled sweet covered in fluff and 20 pence slot machine token.

'Is this it lad? No wallet? No money? No identification?'

Hook said nothing. He wasn't being truculent, The Celtic Fist club rules would not allow him to speak to a law enforcement Officer under any circumstances. If he uttered a single word he could lose his Celtic Fist patch and be ejected from the club as a person of bad standing. The club were very clear on this point.

'I need to take your Kutt lad.'

Hook stiffened. The only person that could tell him to take his beloved club waistcoat off was his club President. Other bike clubs would seek to remove his Kutt as a trophy, this was seen as a massive sign of weakness, a member of an MC and all MC's around the world had the same strict rule, they would, fight, to the death if necessary, in order to stop their club colours being removed.

One of the Guards removed his baton and stepped towards the prisoner knowing that there would be resistance, but after thirty seconds of pulling and shoving Hook relaxed and let him take it. He'd made his point.

'Search him Officer.'

The Guard patted him down with a quick efficiency and nodded at the Sergeant.

'Thank you, cell two please, shoes to stay outside the cell.'

Hook was marched towards the rear of the detention centre where a second Guard opened a series of steel barred gates and steered in him into a cell.

'Shoes.' It was an order, not an enquiry.

Hook bent down and unbuckled his boots, straightened up, stepped out of them and walked into the cell. It slammed shut behind him. It was basic accommodation. The briefest of glances saw a wooden bed with a thin, grotty looking paillasse as a mattress. No pillow. A steel toilet with no lid, bolted to the floor behind a low brick wall. Zero privacy.

This wasn't the first time he'd seen the inside of a cell and he doubted that it'd be the last, obviously if he had a choice he'd rather be elsewhere, but he wasn't uncomfortable with the situation he now found himself in. He stretched out on the bed, yawned and began to gather his thoughts once more.

~THIRTY EIGHT~

'Distraction could work,' offered Gruff.

'So would plastic explosive.' countered Tiger.

'Now now boys,' chided Nina, 'although a distraction would be good, what have you got in mind Gruff?'

'A simple knock on the door would be a start,' said Gruff, thinking on his feet. 'Tiger and I get over the wall and into the barracks and wait until the gaoler comes to the gate and jump him from the shadows.'

'I'm good with that,' replied Tiger, 'who's going to knock?'

'I'll do that Tiger,' said 'Sheila, 'I want to be on the ground when you get our man, positively identify him. I don't want you dragging out some poor paddy that's been temporarily locked up in the drunk tank. '

'Fine,' said Gruff, 'we only want to do this once.'

'How high are the walls?' Enquired Jane.

'Good question Jane,' said Sheila. 'The barracks were built for the British Army in the 1920's, the standard height back then was twelve feet and we're going to go with that until I carry out a quick recce.'

'We can deal with twelve feet,' said Tiger. 'My hire van is eight feet so if I park close enough to the wall, we'll get in easy.'

'Won't that look suspicious?' Questioned Jane. She really wanted to nail down the details.

'It's not Wormwood Scrubs in London,' replied Gruff, it's a backwater Police Station, we'll be fine.'

'I'll be scanning the Police radio transmissions from the back of the van,' interrupted Nina, 'If there is any response I'll let you know soon enough.'

'We are going in armed aren't we?' Asked Gruff.

'Aye,' replied Tiger, glancing at Jane who refused to make eye contact with him. 'We will not be shooting anybody, but this Hook character is in the IRA, he'll respect the fact he's being taken by armed men and won't do anything stupid.'

'Agreed,' said Gruff.

'I'm going on a recce this afternoon,' said Sheila. 'I'll be going into the barracks on a pretext, report a missing dog or something equally innocuous. If you want to join me Jane, you're more than welcome.'

'I'm not sure,' replied Jane, 'but I suppose it's better than hanging around here.'

'That's settled then,' replied Sheila.

'Not quite,' said Tiger. 'What's going to happen after we snatch our target and chuck him in the van?'

'You'll drive him to Clonakilty it's a 20 minute drive, past here and towards Cork City. You drove around the town on your way here. I'll be in my car, just follow me.'

'Er that's not what I meant Sheila. What's going to happen to him?'

'You don't need to know that Tiger, you know the score and it's well above your pay grade.'

'Fair enough Sheila, but if this Callan fellow is the big fish that you reckon he is, will the IRA know that he's currently locked up?'

'I can't answer that Tiger. There might be a Guard that sympathises with the cause, so if any of them recognise Mister Dermot Callan, I am sure they'll know who to call. The IRA have extremely good contacts the world over, this is practically their back yard. So I don't know.'

'So basically the IRA may be planning for a snatch themselves, or they may get there late and see us in action and then ambush us?' Stated Gruff, who was trying to cover every eventually.

'That's the long and short of it Gruff because we just don't know.' Sheila looked grim faced as she replied. She had hoped that this question wouldn't pop up, there was in fact a very good chance that the IRA would be making plans, but she was restricted as to what she was allowed to say. She liked Tiger and Gruff but she was also very good at her job and promotion prospects within her very secret organisation would never happen if she said the wrong thing to the wrong person, she hoped the men knew, understood and respected that.

'Anybody hungry?' Jane lightened the atmosphere.

Everybody nodded.

'So what shall we do?' She was looking at Tiger as she spoke. 'I presume we can't be seen in the village as a group?'

'I'll take you to lunch sweetheart, there is a lovely little restaurant round the corner...'

'There you go again with the sweetheart Tiger, it just pops out doesn't it? Jane interrupted. She was laughing.

'I never said sweetheart Jane,' said a clearly embarrassed Tiger.

'Oh yes you did mate,' said Gruff and everybody joined in with the laughter.

~THIRTY NINE~

Tiger and Jane left the hotel, turned left, walked up the slight hill and into the picturesque village of Rosscarbery. It was a simple square of tarmac of about two hundred yards surrounded by colourful buildings and a large imposing granite church. Parking appeared to be a free for all, but no doubt it worked. There was a restaurant, a café, a small corner shop, and three pubs all displaying hanging baskets of flowers. The pubs were the hub of the village, not only could the locals spend the day drinking and gossiping it was a place where business was transacted, the selling of a horse, the buying of pheasant for the dinner table. Large rolls of money were passed from man to man as often as the Guinness was poured.

'Crikey,' whispered Jane, 'what a beautiful village.'

'It is Jane. Why are you whispering?'

'I never realised that I was,' countered Jane, 'perhaps it's because it's so quiet here. I suppose I was expecting a market place full of hustle and bustle.'

'I don't think there has ever been a market here, not a proper one it's just a simple tourist village now. A thousand years ago this little village was the seat of learning for European scholars and it boasted one of the world's first Universities.'

'You're teasing me Tiger.'

'I kid you not Jane. They taught languages here, amongst other things, the University was built by monks and they taught here.'

'Where is the University now then?'

'Oh that's long gone, fallen into rack and ruin like a lot of things started by the Irish back then.'

'That's so sad.'

'Ireland can be a sad place if you look too deep. Right, on a more cheerful note, let's eat, because the Irish certainly have never lost that skill.'

They walked hand in hand towards the restaurant, called Jingles, for whatever reason. The door opened as they approached, a young couple were leaving and the man held the door open for them and wished them a good day.

'Good afternoon, tourists are ya?'

'Aye, just tourists, thank you sir,' replied Tiger. Jane nodded politely and followed Tiger into the restaurant. It was a sit anywhere place and there were only four other people in the place although it could easily seat ten times that many. Tiger pulled out a seat by the window to allow Jane to sit down at a heavy wooden table, straight out of a farmhouse kitchen, a table that had a thousand stories embedded in the dark oak.

'Thank you Tiger, ever the gentleman,' said Jane as Tiger took his seat opposite.

'You're welcome m'lady,' mocked Tiger.

Jane laughed as she picked up the menu and noticed that Tiger was frowning.

'What's up Tiger?

Tiger pulled back the net curtains slightly and watched a car pull away, memorising the number plate.

'Oh it's probably nothing Jane, the guy that held the door open for us...'

'What about him?'

'He had a West Belfast accent, a really strong West Belfast accent, possibly Ardoyne, the Crumlin road area.'

'Is that a problem?'

'Well, given our present circumstances it may be Jane. The Ardoyne is a hot bed of IRA activity.' The Falls road and Crumlin road is IRA central.'

'They looked so nice, perhaps they are just here on holiday, you did say it's a tourist place.'

'Terrorists come in all shapes and sizes Jane and they don't have their true colours tattooed on their heads, some of the women are beautiful, but they're also some of the most dangerous women in Europe.'

'Did you get the car registration?'

'Aye, I did.'

'Well you can give it to Sheila after lunch, see what she can find out, meanwhile, let's eat, this menu looks terrific.'

~FORTY~

Gruff, Sheila and Nina headed out to Clonakilty where they tucked themselves into the corner of a busy cafeteria.

'What's the latest with Tiger and Jane then Gruff?' Asked Sheila.

'I wouldn't know Sheila.'

'Oh, that's not true Gruff, there is nothing you and Tiger don't talk about.'

'He really likes her and she really likes him, that's it really Sheila. A bit like me and Nina, but with more sex.'

'You won't make me blush Gruff,' Nina smiled, 'if that's what you're trying to achieve.' She winked at him as she spoke.

'Nina, I'm shocked, I'd never do that,' he said and winked back at her.

'Don't tell me you two are playing at lovebirds as well?' Asked Sheila, 'is there something in the water here?'

'All I know, is nothing,' replied Gruff, 'not a thing,' smiling sweetly at a perplexed Sheila.

'I'm going to have the stew and dumplings.' Nina broke the circle of chit chat and got down to the serious business of ordering their lunch.

'I'm the same,' said Gruff.

'Well it's the fish for me,' said Sheila as she caught the attention of the young waitress.

The food was delivered to their table, fresh and well presented, they were all suitably impressed. They waited until the waitress had disappeared before conversing with each other again, a habit born out of necessity.

'The reason I asked,' continued Sheila, 'is for operational reasons, I'm not being nosy for the sake of it, I'm seriously asking myself whether Tiger is up for this, I mean really up for it?'

'Oh, he's up for it,' replied Gruff, 'he did okay last night, didn't he?'

'Last night was a different day Gruff. Words have been spoken this morning and although Jane has said she will support him, I am not sure yet whether that's reluctantly. Tiger may not be willing to take the risks that he once would.'

'None of us take the risks we once did Sheila.' Gruff wasn't just sticking up for his best mate, it was true. Nina nodded her agreement.

'So you give him the green light then Gruff?'

'Yes, yes I do. I wouldn't want to do this with anybody else.'

'Fair enough. Nina?'

'Thumbs up from me Sheila, he's still a top operator even if he is part time and loved up.'

'Right then, that's all I need to know. My chain of command needed a green light from everybody before we proceed tonight.'

'Is everything in place with your people Sheila? I mean if we get ambushed or things get hot at the barracks.' Gruff had his work head back on.

'Well I'm not sure what you expect Gruff, if you see any of my people before you hand Callan over, then things have gone horribly wrong. This mission is totally deniable, it has to be. Kidnapping in a foreign state will get you jail time, kidnapping in a foreign sate with weapons will get you big jail time.' Sheila was laying down the hard facts.

'When you say, you will be getting jail time, you surely mean we, as in us Sheila?' Gruff wanted to be sure.

'Oh yes, sorry, slip of the tongue,' Sheila answered, just a little too quickly.

Nina caught Gruff's eye and she gave an imperceptible shake of her head. Gruff picked it up instantly. Sheila was lying. She would never be going to prison. Invisible hands would pluck her from any trouble. It's how it worked.

'Right,' said Sheila breezily, 'If we're ready, I'll pick up the tab and meet you back at the car.'

Gruff wiped the last of the gravy from his plate with a slice of bread and wolfed it down.

~FORTY ONE~

Back at the Celtic Ross Hotel, the little group had entrenched themselves back in room twenty two. Tiger had given Sheila the registration number of the Northern Ireland registered vehicle and she was in the corner of the room whispering into the telephone. She finished the call and re-joined the group and face Tiger.

'Tiger, what was the colour and type of vehicle that you saw?'

'It was a dark blue saloon, four doors, sun roof, a Ford Taunus I reckon.'

'You're sure?'

'I'd put money on it Sheila?'

'In that case we may have a problem.'

'How big a problem?' Asked Gruff.

'If Tiger is correct and I have no reason to doubt that he isn't, a blue Ford Tuanus with that registration was stolen from Belfast last weekend.'

There was a minutes quiet in the room whilst they let this deadly information sink in. Jane broke the silence.

'Surely there is a border between the North and the South, the Police would have stopped them if it was stolen.'

'Aye, there is a border Jane, but it's not a hard border,' Tiger explained.

'What does that mean? Not a hard border?'

'It means,' butted in Gruff, 'that there are no checkpoints, you can drive between the two countries with no checks at all. Even if the Police and the army put up a temporary checkpoint, word of that soon spreads and there are so many crossing points it's a pointless exercise.'

'Well that's just stupid, 'stated Jane.

'It's Irish, is what it is,' added Tiger. So, Sheila we have an IRA team on the ground here, we know there are two of them so not enough to spring Callan from the barracks.'

'You have seen one vehicle and two people mate,' Gruff stated. 'There may well be another two people and possibly another vehicle. Their trade-craft is good, we know that, they've had a lot of practice at it.'

'So this is bad?' Asked Jane.

'It is what it is sweetheart, and aye, I know I just said sweetheart, but now we know, we can deal with the situation. It's a massive advantage for us because they don't know that we know.'

'Jane, would you recognise them again if you saw them?' Tiger was thinking ahead, 'because if they are out on foot in Skibbereen this afternoon, you may see them when you do your recce later and you can point them out to Sheila.

'I might recognise them Tiger, it was only a fleeting glimpse.'

'Can you recall what they were wearing?

'I think she had black trousers, hiking boots and a grey anorak, he was wearing dark clothing as well, but I think it was all blue.'

'Not bad Jane,' congratulated an impressed Tiger, 'she was wearing a black blouse under a grey windcheater, black tight fitting trousers and brown hiking boots, she was carrying a large brown clutch bag. She had dirty blonde hair, but that could be and probably is a wig. He had short dark hair and piercing eyes, I didn't catch the colour but they were dark so probably brown, he was wearing black trousers and black hiking boots with a blue sweater over a blue open neck shirt and his watch was on his left wrist which could mean he is right handed.'

'Tiger!' Jane exclaimed, 'how could you possibly know that much detail? You saw them for a maximum of five seconds.'

'That's all he needs Jane,' added Gruff, 'the old boys pretty good.'

'Well if they are wearing the same clothes I'll have no problem recognising them.'

'They have no reason to change clothes, they haven't been compromised,' said Nina, 'however don't get too close Jane, these people are just as sharp as Tiger, they have to be, to survive.'

'Should I be worried Tiger?'

'No Jane, you have nothing to worry about, we've got this.' He glanced over at Gruff for confirmation, but his face remained impassive.

Sheila brought the meeting to a close. 'No matter, we go ahead as planned and we'll deal with any problems as and when they arrive. All agreed?'

The rest of the small team in room twenty two of the Celtic Ross Hotel nodded slowly. Despite the unexpected dangerous obstacle that had been placed in their way, this operation was now going to happen.

The time for talking was over.

~FORTY TWO~

He heard the boots of the Guard before he heard the eye hatch slide open and the sound of a key scraping in the cell door lock. He didn't have to open his eyes to know that the guard would be looking at him through the small armoured glass peep-hole, it was S.O.P. Standard Operating Procedure at every cell he'd ever been in. The Guard needed to see the prisoner, he didn't want to be jumped.

The door scraped open and Dermot Callan, alias Hook, lazily opened one eye and then sat bolt upright in surprise, his jailer was a woman.

She entered the cell and leaving the door open behind her, approached Callan.

'So you're Dermot Callan then?'

Hook said nothing.

'I have a message for you Callan.'

Hook said nothing, she was quite a pretty Guard but definitely overweight. He could take her down in three seconds, quietly and efficiently, but what was the point? There were two more locked gates to get through and God knows how many more Guards.

'It's from Belfast.'

Hook was paying attention now.

'It's a message from a Mister Green. Would you be knowing him right enough? Do you want the message Callan?' Her West Coast burr was becoming quite attractive.

Hook remained silent. He knew the rules. She may well be a club informer, it was known to happen.

'Stand up Callan.'

Hook slowly stood. He was at least a foot taller and two stone heavier. He wouldn't kick off though, he wouldn't win in the end, her Dad was bigger than his at the end of the day.

'Drop your trousers Callan, and your boxers.'

By Christ, this is a new one thought Hook, he was obviously being stripped and issued with a paper one piece suit, so his clothes could be forensically examined, however, there are laws regarding same sex body searches and stripping of prisoners. Hook didn't mind, it made a nice change.

What also made a nice change was when the jailer dropped to her knees in front of him and cupped his testicles in a warm hand and placed his penis in her mouth.

Hook spoke.

Well he croaked really.

'What the fuck are you doing?' The sentence sounded impossibly absurd given the circumstances and Hook realised that as soon as the words had left his mouth.

'Shut up and keep still Callan, I haven't got all bloody night.'

Hook felt himself getting hard, she had a skilled, warm mouth. Hook placed his hands behind her head to increase the rhythm and moaned deeply.

It didn't last long.

Quick, dirty sex was always a turn on for him and this was as quick and dirty as it was ever going to get, add into the mix that another Guard could arrive at any second and catch them, he positively exploded into her mouth.

'Oh fuck that was good, what's your name girl?'

The Guard stood up and looked him in the eye.

'It's Guard to you Callan, now do you want this message or not?'

Hook was taken aback, he'd never been in this situation before. Did it actually happen? Unbelievable! And here she was bold as brass wiping her mouth with a tissue and being a Guard again.

'Of course I want the message.'

'Good, I don't know what the fucking about was all about. You could have just said yes to start with Callan.'

Unbelievable.

'What's the message?'

'Mr Green wants you to know, that Mick and Mary are in town and they are not sight-seeing.'

'Uh, is that it?'

'Yeah, that's it, now go and wash your dick. C.I.D. wants to interview you and I don't want you smelling of a bloke that's just had a blow job.'

She watched as Hook washed his privates in the metal sink, pull up his pants and trousers and she escorted him from the cell.

~FORTY THREE~

Sheila was driving her SAAB just inside the speed limit, she would never be found standing in front of a magistrate for speeding, but that wasn't the point, she didn't want to bring any unwarranted attention down on them. Jane sat in the front passenger seat. She was quite fidgety having spent the last twenty minutes scanning the road for blue motor vehicles. Sheila had told her when they started the journey in Rosscarbery not to bother, she herself would spot the stolen Taunus long before Jane, but it was to no avail.

'We'll be at the barracks in a couple of minutes Jane,' said Sheila, as they passed the sign welcoming visitors to Skibbereen. 'As planned, I'll be going into the barracks and all you have to do is sit and wait here in the car. I'll park it so that you have a good clear of the front gate. If you see the characters from Belfast, don't do anything, just observe, I'll be less than five minutes, are you still good with the plan?'

'I'll be fine Sheila, sit here do nothing, walk in the park.'

'Excellent Jane, he we go.' Sheila nosed the car into a parking spot in the carpark at the front of the barracks. As she had said, Jane had a clear view of the front gate. Sheila turned off the ignition. 'I'll leave the keys in Jane you can listen to the radio then. If you like that fiddly dee music, there will be plenty of that. Sheila got out of the SAAB and headed to the barracks, glancing back at Jane who gave her an awkward little wave.

At this time of day the big studded wooden gate was open, a sign on the wall gave directions to the main building where the public could make general enquiries. Sheila reckoned she was correct about the walls, no more than twelve feet tall, there were no clues anywhere that might suggest that dogs were present, nobody had mentioned dogs at the briefing but it was the sort of thing that Sheila would take note of on a reconnaissance mission.

The buildings were as the plans had suggested so nothing to worry about there. Sheila purposely headed to the administration building, ignoring the signs stating that no unauthorised persons were allowed. The outer door was open, but the inner door was locked, access was via a numeric code system, very basic. She peered through the glass window set into the door and saw half a dozen women at typewriters, she was not challenged.

Turning on her heel she left the building and strode over the courtyard to the general enquiry offices. She noticed one marked Police vehicle on her way, it wasn't in an allocated bay so she surmised that it wouldn't be here long. On entering the building she was confronted with a small room with a couple of uncomfortable looking chairs bolted to the floor, the usual array of wanted posters and advice on how to keep your bicycle safe were stuck to the yellow peeling paint of the walls, A short wooden counter separated this room from the main Police station. Behind the counter stood a male Sergeant a member of An Garda Síochána, Irelands fabulously laid back Police service, commonly referred to as simply the Guards.

He was halfway through a tuna and mayo sandwich as Sheila entered, a large dollop of mayonnaise dropped onto his tie and he made no effort to clean it off. Out of politeness to the member of the public before him, he placed his sandwich down on the counter before he spoke.

'Good afternoon madam and what could I be doing for you today?'

'Good afternoon Officer, I am here to report a missing dog.' Sheila's accent wasn't West Cork but it sounded Irish enough.

'Your dog you say? Well Madam I am quite sure we have a form for that here somewhere, no idea where it is to be fair, not much call for missing dogs you see.'

'Oh my poor Rex, perhaps I'll come back later, that'll give you some time to have a rummage around for the form Officer, yes I think that's best, I know how busy you lads are.'

'And the girls Madam, we have girls with us now, we mustn't forget them now must we?'

'Indeed Officer and the girls. Well I'll leave you to your lunch and don't forget to find the missing dog forms, Oh my poor Rex.'

'You'll be having a good day Madam, so you will. Thank you for popping in to see us to be sure.'

Sheila smiled at the incompetence of it all and left the Sergeant to his sandwich.

On reaching the gate she paused, turned around as if she had forgotten something and had a last look round until she was confident that plans matched the reality.

Happy with the outcome of this basic recce she stepped out into the sunlight and headed for her SAAB. But something wasn't right. She stopped and got her bearings front the front of the barracks and then realised with an awful sinking feeling in the pit of her stomach that her car was missing.

Gone.

Not a trace.

Sheila certainly wasn't one to panic, but this was as close as she'd ever been. Nonsensical thoughts flooded her head. She must have exited through a different gate. Jane drove off to get some lunch or a newspaper, yes that was it, a daily paper she would have been bored with the same old tunes playing on every radio station.

She gave it five minutes, regaining her composure and walked back into the barracks.

'Good afternoon madam and what could I be doing for you today?'

It was the same Sergeant but he didn't show a flicker of recognition.

'Hello again Officer, I am here to report a missing car.'

'Your car you say? Well Madam I am quite sure we have a form for that here somewhere, no idea where it is to be fair, not much call for missing cars you see. Wait a minute, weren't you just here about a missing dog?'

'Yes Officer, and there is some urgency with this one.'

'A car and a dog on the same day Madam, well if you don't mind me saying somebody has been a bit careless today.'

'Can I speak to your superior Officer? There really is some urgency here.'

'I am in fact my superior Officer today Madam, so if we start again as if you are speaking to the superior Officer...'

For Christ's sake man, can I use a phone? There's a missing person...

'So, a dog, a car and now a person, if I can just say madam...'

The Police Sergeant had no idea what hit him, he was flat on his back and would awake in five minutes feeling very groggy with little memory of what had just occurred. Sheila vaulted over the counter and grabbed the nearest phone. She dialled two numbers from memory, the first to the nondescript, brownstone offices above a laundry service on a central Dublin side street, the second to the Celtic Ross Hotel.

Vaulting once again over the counter she walked hurriedly across the courtyard, through the barrack gates and headed for the main road where hopefully Tiger or Gruff would be picking her up.

~FORTY FOUR~

'We know who you are Callan.'

Hook was sat behind a desk in a small interview room. On the other side of the desk were two plain clothes cops. The first detective to speak was in his fifties, close to retirement, balding and world weary he looked and sounded as if he wasn't at all bothered if Hook replied to him or not.

'We know who you are Callan.' The old detective repeated himself. 'We know where you come from, how long you've been with the Celtic Fist bikers and what you were doing last night.' He tapped the thin beige file that was sitting limply on the desk in front of him.

The second detective was much younger, couldn't have been much older than twenty five, he had a full head of thick black hair combed back with plenty of gel and looked like a really shit Elvis Presley impersonator. He had no notes, no beige file, but he had the hawk nose and the beady eyes of a man who doesn't need notes.

'So you might as well tell us Callan. Save everybody a lot of time,' the first detective continued. 'We can do this all night Callan, I've got nothing else to do but my colleague here, well Callan, he needs to be somewhere later. He's a singer and he doesn't want to miss his gig, do you Sean?'

The detective named Sean just scowled and looked meaner.

'So what is it to be Callan?'

Hook broke his vow of silence, there was no way either of these clowns would be believed if they grassed him up to his club for speaking to the law and to be honest he was still feeling a bit giddy from his sexual encounter with an overweight, pretty lady Guard.

'Sure lads, my names Callan, so what?'

'He speaks Sean! He speaks.' The old cop had perked up, now he might be able to do some detective work.

'So Callan, are you going to tell us what you were up to last night, just see if it tallies up with what we have in this little file here.'

More finger tapping.

'I was at my club house partying with my brothers, nothing special.'

'But it was special last night wasn't it Callan?'

'Not really.'

'So you are telling me that automatic gunfire, six dead bodies, your fingerprints on a shotgun and you're the only guy standing was a normal party night Callan? Fuck me lad, you should give me an invite some time, I would definitely enjoy that. If this was normal, what the fuck happens at birthdays?

'It was a normal night until some people attacked the club house, I have no idea who they were or what they wanted, but they were deadly serious, I had to defend myself somehow and anyway that poxy shotgun only fired bird seed, did your hot shot forensics tell you that?'

'Oh, our initial forensic sweep told us lots Callan and of course it's still ongoing.'

'So you know who was attacking us then?

'That's the thing Callan, we don't know who they are, or should I say were. What we do know is, they didn't shoot themselves and one poor bastard has his throat ripped out.'

'Well I never shot anybody and I didn't knife anybody, nobody in the club was in a fit state to hurt anybody, all I did was fire a couple of rounds of bird seed blindly from a window and that's the truth.'

'So you keep saying Callan. What about the club member with a spoon up his nose? Just what the fuck happened there Callan?'

'I was unconscious for a bit, they captured me and tied my hands behind my back, I'm the victim here.'

'Sure, sure you're the victim, I tell you what you are Callan, you are the only surviving witness to the worst fucking massacre that West Cork has seen since the fucking potato famine, so even if I believe your fairy tale, which I don't, then as a star witness you aint going anywhere in a hurry, do I make myself clear Callan, seven men dead? And you're saying nothing, pull the other one.'

Hook remained silent, he was hoping that these idiots would give him some idea as to what had happened but they were just as clueless as him, in fact he did know more because he recognised the dead IRA man. Perhaps he should throw that into the ring and see if the bull attacked it?

'I recognised one of the dead men outside.'

'Did you? Did you really? Was it a friend of yours perhaps? Popping over for some tea? A loan shark perhaps, coming to get his pound of flesh? C'mon then Callan put me out of my misery, who was it?'

'I recognised him from some time I spent in Belfast last year, I don't know his name.'

'You don't know his name, that's convenient Callan, where did you meet him?'

'At a meeting.'

'And...'

'It was a meeting of the General War Council for the Belfast Brigade.'

'Really? So this anonymous man was something in the IRA was he Callan?

'Yeah, I believe he was he principle enforcer for all activities south of the border.'

Now Hook was playing a very dangerous game here, if it ever got back to Belfast that he'd identified a fellow volunteer, he would get the chop, a bullet in the back of the neck after some playful torture involving blow torches, but he felt confident that these idiots would never break the code of silence within the ranks of the IRA and he was sure Special Branch north of the border wouldn't be able to put a job description to the man, even now they'll be getting the prints from the Guards in the south. His whole plan was hinged on one of these dopey detectives giving him some information he needed to piece together more parts of the jigsaw.

'That's all I have for you lads, honestly, that's it.'

'Well lad, you're off to West Cork Central tomorrow Callan. You won't get a free ride there you know, hard bastards work out of Bandon and when their done with you It'll be jail time in Cork City.

Hook knew he wouldn't get that far up the chain. Mick and Mary were out and about in West Cork and were going to spring him well before that.

'Well, can you give that lovely lady a Guard a shout and let her know I'm ready for my cell now.'

'Looks like you'll make you gig Sean because Callan here is having an early night.'

Sean attempted a smile, but it just made him look sick.

'We'll see you in the morning Callan, before you go to Bandon.'

And that was that, interview over, the same lady Guard escorted him to his cell and made zero contact with him. Never said a word, it was if the little episode in the cell earlier had never actually happened.

He lay back on the poorly filled mattress, closed his eyes and started putting some of the pieces together.

~FORTY FIVE~

Tiger was beside himself, what the fuck was he thinking bringing Jane on this operation, it was reckless and now she's gone, kidnapped at best. Raped and dumped at worst, it was a dreadful, heart-breaking, shambolic state of affairs and the responsibility lay firmly on his shoulders, his alone.

'It's not your fault Tiger, it's mine,' said Sheila softly, once they were all back at the Celtic Ross Hotel, 'It was my decision to take her to Skibbereen and my decision to leave her in the car, I take full responsibility Tiger, me and me alone,'

'With due respect Sheila, that's horseshit. Let's go back in time a time a bit, I let her talk me into coming over here, I drove her over here, I never fully explained the dangers we may face, it's my fault.'

It's nobody's fault.' Gruff was acting as the referee, the arbiter, the voice of calm.' It's happenstance, completely unforeseeable, we didn't take her into a firefight Tiger and to put it bluntly, if and I mean if, there is any blame, we can all shoulder the burden, what we need to do now and with the utmost speed is find out who's got her and start negotiating.'

'The IRA have her, I am certain of that,' said Sheila, adding, ' those bastards in the stolen Ford Taunus recognised her in the carpark, they were bound to be in the vicinity, checking out the lay of the land. It's the IRA.'

'Okay,' said Tiger. How do we find out who they are?'

'My people are working on it right now Tiger. Everything in Dublin has stopped, they're all on this, I expect to get a call here within the hour, so until then we sit tight and wait,'

'Wait? Really?' Tiger was getting angry, he knew how these things worked, it was pointless rushing around like a headless chicken, he had to have trust in the guys and girls in Dublin to come up with the answers, there really wasn't any other way, but his anger wouldn't subside, he couldn't get Jane out of his head, the horribly dangerous situation she was in, if in fact she was still alive? Was she taking it well? Shit! Of course she wasn't taking it well. Was she terrified? He would have traded places with her in an instant, but of course this was foolish talk, he needed to concentrate and have trust.

The phone rang, everybody looked at the phone as if it was something they'd never seen or experienced before. Sheila grabbed it and held it up to her ear for a couple of seconds before crashing it back down again.

'Reception, that was reception downstairs informing us politely that due to the chef falling ill, the restaurant will be closed this evening and may not be open for breakfast in the morning.'

'Bloody hell!' Exclaimed Gruff. 'Here we are in the middle of a massive catastrophe and all around us life just goes on as normal, yet it's so abnormal.'

'Hang on a minute!' Yelled Tiger. 'Sheila phone reception and get the name of the chef that has just fallen ill.'

Sheila knew better than to argue, picked up the phone and dialled zero for reception. Twenty seconds later she had the answers she wanted to her gentle questions.

'His name is Patrick O'Regan, he lives alone in a cottage at the edge of the village, it's called Whitestone on Main Street.'

'You got his address as well Sheila?' asked Gruff.

'Yep. Just a subtle piece of social engineering. I told reception I was so pleased with his food and it would be good idea to send him a get well card. They thought that would be a nice idea as well.'

'Great work,' said Tiger, 'now feed that gen into your pal's network and let's see what pops out.'

'Really Tiger? You have a hunch?'

'I don't like coincidences Sheila. Simple as that.'

Sheila was back on the phone to Dublin, within five minutes she had those answers as well.

'Patrick Seamus O'Regan, born may 3rd 1948 in Belfast, the son of Patrick John O'Regan who is currently under lock and key, at Her Majesties pleasure, for handling explosives, where he shouldn't have been handling explosives. He drives a red Mini Cooper on a Cork County plate, he visits the North twice a month, he's a chef at this very hotel, and get this, he's on a watchlist for chrissake, a Government watchlist and they never bothered to tell me at the briefing last week. Unbelievable.'

I'm going to fire up the Triumph and put him under surveillance right now,' said Tiger. We need the van here for you lot so I'm the obvious choice. Sheila, can you sort out another hire car please? Something bland but fast. There's a Hertz rental in Clonakilty, Gruff and Nina can collect in the van once you sort it. We'll meet back here in two hours at the latest, Sheila you've got to stay by the phone, that's a given. Is everyone okay with that?' Tiger had grabbed his leather jacket and was halfway out of the door before anybody could voice an objection, there weren't any.

Tiger took the stairs, with his luck the lift would jam with him in it. His helmet was in the van and it wouldn't take him more than two minutes to wheel his bike out the back of it.

In fact it was ninety seconds later that he accelerated out of the car park and headed for Main Street. It was less than a mile away.

He slowed right down as he reached the outskirts of Rosscarbery, He moved his head to the left and right, not looking for property names, that would take too long, just white cottages. There, on the left. He slowed right down as he passed it. Yes definitely Whitestone cottage although it was more of a bungalow than a cottage, with a red Mini parked on the gravel driveway. The front garden was laid to lawn and totally over grown, it obviously hadn't seen a lawnmower in months. The curtains to the front were drawn shut so there was no way to see if anyone was at home without getting far too close. Even an innocent pretext could spook them, they probably didn't believe in coincidences either. He spotted the lone telephone wire coming from the bungalow to a pole holding another three or four lines of communication, a plan formed.

He turned the bike around and rode back to the hotel just in time to see Gruff and Nina at the van in the carpark.

'What's the story Tiger? Asked Nina. 'We've secured a hire car in Clonakilty, on the way to collect it now. That was a good call mate.'

'Cheers Nina, have you got your wiretapping kit with you?'

'Yes Tiger, it's all up in the hotel room, grey satchel with the words telecom on it in faded letters.'

'Excellent, I'm borrowing it for a bit, Gruff can you drive the hire car and Nina I need you and the van at the target cottage as soon as you get back from Clonakilty. Is that okay?'

'Sure thing Tiger,' replied Nina.

'We have a plan, I like plans,' said Gruff as got into the van.

Tiger walked casually through reception nodding at the lass behind the counter and took the stairs three at a time to the second floor, bursting into room twenty two and grabbing Nina's bag of tricks as an astonished Sheila watched open mouthed.

'You okay Tiger'

'I'm great, but I'll be even better when I get this lot rigged up. I suppose there is no news from Dublin yet?'

'Not yet Tiger, be careful out there, I never had a chance to say that earlier, I mean it Tiger, these are professional animals we're dealing with.'

'I hear ya Sheila, gotta go.' And with that, Tiger hauled the grey bag over his shoulder and was out of the door again.

Back on Main Street Tiger had figured out the wiring loops to the listening set, it was a bit more modern than the one he last used, many years ago, but the principle was the same. Inductive loop crossing the target line, this involved shaving of quarter of an inch from the plastic insulation, there was a tool in the kit for this purpose. He slipped on the tatty looking yellow reflective vest and rode the one hundred yards to the telegraph pole near Whitestone cottage. He was relieved to see the Mini still on the drive. Now to get up the pole, the first handholds were ten feet up, this to deter children climbing them, but he wasn't a child, he was a Tiger, piece of cake. He leaned his bike against the pole and at full stretch he grasped the lowest hand holds and within the minute he was at the top, braced onto the pole with the supplied wide leather belt.

From a distance or from a passing motorist it all looked quite kosher, it would only get problematic if one of the homeowners came out and asked what the hell he was doing.

He scraped away the insulation on the wire that led to Whitestone cottage, clamped on the induction loops with little crocodile clips. He then placed the head set over his ears and began listening, if any call was made to or from the property he would have access to it. He didn't have time to set up the recording device, but he wasn't looking to collect evidence, if his hunch was correct he would be collecting intelligence, a whole different ball of string. He really wanted Nina here, she was the expert and with a large white van it gave this snooping operation a thin veneer of legitimacy.

After just ten minutes a series of clicking noises started in his headphones. Tiger had no idea whether this was an incoming or an outgoing call. Was it the phone ringing? Or was it the dialling tone? No matter, it was a call.

'Hullo Pat.' A strong Northern Irish accent, not Belfast, not Londonderry somewhere in the countryside, border territory.

'Hullo yourself, who's this?'

'It's Mick, from the North, you should be expecting my call.'

'I was expecting a call from Mary.'

'Well she is baby sitting at the moment and can't come to the phone, so you'll be talking to me so you will.'

'Suits me.'

'Grand, so you managed to get the night off Pat, What about tomorrow morning?'

'I'm good for tomorrow as well.'

'That's grand Pat so it is. What about the Brits at the hotel? Did you see any Garda snooping around, asking questions?'

'No Mick, no Garda. I don't even know if the Brits are still there.'

'Oh they're still there Pat old son and they won't be fecking off home just yet ya hear me.'

'I hear ya Mick, so what's the story?'

'Mary and I will be leaving Skibb in the early hours of the morning and heading down to you, it'll be breakfast for four of us at yours Pat. Are you all set for us now?'

'Yeah. I'm all set Mick. How long are you intending on staying?'

'That depends Pat, just you worry about tonight. Okay?'

'Yeah that's fine Mick, see you all later.'

The phone went dead.

Tiger couldn't believe it, what a massive slice of luck. He gathered up the wires and headset and made his way down the pole, he couldn't be bothered making good the damaged wire, that'd get sorted soon enough by a legitimate engineer when the salt from the Irish sea started eating through it.

Tiger made his way to the main Cork road in order to head off Nina because her services were no longer required at Whitestone cottage.

Nina saw Tiger coming the other way and flashed the head lights and slowed down. Tiger did a U turn behind her, overtook the van and pulled into a layby, Nina followed.

'What's up Tiger?'

'I have great news, let's get this bike in the back and I'll bring you up to speed on the way back to the hotel. Where's Gruff?'

'Oh he's still sorting out the paperwork for the hire car so I left him there and hightailed if back here Tiger.'

With Nina's help the Triumph was securely lashed down in the back of the van.

'That's going nowhere that,' Said Tiger mostly to himself.

'I heard that Tiger, why do blokes always say that after you lash something down with straps or ropes.'

'Say what Nina?'

'Say 'That's going nowhere.'

'Did I say that?'

'Yeah, you said it, you know you said it, all blokes say it. It's weird, you must have been taught it at school or something.'

'Whatever Nina, are you still good to drive? I need to scribble down some notes whilst they're still fresh in my mind.'

'I can drive mate, hop in sit back and relax.'

They set off back towards Rosscarbery, and Tiger started taking notes. He stopped when he heard Nina, mostly talking to herself with a smile on her face.

'I'm driving the Tiger.'

For the first time that afternoon Tiger smiled as well.

~FORTY SIX~

It was quick. Jane never even had a chance to call for help. One second she was sat in the passenger seat of the SAAB, head down trying to figure out how to tune the damn radio, the next second a bloke was in the driving seat starting the car and her hair was being tugged viciously from behind, pulling her head back before an arm was clamped around her neck.

She estimated it as less than three seconds and it took another three before she realised who it must be. From the corner of her eye she had a blue sweater beside her and the faint whiff of perfume from behind. That's when she pissed herself, really, properly scared, the warm urine shamelessly trickling through her flimsy panties, through her dress and slowly soaking the car seat and her buttocks.

The driver accelerated hard and was no stranger to high speed cornering, the SAAB was a powerful car and blue shirt knew how to drive it. They drove north away from Skibbereen, narrow country lanes, twisting and winding. Short of breath from the arm across her throat and the speed of the car soon threw her off track with time and distance. She had read a story about a kidnap years ago, in Sussex she thought it was, the woman thrown into the boot of a car, she later escaped and knew where she was within two hundred yards. She had silently counted the seconds and the bumps in the roads gave an indication of speed as she memorised the left and right turns and built up a virtual map in her head.

Well what a load of bollocks that story was, it was impossible, Jane was so scared she could hardly fucking think, let alone route out a map.

She had no idea how long they'd been driving but was so glad when it stopped. The arm across her throat relaxed just a bit. They were in a built up area, old garages and run down commercial units.

Then the girl behind her spoke.

We're getting out here bitch. I'm going to release my grip and when I say so you are going to get out of the car. Nod if you understand.

Jane nodded. She was going to cause no trouble to these people. She would do anything they asked.

Once you are out of the car you will not scream, shout, talk or run so if you attempt to do any of those things we'll kill your boyfriend, nod if you understand.

'You have my boyfriend?'

The pressure was instantly back on her windpipe, it was impossible to breathe and the pain was excruciating.

'Yes we have your fecking Brit boyfriend and if you speak again we'll fecking kill him. NOD YOUR SLAG HEAD IF YOU FECKING UNDERSTAND. Each word yelled in her ear and punctuated with little jabs of increased pressure on her throat. Jane thought she was going to die right there. It was a shit way to die, she hadn't planned for this. Who plans to die this way? Staring out of a car windscreen whilst a homicidal Irish terrorist woman slowly strangles the life out of you whilst screaming obscenities in your ear.

Even the view was fucking shit.

Jane managed to bob her head up and down.

'That's fucking better bitch.'

Jane could not believe they had Tiger, not her Tiger, the Tiger. If they had him she was surely doomed.

The strangle hold was released, the passenger door was opened and she was dragged out by blue shirt. One of her shoes fell off and remained in the car footwell as the door was kicked shut and she was half dragged, half carried a couple of metres into a ruined garage.

Jane was pushed to the floor and ordered to lie face down, her arms were pulled behind her and her wrists were tied together by some unseen method. Jane didn't fight, she didn't argue, she didn't cry out, she was totally subservient.

Strong arms lifted her back up and threw her against the wall, she slid to the floor into a sitting position, her hands cut and crazed as they dragged down the rough concrete wall. She was beyond scared, sat in a puddle of her own piss on a stinking concrete floor, arms bound behind her and no inkling as to why she was in this situation. This is what no hope looked like and it was terrifying.

She looked up at her female captor, no tears just defiance from deep within her soul and whispered.

'Tiger.'

'What's that bitch? What did you say? You know what will happen if you open your fecking whore mouth one more time.'

'Water, please, just a drop of water.'

This simple request simply earnt Jane a kick in the face. Blood from her nose streamed down her face, the salty liquid offering no respite to her dry lips and parched throat.

She couldn't give up. There is no way on Gods little green earth these wankers could have captured Tiger. Even if they had, they didn't have Gruff, and he would go to the ends of the earth for his best mate, they had no idea of the shit storm headed their way.

Jane tried to relax but it was so difficult to break through the pain. She would be signing up for yoga classes when she got out of this mess, she'd be all over the relaxation and deep breathing next time.

She heard the terrorists whispering to each other but couldn't make out the words, why was this so fucking hard? It was a piece of piss in the films.

She watched as they left the garage and thought for a moment she was being abandoned when she heard the car start up, but no, the grey anorak bitch came back in and pulled her to her feet. She was walked further into the darkness, a plastic bag was rammed over her head, this is it Jane thought, the end, but no the bastard was tormenting her, she wasn't using to kill her, it was just a makeshift hood. Rope was forced between her arms, it may have been the towrope from the car boot and she found herself being lashed to what must have a broken ceiling beam. Once grey anorak cunt was satisfied it went quiet and then Jane heard the SAAB accelerating away. She daren't cry out, being kicked in the face whilst wearing a hood was a petrifying thought.

Time was nonsense now. Jane couldn't tell if she had been there ten minutes or ten hours, she had no recollection of sleep but she must have dozed off because she woke with a start when her body weight forced her cuffs behind her to cut off her blood flow.

She risked a whisper.

'Tiger.'

Jane immediately flinched after the word left her mouth, she had been conditioned in such a short time it was frankly astonishing.

Nothing happened, completely quiet and utter blackness. She tried again.

'Tiger.' Louder this time, she couldn't shout, her throat wasn't up to that, but it was a very loud whisper.

'Tiger.' She refused to believe this was a pointless exercise, firstly it proved her tormenters were not there to cause her any more pain, secondly some passer-by, some kids perhaps, they dicked about in places like this, might hear her and investigate and thirdly but much more importantly it gave her comfort. If she was going to die in this shit state then it was his name she wanted as her last breath.

~FORTY SEVEN~

Back at the Celtic Ross hotel, Tiger recounted his conversation with the others, his notes helped, it was on the face of it a fairly bland conversation he'd overheard, but it was laced with clues, plus of course Tiger was in no way ready, or in fact expecting a call, let alone so soon after scrambling up the pole. He just had an idea. He wanted to do something, anything was better to him when the alternative was to sit around this bedroom waiting for the phone to ring.

Nina was the first to interrupt.

'Tiger, these clicking noises you heard immediately before the conversation took place, do you reckon you could recall them. Properly I mean. Can you recall the groups of clicks?'

I'm not sure what you mean Nina, I certainly heard a series of clicks.'

'Tiger those clicks relate to the incoming phone number, they will be in short groups between one and nine. A bit like Morse code, here you go, click click click, pause, click click, pause, click. That's three two one.'

'Easy as that Nina?'

'Yep, it's as easy as that Tiger, but we use a tape recorder and slow it down a bit to make it easier, I just thought with your memory you might be able to pull this off.'

'Okay, I'll go somewhere quiet and work on it, in the meantime can someone come up with an idea of where we go from here? Even if I crack this clicking thing, there is no guarantee that anybody will be at the end of the phone line then and we know that they are coming to Rosscarbery in the early hours so we could wait until then and ambush them. No? Any takers?'

'I'm thinking about Jane mate, the longer these wankers are holding her the worse her condition will get, they absolutely will not give a toss for her welfare, if she dies on them it's just collateral damage, they'll come up with another plan, kidnap somebody else, they're smart and their fucking ruthless, you know this old boy, how many times have we dealt with these type of fuckers?'

This, a speech from Gruff was probably the most anybody had heard him say in a long while and although It might have been long, it was deadly accurate and hit Tiger hard.

'Gruff, with me downstairs at the bar, I need you to help me concentrate.' Tiger was all action again. 'Nina, set up your long range comms set from here, this is our base, Mick and Jane the terrorist duo know we are here, it's pointless moving again, that will only alert tem that we know something. We are supposed to sit tight and wait for these fuckers to call, a ransom or whatever, so we stay here, Sheila you're staying on the hotline to Dublin although it's not very hot at the moment.'

People started getting busy.

Tiger and Gruff sat at a table in the bar/lounge, they both had their backs to the wall with a view of entrance to the room and crucially, given the information that they had, the waiter's entrance to the kitchen. Most bars that served food had immediate access to the kitchen. Chefs always needed port or red wine or a bottle of stout, sometimes it was for the food they were preparing, but sometimes they just wanted a drink.

'Gruff mate, I know what these fuckers want.'

'Can I take a wild guess Tiger?'

'Sure.'

'They want Dermot Callan.'

'Bingo mate, that's exactly who they want, but here's the thing. Sheila Brown also wants Callan, she needs to hand him over to the spooks in Dublin for God only knows but we need him to hand over to two terrorists in exchange for Jane.'

'Tiger it's a no brainer if you're going to ask me if I trust Sheila to do the right thing for you, she won't, she's good and she wants promotion, she wants out of the field and into an office.'

So we need to spring Callan, without her knowledge and put him on ice until this Pat the fucking Chef character calls us, right?'

"That's about the long and short of it Tiger.'

'Good, because I am buggered if I can remember the sequence of those bloody clicks, they were fast, I wasn't expecting them plus of course I didn't know what the fuck they meant.'

'So the question is old boy, when do we spring Callan, we can't leave it too late, we certainly can't stick to our original timing, we have to go in earlier Gruff, before midnight at least.'

'Okay, we can do that, just me and you, in and out, speed and aggression.'

'The bad old days mate. Next problem is, how are we going to slip this past Sheila, we can't just tell her we're off for a stroll, she'll see right through that.'

'Let me have a think Tiger.'

'Too late mate, I've got it.'

'C'mon then give.'

'Whilst we were down here, I received a telephone call from Pat the Chef, he tells me I need to be at a certain address in Skibbereen at ten tonight, just me, no cops, no back up, the usual crap.'

'Obviously I will be going with you as back up, because that's what we do, right?'

'Obviously. We'll get Nina to set up a comms suite for us, an HF radio each and we'll let her know ASAP, as to what the sketch is.'

'Will she buy it Tiger?'

'I have to sell it to her mate, I reckon we get one go at this.'

'Okay, I'm good so far, where are we putting Callan?'

'Back of the van.'

'Right, what about the actual hand over? You don't trust these fuckers right?'

'Nope, I am going to do the long walk up the driveway with Callan under control, you're going to be five hundred yards away, covering everybody through a sniper scope.'

'I'm not liking this bit Tiger.'

'There is a pretty good rifle attached to the scope mate.'

'Okay, it's getting better.'

'It's an L115A3.'

'The standard issue British army sniper rifle, bolt action, 8.59mm, good for a thousand yards and change. I'm liking this more mate. Scope?'

'Standard glass Gruff, Schmidt and Bender 5-25x56, that's twenty five times of magnification.'

'Great. Ammo?'

'Ten rounds of Lapua Magnam, hand filled.'

'Okay, you have me drooling and dangling like a puppet, so the bad news is you haven't got one of those so what am I actually going to get?'

'Gruff mate, have a little trust in the old man. It's upstairs under my bed in a hard case.'

'I aint even going to ask Tiger.'

'That's usually the best way. Now you won't have a spotter obviously, but you're not hunting, you'll know exactly where your killing ground is so you won't need one. The weapon should be zeroed obviously, but we don't have the time or the ammo for that, its set up as factory setting and it's only five hundred yards, you'll piss it mate.'

'Let's go and sell this to Sheila bro.'

~FORTY EIGHT~

God knows how long she'd been there, she'd obviously managed to sleep but that was nervous exhaustion kicking in, not proper sleep, how could she have proper sleep trussed up like this. The only bit of good news was the bag had slipped off as her head lolled over in her sleep. Small mercies, but she would take anything good at the moment, however small.

The pain had slowly ebbed away. She didn't know if that was because the pain had actually gone or her whole body was so numb she couldn't even feel pain, she guessed the latter.

She had no idea if it was day or night, it was pitch black and completely silent, no passing traffic, no animals scurrying about and unfortunately no Famous Five children with a smart dog to sniff her out and save her. Damn you Enid Blyton.

~FORTY NINE~

'So you had a phone message whilst you were at the bar?'

Tiger had given his pitch to the Government super spy, would she go for it? He glanced at Gruff and he was very slowly nodding his head, he thought it was going well.

'Did it sound genuine Tiger?' Nina was convinced, or at least she was getting there.

'Aye Nina, it was a broad Belfast accent, the man asked for me by name and gave me directions.'

'And he never gave you an address, just a rather vague location of a telephone kiosk on Skibbereen Main Street.' Sheila had resumed her questioning. She was covering old ground now so she was testing his narrative, basic interview technique, check if he kept to the same story. It wasn't difficult for Tiger, A. he had a superb memory and B. the story was short and sweet.

'Aye Sheila, I am to be at that phone box at exactly ten tonight, I am to be on my own, but obviously that's not going to happen, Gruff will be there in the shadows somewhere looking after my back.'

'And what will happen at ten o'clock?'

'Sheila, I don't know, the bloody phone might ring and he'll give me five minutes to be somewhere else, try and check that I am on my own. Perhaps he'll meet me at the phone box, Sheila listen, this is a good lead, we can and we must follow this through.'

'Okay Tiger, give him the radios Nina. I want an update as soon as you can after ten tonight Tiger, if I don't hear from either of you I'm going to hit the panic button, understood?'

'Yes Ma'am.'

Tiger grabbed the radios from Nina who had a non-committal expression on her face. Had she twigged? If she had where did her loyalties lie? Questions that will surely be answered tonight, one way or another.

'Are you tooled up Gruff?

'I'm good to go Tiger, just need the long, just in case.'

Gruff was talking about the sniper rifle under the bed, soldiers referred to rifles as longs and hand held side arms as shorts. It made for quicker radio procedure when describing weapons related incidents.

Tiger crouched down and dragged the sniper rifle from under the bed and handed it over to Gruff.

'Is that what I think it is Tiger?' Another question from Sheila.

'It might be Sheila, it's only for when things go tits up.'

'You know what will happen if you get caught with that Gruff?'

'Will I get a slapped arse? C'mon Tiger lets save the day.' Gruff was in no nonsense mood.

Both men made it down to the van in the carpark without further interrogation from Sheila.

'Well she fell for it old man.'

'I'm not so sure Gruff, she's canny that one, no flies dare come near her.'

Gruff opened up the rear, stowed the rifle and joined Tiger up front in the cab as he started the engine.

'Operation let's make it up as we go along.' Quipped Tiger as they left the hotel carpark and turned onto the road to Skibbereen.

'What? You mean an operation organised by any commissioned Officer in the Regiment mate?'

They both laughed. Officers in every part of the British Army had experienced major fuck ups, it was a standing joke, and had been since Mr

Geradus Mercator was at school in the middle of the 16th century, that Officers couldn't read a map to save their lives.

The traffic was light and it only took the men twenty minutes to reach the Guards barracks. Gruff hopped out in the car park and took a walk around the perimeter. The Eastern wall abutted the rear of a row of shops so it was a fifteen minute journey. Neither man complained because time on reconnaissance was never wasted time, a military adage that had stood the test of time.

'Front gates are shut and locked Tiger, I tried the handle. I can't see in so you're going in blind. I'll give you exactly five minutes to get in and find a hidey hole near the gate, that's when I'm going to hit the doorbell and insist on seeing an Officer.'

'That's grand mate, plenty of time, let's do the watch thing. On my mark it is 21.40 hrs...Now.' Both men hit the button on their respective watches.

'Outside. Jump test.' Both men jumped up and down, no clanging, no loose coins jangling, perfect.

Tiger got back in fired up the van and nudged it right up against the Western wall. He clambered out of the passenger door and onto the roof of the van, it was only a hop and skip and he was inside the wall and standing on the roof to the admin building. He waited there for a full two minutes, standing perfectly still and listening. It was a quiet as a graveyard, which was quite apt, as that's exactly what this place will be if this goes wrong, thought Tiger.

He crawled along the low roof and peered down, it was an eight foot drop. He was six feet tall so by hanging off the gutter, it was just a case of hopping to the ground. He did this and crouched for a further minute stealing a quick look at the luminous dial of his watch. 21.43 and the second hand was sweeping quietly towards the 21.44 mark.

He decided to stay where he was, there was no time to find a place near the gate, he was good here, with the noise Gruff was going to make on the door bell he would step in behind the Guard as they made their way to the gate.

21.45. The doorbell started clanging, echoing across the courtyard, Gruff would be on the gate phone as well, pushing along a cock and bull story, some dire emergency that demanded attention.

Sure enough, a minute later, Tiger heard the door to the Jailhouse open and close, footsteps crunching across the tarmac towards the gate, an exasperated copper concentrating on one thing only, the massive bollocking he was going to give the person on the other side of the gate.

Tiger stepped in behind the Guard, softly following in their footsteps, it was a woman. Blonde, could do with laying off the pies for a bit. He had no qualms about decking a woman, she was armed, all Irish coppers, An Garda Síochána as they were formally known, carried a side arm. She could do some damage even accidently.

The Guard pulled back a large iron bar across the gate and inserted a key into the lock.

Now! The Tiger pounced and with a single chop to the side of the neck the poor woman was in his arms being lowered to the floor. She would out cold for around fifteen minutes. He finished off the key turning and pulled on the door, it opened easily on well-oiled hinges.

'Nice work Tiger,' said Gruff as closed and locked the door behind him.

They both ran across the courtyard towards the Jailhouse. The door was open just a crack, really slack security drills holding a prison door open with a stone, because you can't be arsed to use a key or a code every time you go in and out. Very poor drills, but on this occasion very handy.

'In we go Gruff, I'm going in first and sweeping left, both men drew their hand guns and slipped into the light of the Jailhouse.

They worked their way right into the office that controlled the cells, left and right arcs of fire covering as many angles as they could, every move precise and not rushed. It was a deadly ballet.

There he was, a big fat sergeant sat at a desk eating what looked like a large pork pie.

'Good evening Sergeant', said Tiger, minding his manners. 'Would you mind awfully standing up and moving away from your desk, very slowly if you don't mind, take your pie if you must.'

The Custody Sergeant was so close to retirement he could actually taste it, there was no way he was going get hurt, or hurt anybody, not with his short time do.

'Don't shoot me I'll do what you want. What have you done with my Officer?' He slowly rose to feet as he spoke.

'I'll be asking the questions if you don't mind Sergeant, we are not here to hurt you and we do not plan on hurting anybody else, so be a good Sergeant, turn around and face the wall.' Tiger kept his voice low and calm.

The Sergeant duly complied. Gruff walked behind him and relieved him of his handgun. The big Sergeant didn't appear to be frightened, the pork pie in his right hand was rock steady, he just wasn't involved in a bun fight, their intelligence was good in that regard.

'Thank you Sergeant, now I need two things. I need to know the cell number of a certain Mister Callan and secondly I need the keys to get to him. Provide both to my colleague now if you please.'

The Sergeant answered immediately.

'Callan is in trap two and the keys are next to on the wall, you need the yellow tag to open the gate and the red one for the cell door.'

Gruff grabbed the keys and made his way past the Sergeant. Tiger heard the key going into the outer gate, he glanced at his watch. 19.50. They had five or ten minutes before the unconscious Guard at the gate recovered her senses. Callan better not start dicking about. Tiger heard the key turning the lock to cell number two, or trap two as the Police referred to them the world over. Then it got noisy, speed and aggression, Gruff at work, the angry machine that nothing will stop.

'ON YOUR FEET, ON YOUR FEET NOW, TURN AROUND, NOW, HANDS BEHIND YOUR BACK, DO IT NOW.'

Gruff appeared with a half-naked Callan, poor bloke, he was tired and confused and he had no idea how his wrists were cable tied behind his back. Gruff hustled Callan ahead of him and started towards the Jailhouse door.

'C'mon Sergeant, you're coming with us as far as the main gate, c'mon man, were going now, bring your pie if you want.'

The Sergeant passed Tiger without a second glance. He had probably read somewhere that you shouldn't look at bad guys faces in the commission of a crime, because they are more likely to let you live if you can't recognise them. Something like that anyway.

Tiger was the last one out of the Jailhouse, he made sure the door was closed and locked, it was all get away time now. They reached the front gate, the woman Guard was still on the floor but beginning to stir. Tiger asked the Sergeant to lie down next to his colleague, his pie had disappeared and it hadn't been thrown away. It took the big man a while to get to the floor, Tiger considered chopping him at the knees with a kick, he'd go down like a sack of spuds that way. But he made it to his stomach and Tiger crouched down beside him and cuffed his arms behind his back.

'Have a nice retirement Sergeant.'

Tiger sprinted to the West wall dived into the van and fished the vehicle keys from the door pocket where he'd left them, he started the engine as Gruff reached the rear of the van, opened the door shoving Callan in face first, he jumped in after him and slammed the rear door. This was the cue for Tiger to go. Steady drive out of the carpark, through the quiet streets of the town and onto the main Cork road. He knew it would take him twenty minutes to get to the Celtic Ross Hotel if he drove with a steady right boot. He also knew that in less than five minutes the woman guard would free the Sergeant and three minutes after that they would be back in the Jailhouse to raise the alarm. The alarm would sound in the barracks in Bandon, the Headquarters for the West Cork division. There were fifty or sixty Guards available there. The good news was that even in a fast patrol car it was a thirty five minute journey to Skibbereen twenty minutes to Rosscarbery. That gave Tiger a total of eighteen minutes to do his journey.

He pushed his right foot down on the gas and increased his speed, it only took the chance of one patrol car to be patrolling between Bandon and Clonakilty and the travelling time was reduced to fifteen minutes, There was a slight, but real possibility that an armed Bandon patrol car would reach Rosscarbery before him and a hard stop routine would be guaranteed.

No half decent criminal committed crime in West Cork and headed South, there wasn't anything there, one had to go North keep heading towards Cork if you can, use the hundreds of narrow dirt tracks if you must and you must have researched your route in the finest detail, those tracks all looked the same, some came to an abrupt dead end, some just looped back on themselves. These are the tracks that kept the likes of Michael Collins alive in the 1920's when the infamous Black and Tans seriously wanted to hang the man.

Most criminal enterprises in West Cork get caught, that is why it is such a safe place to live.

Tiger turned into the carpark of the Celtic Ross Hotel, he hadn't seen a Garda car. As soon as the van stopped, Gruff was out the back of the van.

'How's our man Gruff?'

'He's fine old man, he is tied to your motorcycle and is currently having a little sleep.'

'Righto mate, let's go and face the music upstairs then, its 22.20, it's such a shame that this was, in all probability, a hoax.'

Gruff smiled, he loved working with the Tiger.

~FIFTY~

'A hoax you say? Mmm, that's interesting Tiger, I'm intrigued as to why you think it was a hoax call and yet two hours ago you were mad keen to follow it up?'

'Sheila I have just explained all that.'

'Just humour me Tiger.'

'I was downstairs with Gruff earlier and he was helping me with my power of recall regarding the phone clicks on my impromptu wiretap.'

'Gruff does that does he Tiger, help you with your memory?'

'Aye he does, anyway we were chatting…'

'How exactly does he help Tiger?' Sheila interrupted him mid flow, 'in fact I'll ask Gruff the same question. How exactly do you help Tiger with his power of recall? I'm intrigued as to that would work.'

'I've known Tiger a long time Sheila.' Gruff was on the defensive.

'I know that Gruff, you followed him into 'G' squadron, the squadron allocated for men who pass the selection process for the 22nd Regiment of the Special Air Service and were former Guardsmen. You had both been Grenadiers. You saved his life, twice, in the Radvan valley, there is very little I don't know about the pair of you Gruff, what I am interested in is how you help people, Tiger in particular, with memory?'

'We talk.'

'Talk? What do you talk about?'

'We just chat, nothing in particular, it eases his mind.' Gruff was floundering, Sheila knew it Tiger knew it and Gruff knew it.

'Sheila, can I just…'

'No Tiger, you cannot just anything. '

'I refuse to tell you what we talk about Sheila, it's personal shit, stuff you don't know about, stuff that I'm not going to talk about, not to you anytime soon.' Gruff stuck his chin out, defiant.

'Look Sheila.' Tiger tried a different tact, 'we know this whole operation, my bike recovery, for which I am grateful, the snatching of Callan that is now on hold because of the Jane kidnapping, everything is your job, you are in charge, you make the big decisions, we are just subbing for you.'

'Really Tiger, you flatter me, so I make the big decisions do I? You lot are just the underlings, right?'

'That's right Sheila, you say jump, we ask how high?'

'Are you a team player Tiger? Are you on my team or are you in a double secret team with your mate Gruff?'

'I'm on your team Sheila.'

'That's good to hear Tiger, really good because I was beginning to believe that you and Gruff and possibly the fragrant Nina have gone rogue on me...'

'Hang on Sheila, I've been here with you, I'm not rogue on anybody.' Nina was appalled by the accusation.

'Nina darling that sentence doesn't even make sense. I am beginning to think that I am dealing with idiots and breakaway crews.'

'Sheila!..' Tiger was getting angry.

'You doth protest too much my little Tiger, now riddle me this...Where the fuckity fuck have you got Callan? He's on ice somewhere and you fuckers have got him. Riddle me that Mr Stripes, the team playing Tiger.'

Fucking hell, thought Tiger, she knows, she knows everything, he had no idea just how fast her organisation could work, she must be plugged into the Garda network, she is getting up to the minute classified information, there is no way, no fucking way at all that the Police have released the fact the a secure barracks was breached and a high value prisoner had been spirited away, to the press or any other security agency. It was too damned sensitive, too damned embarrassing. He stole a look at Gruff and he just shrugged. He didn't know what else to do.

'Sheila, before I tell you anything I have a couple of questions for you. I want an honest answer and if I deem it to be dishonest then we clam up and tell you nothing. Ever again. My Jane's life depends on this, I am going to try and save her no matter what it costs me personally and I include my life in that.'

'I feel the same as Tiger.' A simple statement from the ever faithful Gruff.

'What's the question Tiger?'

'Callan, what do you intend to do with him?'

'I thought these were going to be tough questions Tiger, the way you waffle on. I intend to present Callan to my chain of command to do with as they see fit, I would never question their motives. Next.'

'We thought as much, here's my next question. Do you realise that the IRA couple, Mick and Mary, together with Pat the Chef are going to ask for Callan in a callous prisoner exchange?'

'Yes I do know that, not only do I know that, I know where and when. You are thinking that the IRA are bringing Jane to Rosscarbery, to the Whitestone cottage to be exact. Well you are wrong.'

'What?' Exclaimed Tiger, how do you know that?'

'Is that your next question Tiger?'

Tiger was silent for a moment. He wasn't hugging enough cards to his chest, he had a couple of poxy Jacks and Sheila appeared to have the rest of the pack. He needed time to think and time wasn't on his side, It was getting for 23.00 now, he was thinking he had a bit more than an hour to play with, for fucks sake, Gruff should be out at his hide now setting a firing point, they shouldn't be sat around a hotel bedroom firing questions at each other, it would be real bullets that will be firing shortly, what a fucking mess. Think man think...

'No Sheila that is not one of my questions, I want to know if you have a plan to save Jane or is she going to be a pawn in whatever game you're playing?'

'Yes I have a plan, it's been in place for some time now and it's actually going like clockwork, which makes a bloody change Tiger.'

Tiger paused again, she really did have all the fucking cards now and he was totally in her hands. He looked across at Gruff.

'Mate, last question is for you, it's a fucking biggie Gruff, do you trust Sheila? Take your time.'

Gruff looked relaxed but Tiger knew for a fact that his mind was racing. It took him twenty seconds.

'Yes, fuck it. She has a plan bro.'

'Callan is in the back of my van.' Tiger jumped straight into the deep end. He had just chucked away his last card.

'Is he alive?'

'Yes he's alive'

'Good, now before I continue, I need to see him with my own eyes and make sure he's lucid, is the van unlocked Tiger?'

'No, of course not.'

'Well I'm going to need the keys.'

'Not a chance Sheila, I give you the keys and you drive off into the sunset with our hostage? No, that's not going to happen.'

There was an uncomfortable silence in the room until Nina spoke up. She addressed Sheila.

'Okay, listen, how about if you go down to the carpark with Tiger, he unlocks the van with his remote from a distance, you check on Callan and then Tiger relocks the van, that'll work.

So that's what happened.

Back in room twenty two, Sheila started the conversation.

'Listen, all of you, I understand that you are upset with me, I can even understand the luck of trust, it was my mistake that got Jane snatched, that has been playing on mind since it happened, so I put a plan together to get her back, now admittedly we have no idea exactly where she is at the moment, but we know where she is going to be at 01.00 a little over two hours from now.'

'I thought she was going to Pat the chefs place? That's what the wiretap gave us.' Tiger was grateful that Sheila appeared contrite and she was taking some weight off his own shoulders but he still didn't see any concrete plan.

'I had a team come down from Dublin, in a black ops helicopter. They landed on the playing fields behind Rosscarbery School about an hour ago. They have completed a CTR of Whitestone cottage, it's a really crap location, to many escape routes, too many variables and certainly too close to innocent civilians.'

'What's a CTR? Asked Nina.'

'It's Close Target Reconnaissance,' answered Gruff. 'It's my speciality.'

'You didn't visit the cottage in question though, did you Mister Specialist?' The old Sheila, back to having a sly dig.

'We, I mean I, didn't have time, we had to get our bargaining chip out of Skibbereen nick.'

'Well yes, there is that. I was counting on you two cracking on with that job whilst I organised the Rosscarbery end of things.'

'Wait! What?' Exclaimed Tiger. 'You mean to say you knew we'd be pressing on with the snatch in Skibb?'

'I was counting on it Tiger, if anybody could do it you and Gruff could. You two are world class when you're under pressure and the original plan was far too complicated any way. Too much faff.'

'Faff?' It was Gruff's turn to question Sheila's motives.

'Yes Faff, aerial plans, building plans, sewage systems, height of walls, decoys, all that faff.'

'How did you know we'd definitely go and do it Sheila?'

'Well let's put aside your desperation to do something positive relating to Janes kidnapping, we'll also put aside the rogue element that you both carry, it was simply dogs, or more accurately the lack of questions about dogs at the initial briefing.'

'Dogs?' Asked Gruff.

'Yes, dogs Gruff, you were not bothered about dogs, it's one of the first questions after armed guards, its asked at every briefing, neither of you raised the question which told me you were going in anyway, anyhow. If you came across an armed guard you'd shoot him or slice his throat, if you came across an attack dog you'd kick its head in, nothing was going to stop you, you just didn't ask the question.'

'Well bugger me, she knew all along. No wonder you're a spy and I'm still a grunt Sheila.' Gruff sounded impressed.

'Okay Sheila where are this CTR team now?' Tiger wanted the conversation moved along.

'Oh, yes, the plan, well the Whitestone cottage would have been perfect for the terrorists and a nightmare for us so we had to move the venue, somewhere we preferred.'

'So you just phoned Mick and Mary and changed the venue and they were happy?'

'In a broad sense yes, in a more detailed sense we eliminated Pat the Chef and put a man in his place, similar build, exact same voice. Our man, not their man, makes planning so much easier. Oh Gruff, try not to shoot him, there's a good fellow, he's on loan from The Royal Ulster Constabulary, I suspect they'd like him back at some stage.'

'Jeezus,' whispered Nina, I've worked with some funny named groups before in the alphabet soup that is security services, but really? Elimination? You eliminated Pat the Chef?'

'He was a terrorist sympathiser Nina, he was involved in the kidnap of Jane, among other things, he somehow slipped through the net before today, but he won't be doing any more slipping for a bit. Well forever actually.'

'So we have a man in Whitestone cottage and he's talking to the kidnappers?' Asked Tiger, just to make sure he'd heard it right the first time.

'Yes, that's correct, I persuaded them that there is far too much Police activity in area following the Jailhouse snatch, door to door enquiries and such like, and they went for it.'

'So where is it happening now?' Asked Gruff.

'There is an all-night café on the Cork road between here and Clonakilty, it's owned by, er, a friend of the service, it's a popular hangout for neer-do-wells, including known IRA men. It's perfect, it won't be busy tonight because we have ensured that it won't be busy tonight, I am afraid you don't get the skinny as to the reasons that happened, it just is what it is. Two of our men are already inside but we are expecting them to get moved outside when Mick and Mary turn up. They are just there for decoration and they look the part, they can walk the walk and talk the talk if they get questioned. One of the CTR crew has made you a nice little hide Gruff, he's not a marksman he's a spotter and knows the score. It's only four hundred yards away though, that shouldn't be a problem for a man of your calibre Gruff. Excuse the pun.'

'When am I expected there?' Asked Gruff.

'Grab your long and take the new hire car, park up in the café carpark as anybody else would and you'll be approached, they know what you look like, once you're in place the spotter will disappear, his skills are required elsewhere tonight. Don't get all chatty with him, he will not respond. Nina please give him a radio.'

'Roger that boss, cheers Nina, I'm out of here. I'll see you on the other side.'

'Oh Gruff, you know who your targets are don't you?

'I do Sheila, extreme prejudice and all that.'

'Tiger you are going to be point man, you'll be in your van with Callan in the passenger seat. You are carrying out the exchange so I trust that you're good with arrangement?'

'I wouldn't want it any other way,' said Tiger quietly.

'Excellent Tiger, you'll have a radio as well, keep it under the dash, if get the message 'abort abort abort,' you will do as ordered, you will leave the area immediately regardless of how you think things are going. I have the big picture not you. Do I make myself perfectly clear?'

'Perfectly clear Sheila. If I get the abort message three times I bugger off regardless.'

'Right were all set. We are not synchronising watches Tiger, that's bullshit on this job. It's a very dynamic situation, very fluid you understand?'

Tiger glanced over at Gruff, who returned his look and raised an eyebrow.

'Sure thing Sheila, what about the jump test? We always do that.' Tiger was being flippant.

'Yeah, knock yourself out, nobody cares Tiger, just be at the café at 00.45 and it'll play out as its going to play and remember Pat the Chef is my man.'

Tiger still had his radio as he hadn't turned it on in Skibbereen so it still had a full charge.

'Quick question Sheila, all the Guards in Ireland will be bombing up and down the Cork Road looking for the Jailbreakers, what's the drill if I'm stopped? Do I drop your name?'

'You won't get stopped Tiger, you won't even see a copper, they are all confined to barracks until 02.00 so relax, do your bit to get Jane back and we can all fuck off home.'

~FIFTY ONE~

Jane was wide awake, they'd returned.

Every sense in her body was screaming at her, her nerve endings were scrambled but the overall message seemed to be, make this shit stop. She was covered in pain.

'Up, get the fuck up whore, if I have to get you up it'll fucking hurt you so get the fuck up.'

Jane couldn't get up if her life depended on it and this evil piece of shit knew that. There was one more slim glimmer of hope shining through though, if these fuckers wanted her dead she'd be dead by now, they could have just left her here, she'd have been dead by the morning for sure.

Blue sweater grabbed her armpits and lifted her up while Bitch woman cut through the tow rope holding her to the beam, she hacked at it cutting deeply into Jane's wrists. Christ the pain was unbearable, Jane was sure she was going to pass out. Blue sweater dragged and kicked her outside to the car, it was definitely night time, she was bundled unceremoniously onto the back seat where she lay, racked with pain but so grateful for the scant comfort the seats offered. The door slammed behind her.

Bitch woman and Blue sweater got into the car, Jane had no idea who was driving she just heard the two front doors opening and slamming shut. The engine was started and they were on the move. Jane was in too much pain to care where they were going.

~FIFTY TWO~

Gruff was in his hide, his firing point, his temporary home. His silent guide knew exactly who he was and how to make a hide. No conversation has taken place during the ten minutes it had taken to get him to where he needed to be, but Gruff was grateful for the pat on the back he received before his host fell back into the night. It was good luck pat, a mark of respect pat, it was what Gruff would have done had the roles been reversed.

His weapon was out, lying so it naturally pointed at the kill zone, the short bipod legs were unfolded and the Schmidt and Bender sight had been switched to night vision. He had slammed a round into the breech and felt a chill of excitement as the bolt locked the round into place, its deadly tip ready to burst from the barrel at three times the speed of sound. This was the end game, the home straight, his best mate would be on the ground shortly, part of the team and they could be home in fourteen hours from now.

From his position precisely four hundred and twenty three yards away from the front door of the café, the bullet would reach its target in less time it took a man to blink. He placed his right eye to the scope and gently scanned the café carpark for the tenth time, with the butt of the rifle pulled tight into his shoulder he really didn't want to be anywhere else right now.

~FIFTY THREE~

Tiger wasn't quite as comfortable as Gruff was at the moment. He was sat behind the steering wheel of his van and Callan with his hands cuffed behind him sat locked into place behind the seatbelt in the passenger seat.

At least Gruff was doing a job he loved, a job he was exceptionally good at and Tiger knew that he'd have his back if the shit hit the fan, but Tiger was going into unknown, the massive uncertainty of it all, Sheila Brown running the show with her gang of super sneaky guys and girls and she definitely had an ulterior motive. All this planning, Pat the Chef, the Café clearance, the contacting of the kidnapers, the Close Recce team coming in by chopper, all of this took weeks to plan not three hours.

No organisation is that good surely? All those niggling doubts paled into insignificance though when put against the future of Jane. Was she still alive? How would he cope if she'd been raped, how would she cope? Some selfish thoughts but these things needed to be addressed.

He was stepping into a void here and it didn't feel right, it didn't feel good. It didn't feel good at all.

~FIFTY FOUR~

Jane had estimated that they'd been travelling for twenty minutes, that was just SWAG though, a stupid wild assed guess. It could have been an hour. What she was sure of though is they were on a smooth tarmacked road, there was only one in West Cork, the Cork road, so they must be travelling East and North, that meant the villages of Leap and Rosscarbery, the towns of Clonakilty and Bandon and eventually Cork City. She knew that it was a twenty minute steady drive from Skibbereen to Rosscarbery, they had to pass the Celtic Ross Hotel with its grand old turret and cross the causeway at sea level, they hadn't got that far yet, if in fact she had been held in Skibbereen to start with. It was all so confusing and she missed the strong arms and warm scent of John Stripes her friendly Tiger. She felt the car slowing down a bit that must mean the causeway crossing at Rosscarbery, if only she could smell the sea she'd know for sure.

The car had come to a complete stop for a moment as Bitch woman and Blue sweater quietly discussed something, their options perhaps? They jolted forward again, was that a kerb? The tyres hissed as they passed over gravel at walking speed. A carpark? Oh Christ she was crap at this.

~FIFTY FIVE~

Gruff saw movement in the café carpark, right at the far end. It was four hundred and eighty yards to the windscreen that his sights could not penetrate. He couldn't work out the colour either, but it was a fact that he was looking at a Ford Taunus.

He swung the scope very slowly to the left, movement was a big no no in the world of camouflage, Gruff's world. The scope settled on the bonnet of Tigers van, he could only see the bonnet, nothing else. He glanced down at his watch, 00.50, ten minutes until the exchange. He thumbed the radio send prestle and whispered.

'Hello Zero, LONG here, do you copy? Over.' There was a faint hissing in his ear and the reply came back loud and clear.

'Hello LONG this is ZERO send message. Over.' This was Nina, on the ball and great at communications.

'Hello ZERO his is LONG can you relay to STRIPES, I need another ten feet. Over.'

'LONG, Wait out, Hello STRIPES this is ZERO. Over.'

'STRIPES go ahead. Over. '

'ZERO, relay from LONG can you give him another ten feet. Over.'

'STRIPES, Wilco, moving now. Out.

Gruff watched as Tiger drove forward the requested ten feet and stop, he now had an excellent sight pattern.

'ZERO. This is LONG, I am very much obliged, LONG standing by.'

'ZERO. Roger that LONG. ZERO OUT.'

Such is the way of radio comms, it would have been much easier for Nina to throw a switch and all call signs could talk directly to each other, this was called 'talk-though' But Sheila obviously had a hand in that decision as she wanted full control of the airwaves. No matter, Gruff now had what he wanted.

He watched as Tiger exited the van, it was 00.55, Tiger walked around to the passenger side and released Callan from the seatbelt and helped him to the ground. He then walked towards the café, keeping a grip on Callan and ignoring the Ford at the far end of the carpark. Tiger and Callan entered the café and took a seat at a bench table, Callan next to the window, Tiger blocking him in, they were not talking.

A slow sweep of the café with the powerful scope and Gruff spotted the two undercover guys, Jeez, they looked like a right pair of scruffy bastards. He switched his view to the Ford Taunus. It was moving very slowly across the gravel, he still couldn't penetrate the windscreen with the scope. He really would have liked to look in that car, he couldn't fire blind, Jane may be in there and it might not be the terrorist kidnappers, they might be a couple of saps acting as a proxy, these things do happen. It's all a massive mind game, who breaks sweat first, loses.

The Taunus was about ten yards from the front door now and was stationary. The engine was still on Gruff could see wisps of emissions from the exhaust pipe. It was four hundred and eighteen yards to the windscreen.

An easy shot.

Somebody was getting out of the front passenger seat, female, blonde, confirmed as Mary. She walked slowly towards the door to the café, opened it and stepped in. She was the immediate threat so he tracked her, she walked over to the table where Tiger and Callan were sitting and slid onto the bench seat facing them. Her hands were resting on the table, not threatening. He shifted his scope slightly right, no change at the Taunus. He had no idea what was going on.

~FIFTY SIX~

Tiger was sat next to Callan in the café, they were facing the door. Neither man had spoken a word since Tiger had told Callan in the van that if he uttered one single word any deal was off and he'd break his scrawny neck. Hook had seen these guys in action and knew they wouldn't be fucking about so he wisely stayed quiet, biding his time.

Two other men were in the café, sharing a table at the back of the room, they were over Tiger's left shoulder, so he would have to turn his body around to see them but he knew, or at least he'd been told that they were friendlies.

Five minutes later Mary with the grey windcheater turned up at the door, she let herself in and walked slowly towards their table. She plonked her skinny terrorist arse on the seat opposite, put both hands on the table and stared directly at Callan, and she blanked Tiger completely, all her considerable focus was on the man sat next to him. It was quite unnerving.

It was another two minutes before the door opened again, a large man with a grey beard aged around forty entered and sat down at the adjoining table. He hadn't been in the Taunus, Tiger wondered where the hell he'd come from. The bearded man spoke first in a heavy West Belfast accent.

'So you're Callan then?'

Hook said nothing, he wasn't sure if the big English bloke next to him had relaxed the no speaking rule. Oh, apparently not as he spoke next.

'Yes this is Mr Callan'

'Ah the fucking nosy Brit from my hotel. What's your fecking business here Mister Englishman?'

'This lady here has one of my friends and I'd like to see her.' Tiger turned towards Mary. 'Anytime about now would be good.' Mary sat motionless, still staring at Callan, still ignoring Tiger.

'If I do not get to see my friend in sixty seconds then me and Mr Callan here are walking. I am showing you proof of life, you need to reciprocate. Where is my friend? Forty seconds.'

The man on the next table, who Tiger had assumed was the false Pat the Chef, spoke.

'You have no control over this situation pal, I suggest you stand up and fuck off and let us have a wee word with Mr Callan alone.'

'Thirty seconds'

'Twenty seconds.' Tiger grabbed hold of Callan's arm and started sliding him along the bench towards him before standing up and dragging Callan with him.

'Times up folks, this fella is coming with me, if you cannot produce my friend, I have to surmise that you've killed her, and if you have I am going to lock Callan in my van, come back in here and kill both of you. It's all fairly straight forward, c'mon Callan.' Tiger headed towards the door when Mary spat out her first words.

'The fucking bitch is in the car, back seat, leave Callan here and go and have a look see.'

'You must think that I was born stupid, that's not even a deal is it? C'mon Callan let's get you off to Bandon and get you back in custody.' Tiger was halfway out the door when the Taunus headlights came on, full beam and he was momentarily dazzled and loosened his grip on Callan's arm. Callan tried to struggle, why? Perhaps it was a futile escape attempt, a bid for freedom? Where was he going to go with his hands tied behind his back?

These clowns didn't seem to give a toss about him, not really although he obviously had something that they wanted, but once they got that out of him, he was dead meat. He put his free hand up to shield his eyes and started walking towards the Taunus, moving at a tangent he eventually was back in darkness and alongside the passenger side of the vehicle, he couldn't see the driver, he may have a gun pointing at him, he hoped that as Gruff wasn't unleashing hell, that he at least could see into the damn car.

The headlights were switched off at the same time as the ignition, darkness descended once more. A bit of fluorescent light was leaking from the café, not much though, not enough for him to have a good look on the back seat.

The driver's door opened and a male got out, the same bloke that had held open the door at Jingles yesterday lunchtime, a life time ago now.

'Who is in the back Mick?' Tiger needed to sort this bloke out. Calling him by his name might throw him off his stride for a bit.

'Your wee skinny whore, that's who.'

Perhaps not then, still it was worth a go, he didn't want to draw his weapon, not yet, if Jane was alive in the back of this car she'd die in a shit storm of hot lead.

'Why isn't she moving Mick? What have you done to her?

'I haven't touched her. She's cuffed up same as our man there.'

'I want you to lift her out of the car Mick, show me that she is living. I'm holding your proof of life, you show me mine, that's how it works Mick.

'You can fuck off with your proof of life bullshit. I'm telling you she's alive, are you doubting my word?'

'Of course I doubt your word, so here's what's going to happen. I'm getting back in my van with Callan and I'm driving him to Bandon unless you open the back door and prove she is alive right now, I'm gone Mick and so is this fella.'

Mick never moved because this playing at silly buggers was going to get someone hurt.

'I'm gone Mick, nice meeting ya.' Tiger moved towards his van, his left hand squeezing Callan's right bicep, his right hand under his jacket on his handgun, he moved past he front door of the café and grabbed a glimpse in. Nobody had moved. Why was that? Just what was going on?

It was a disturbing tableau.

'I'm not armed.' Mick was trying to reassure him.

'I don't believe a word you say Mick and I won't unless you open the back door. Tiger was a yard away from his van when Mick opened the off side passenger door and dragged out a sack of potatoes, dumping it on the ground.

'Here you go, she's all yours, now put my fucking man into the back of my car and we'll be off.'

'Is that a joke Mick? You drag a sack of shit out of your car and think that's it?

The sack of potatoes began to stir, slowly at first, as an outstretched arm grabbed hold of the passenger door and started to drag itself upright.

~FIFTY SEVEN~

Gruff had been watching the whole show in close up detail but he had no reason to pull the trigger. There appeared to plenty of talking but no action, certainly no sign of Jane.

Tiger was outside now standing in a blaze of light, the driver of the Taunus was trying to blind him. Gruff considered shooting out the headlights, an easy enough task but he had no idea what Tiger was planning to do, although judging him by his actions he looked like a man without a plan.

There were plenty unanswered questions going on here, why was Pat the Chef and Mary still in the café? Why hadn't Mary questioned the two scruffy guys in the café? Why wasn't Jane being produced? It was all wrong. He couldn't shake off the feeling that every single person in this sketch was being played, including himself.

Mick was out the car now and taking to Tiger, it looked like a Mexican standoff, neither side wiling to back down. Tiger was edging away from the car and it looked from his perspective that Tiger was moving towards his van, still clutching Callan.

Mick had opened the rear passenger door and was dragging something out, it was on the opposite side of the car and Gruff had no idea what, or who it was.

He started concentrating on glass reflections, trying to get a better view behind the car, he ramped up the magnification to eighteen, a daft idea at this range, the higher the magnification the lower the depth of field and the harder it was to keep a steady viewfinder. He managed to get a spot on the driver's door mirror, there was something there, so he concentrated on his breathing, a basic marksmanship principle, he steadied his grip and concentrated on the door mirror, something was there and it was moving. Was it an arm?

His radio hissed in his ear. What? Now? Christ he hoped it was the abort message, something had to break this deadlock.

'Hello LONG, this is ZERO, do you copy?'

Bollox, Gruff rested the rifle and hit the send prestle.

'Hello ZERO this is LONG, go ahead over.'

'Gruff it's a trap.' Nina's voice sounded urgent and she had resorted to plain speech. That broke every rule in the book.

'LONG. Say again over.'

'Gruff it's a trap, every single person there is a target, the café has been rigged to explode, it's a massive bomb, the only friend you have there is Tiger and Jane if she's there, you are not going to get an abort message Gruff, you're all going to get blown to Kingdom Come...'

Nina was abruptly cut off. This was now sinister.

'Nina, Nina, this is Gruff, hit the talk through button if you can. Nina, Nina...'

Gruff was getting seriously alarmed, the situation on the ground, Nina's message and now the radio was silent what the fuck was happening?

He took another slow sweep of the killing ground with the scope magnification reduced to four, the two friendlies in the café had moved. Where the hell were they? He shifted to the far left of the café and there they were. Both of them in the darkness, bent over. Ramp up the magnification to ten, they were fucking about with the café's gas bottles. Fuck!

He made a decision.

He pulled the trigger, the recoil hardly noticeable as the deadly little cargo sped into the night. Shifting the barrel a couple of millimetres to the left he snapped the bolt open and pulled it back, the ejected round left the breech and skittered away. He pushed it forward again causing a new round from the magazine to enter the breech block and be rammed it into the barrel. He snapped the bolt handle down and fired again. Two shots, two kills, the entire process had taken less than two seconds.

He placed the butt of the rifle on the floor, removed his handgun from his shoulder holster, kneeled and then burst from his hide. He had four hundred yards to cover, down an incline across rocks and shrubbery at night.

~FIFTY EIGHT~

Tiger watched with growing incredulity as the thing on the ground dragged itself to an upright position leaning heavily against the car. He whispered to himself, 'Jeezus Christ is that Jane?'

'Jane! Jane is that you? Damn you Mick what the have you done to her? You fucking animal' Tiger was enraged. He kicked Callan behind his knee that instantly dropped him to the floor. He pulled his gun from his pocket, cocked it, aimed it at Micks and strode towards him, the weapon not wavering in his hand. Mick didn't move, Tigers actions had so fast and so decisive he didn't have time and now he did have time, it was too late.

'Support her and put her back in the car. NOW'

Mick didn't move

Tiger jabbed him in the forehead leaving a small round indentation. It would have hurt but the Irishman didn't flinch.

'I will not ask you again.'

Mick turned and starting putting Jane into the rear of the Taunus. He wasn't a threat in that position so he grabbed a quick look in the café. Sheila's men had gone and Mary was still sat on the table next to Pat the Chef. No threats from that direction either.

Two high velocity rounds screamed though the air follow by the double retort of a rifle. Mick dropped to the floor as if he had been hit. Tiger knew he hadn't, the crack of the shot was nowhere near them, he'd been at the receiving end of effective enemy fire and this wasn't it.

He sensed movement, there, coming down the scree a couple of hundred yards away, a man with a handgun, jumping over boulders, tripping and rolling, sliding back to his feet. Shit, it was Gruff, in a hurry, something was badly wrong. His radio was in the van so he wouldn't have heard the abort order. That must be it. Well fuck that, he wasn't aborting anything now. Jane was going to hospital. End of.

He turned his attention back to Mick.

'Get up you cunt.'

'It doesn't matter what I do, it doesn't matter what you do, It doesn't fucking matter what any of us do. It won't matter.' Mick had finished loading Jane. He stood up and looked straight down the barrel of a 9mm semi-automatic when he spoke.

'What? Are you talking in riddles?'

'I suppose this ragged fella coming down the hill, is one of yours.'

There was no way on earth that little trick will work so Tiger kept him pinned down with his eyes.'

'Tiger, TIGER!' That sounded like Gruff shouting. Tiger kept his weapon on Mick and walked around him, he wanted him between him and the café and more importantly he wanted him between him and Gruff.

'Face your front,' Tiger ordered as Mick started to turn. He obeyed.

'Shoot the fucker Tiger, SHOOT him!' Gruff was deadly serious Tiger thought, this wasn't a polite request, he absolutely trusted Gruff's call and he pulled the trigger.

A surprisingly muffled bang and Mick dropped to his knees and stayed there. Half his face missing.

Gruff veered away from Tiger position and ran behind the café. Two shots, both from a British Army issue 9mm semi-automatic. Gruff's weapon. Ten seconds later Gruff reappeared.

'What the fuck is happening mate?' Asked Tiger.

'No time Tiger, just get in the Tuanus, get to the hospital, I've got business in Rosscarbery, I'll take the van, are the keys in it?

'Aye, in the ignition mate, what about those?' Tiger nodded in the direction of the café. 'What about Callan?' He was still on the ground.

'Fuck em, we're going now Tiger and I mean fucking now.'

Tiger needed no more encouragement, he was in the car, engine started and wheels spinning in the gravel exactly five seconds later. He had turned onto the road when an almighty explosion rocked the car and the night turned to instant day. A sonic boom reverberated in his ears, he automatically flicked his eyes to the rear-view mirror, what? The fucking carpark was on fire!

His van, with Gruff at the wheel, careered maniacally onto the road with the steering wheel on full right lock, as the back end swung out to the right. A small fire was blazing away on the roof as he roared away. He was definitely a man in a hurry.

Then it started raining debris. Glass, lumps of concrete, a plastic chair and lots of unidentifiable detritus hammered down. Tiger metaphorically crossed his fingers and accelerated through it.

The small hospital in Clonakilty didn't have an A&E unit but the duty Doctor took one look at the unconscious Jane and had her transferred to an ambulance. He asked Tiger to follow him to a small office. Tiger got the questions in first.

'Whadda you reckon Doc?'

'What happened to her? Did she fall from a moving car or was she run over by a truck?' Retorted the Doctor.

'It's complicated.' Tiger peered at the Doctors name tag on his left breast. O'Brien. 'Doctor O'Brien.'

'They always are. What's the patient's name? Asked the doctor as he scribbled notes onto a form on his clipboard

'Jane, Jane Albright.'

'Address?'

'Donington-on-Bain, Lincolnshire. England. We're here on holiday Doc.'

'How's that working out? Said the Doctor, with a wry smile adding, 'your name?'

'John Stripes, same address.'

'And a contact telephone number, an Irish one.'

'We're staying at the Celtic Ross Hotel in Rosscarbery.'

'Very nice...'

'We're booked in as Mr & Mrs Smith.' Tiger interrupted.

The Doctor raised an eyebrow but didn't say anything. The sound of an emergency two tone horn started up and the office was temporarily bated in blue flashing lights.

'That'll be Jane off to General in Cork City, we have a world class team there Mister Stripes, she'll get the best care possible, is that a gun in your pocket?'

'Yes, yes it is but I'm authorised to have it.'

'On holiday?'

'Everywhere I go Doc.'

'Ah, okay. There is no point going up to Cork for at least twenty four hours, you won't get to see her, but a bit of advice Mister Stripes, when you do visit, leave the armoury behind, you here?'

'Aye, sure Doc.'

'And another thing before you go, I would be surprised if the Garda didn't start taking an interest, some questions will need answering.'

'I bet they will,' thought Tiger as he said goodnight to the Doctor and made his way back to the Taunus.

~FIFTY NINE~

Tiger was deep in thought as he left the small hospital in Clonakilty. There were so many questions, least of all whether Jane would pull through. Or Not.

What the hell was Gruff doing shooting friendlies and breaking cover? What happened at the cafe, and who blew the fucking place up?

He slowed down as he approached the carpark where the café had been, it was awash with blue flashing lights from at least six fire appliances. There didn't appear to be any Police. He remembered that Sheila had said they'd been confined to barracks but surely they would have turned out for this? Apparently not.

A fireman in a white hard hat raised his hand indicating that Tiger should stop and he obeyed. The fireman approached his car and Tiger wound down the window a notch, his handgun in the door pocket, loaded and ready to fire. Tiger didn't know who he could trust.

'You'll not get past Sir, dreadful mess,'

'What happened?'

'Some sort of explosion Sir.'

''Wasn't there an all-night café here?'

'To be sure there was Sir, but's gone now.'

'Was anybody hurt?'

'I cannot disclose any information at this time Sir, it's still a bit hot to get around properly. Are you English? Here on holiday?'

'I am yes, I wouldn't want to anywhere else to be honest because it's a beautiful part of the country, notwithstanding exploding cafes!'

'Where are you headed at this hour then Sir?'

'I'm trying to get back to my hotel in Rosscarbery.'

The Celtic Ross is it Sir?'

'Aye, that'll be the one, is there a way around this mess?'

'There is but its narrow roads and if you don't know the area you'll soon get yourself in a right tangle so you will. Look, hang on a minute I'll see if I get a couple of lads to make a path for you.'

'You're very kind.'

The firemen looked over his shoulder at the devastation behind him, a fully floodlit scene with about ten jets of water arcing high into the night and dropping on to what was left of the café.

'We do what we can for our visitors Sir, enjoy your stay.'

He wandered off to sort out the road and Tiger remembered why he actually liked coming to West Cork. It was a wonderful place with warm friendly people, it was a shame he was visiting the ugly underside.

The fireman appeared in his headlights and beckoned him forward. Tiger pipped the horn and got a friendly wave in response, and then a series of other fire fighters took over, guiding him through the maze of rubble.

Tiger reached the Celtic Ross Hotel ten minutes later, the carpark was empty. Where was his van and the hire car? He parked up and went into reception, nodded at the duty clerk and made his way up the stairs to room twenty two.

He put his ear to the door and listened. Nothing. He tried the door handle ant it moved easily, the door was unlocked. He reached for his weapon and holding to his chest, he took a deep breath, swung the door open and entered the room at speed, his gun swinging from left to right and covering every arc.

Nobody shot at him because there was nobody in the room, well, nobody alive anyway. Nina was slumped on the floor with a small round hole in her forehead. Tiger crouched and checked for a pulse at her neck despite knowing it was a futile gesture. He stepped over her lifeless body, moved to the bathroom and pushed it open with his foot, gun at the ready. That too was empty.

He sat on the bed and stared at the bank of dials and switches that made up Nina's communication set up. 'What's the point of having thousands of pounds worth of radio equipment and leaving me in the dark?' He spoke out loud. Then he had a thought. He stood up and picked up a headset from the panel and hit the transmit button.

'Hello Gruff, this is Tiger, over.'

To his astonishment he received an immediate reply.

'Now then old man, you made it back then?'

'Aye mate. Jane's been taken to Cork, what's happening? Where are you?

'I'm on my way to you now my old mate. You need to pack your stuff and wipe down anything you've touched. I'm picking you up in the van.'

'Wait, what? Nina's here she's been shot, where's Sheila?'

'I know about Nina, I've got Sheila, we haven't got time for this chit chat Tiger. Get packing, wipe the room clean and go down to the carpark. Gruff out.'

Tiger removed the headset and set about packing, luckily they'd travelled light, it only took five minutes. He used some baby wipes from the bathroom and cleaned up, that took another five minutes.

He had a last glance around the room before he closed it behind him and headed for the stairwell.

~SIXTY~

Tiger hadn't been in the carpark long when his van pulled in. He opened the passenger door, chucked his bag on the middle seat and clambered in. He hadn't closed the door before Gruff was on the move. It slammed shut as they left the carpark for the last time. Tiger somehow doubted he'd be welcome back.

'What's the hurry Gruff?'

'We need to get to Cork mate and lay low, the shit has hit the fan and the brown stuff is headed our way.'

'Where's Sheila?'

'She's in the back.'

'In the back? Is she okay?'

'If you mean physically okay, then yes, if you mean is she okay in the general sense, then no she aint okay, she is as far from okay as you can be.'

'You're speaking in tongues Gruff.'

'I'm surprised I'm speaking at all. I am so fucking angry Tiger.'

'Nina?'

'I'm not ready to talk about Nina yet mate,'

'Well you have to talk about something, I am completely in the dark here, I have no idea what's happening Gruff,'

'Hang on we're turning here.'

Gruff turned left onto a single track road signposted 'Reenascreena 5 miles' and pulled into a passing space. He switched off the headlights and killed the engine. It was pitch black and the only sound was the motor ticking as it cooled down. He turned to Tiger in the dark.

'It's difficult to know where to start mate.'

'Let's start at the firing point, your hide, that's where things started getting noisy.'

'Right, fasten your seat belt Tiger it's a bumpy ride. I'm tucked up in the hide, it's all good, I have a perfect field of fire, I saw you arrive although I couldn't see into the cab, so I gave Nina a shout on the radio and I presume she contacted you because the van moved forward ten feet.'

'I got the message and moved but that was the last thing I heard, why didn't you give me a call on talk-through? It would have a hell of a lot quicker mate.'

'That feature was switched off, it's obvious now but Sheila didn't want us talking, she wanted to monitor everything. Anyway I saw you take Callan into the Café, I saw the two odd looking guys in there that Sheila said would be in there and I saw Mic and Mary turn up but I couldn't get a view into the car. I saw Mary sit down with you and I saw the Pat the Chef stand in sit down, but I haven't got a Scooby Doo how he got there. You got up and dragged Callan out and confronted Mick and that's when I get a call on the radio from Nina, clear speech, no procedures'

'Bloody hell that's weird, Nina was a pro.'

'She was mate, but it's what she said that frightened me. She was literally screaming at me, warning me that the café was rigged to explode, you were all going to die, there were no friendlies in that café Tiger.'

'Jeezus, what happened next? What else did Nina say?'

'That was it Tiger, then nothing, just radio silence. Then I saw that Bill and Ben the odd job men had left the café by a rear door and were fucking about with the gas connections, I slotted both of them and legged it down the hill to you. I wasn't one hundred percent sure of the shots because the weapon wasn't zeroed, I had no time to get to a range and fire a dozen rounds to get the scope set up for my eyes, so I made sure with a head shot each.

'And then it was kaboom. The lot went up, we only just made it. But immediately after that, I went to Clonakilty to get Jane sorted and you buggered off back to Rosscarbery, I presume to see what the hell was going on back there.'

'Correct, I was really worried about Nina.' Gruff paused. 'I really liked her Tiger.'

'I know you did mate and I am truly sorry, but what the fuck happened? Who shot her? Do you know?'

'Sure I know Tiger because she's trussed up in the back of this van. It was Sheila.'

'Sheila? What? Jeezuz Christ Gruff, really? You know this for a fact?'

Gruff nodded in silence, Tiger said nothing because Gruff's emotions were running high. It took a full minute before Gruff resumed.

'Yes, unfortunately I do. I got back to the Celtic Ross and Sheila was getting in the new hire car in the car park, she saw me and looked horrified. I ran up the stairs and noticed door to room twenty two was open, Nina was on the floor, Dead. I knew then. I was out of the hotel and back in the van within a minute and I headed for Skibbereen on a hunch, caught up with Sheila and rammed her off the road. I dragged her from her car and put a gun to her head and she told me to get fucked and that I should already be dead. I put a round in her kneecap and that's when she realised that I was not dicking about.'

'You shot Sheila? Fucking hell mate, what did she say next?'

'She started boasting that we're dead whatever happens, we, that's me and you Tiger. She is a double agent giving information to the IRA as well as collecting it. She was under orders from Belfast to stop Mick and Mary by any means possible, they had gone rogue and were a massive liability.

'Okaaay,' Said Tiger slowly, 'but what the hell has that got to do with us?'

'Sheila lost Jane to Mick and Mary, Belfast were livid and told her in no uncertain terms that if she doesn't get her back she is under the cosh as well. When you and I sprang Callan from his cell, well that little exercise put us in the frame as well. We were all potential witnesses to IRA activity in West Cork and we all had to disappear. Jane was an innocent civilian and the IRA, for reasons beyond me were pissed off that Mick and Mary had grabbed somebody that wasn't a player and certainly it wasn't an authorised snatch.'

'So Sheila concocted the café plan herself? It wasn't a Government sponsored event?'

'Correct old boy.'

'But the helicopter? The IRA hasn't got choppers.'

'Did you see or hear a chopper Tiger? No. Because there wasn't one.'

'So the CRT team didn't take out and replace Pat the Chef?'

'Nope. The Pat the Chef we saw in the café was actually Pat the Chef Tiger. There was no CRT team'

'Bloody hell Gruff, and the two friendly stooges in the cafe? I suppose they were IRA as well, not friendly to us?'

'Correct again Tiger, you're catching on. Sheila got access to a South Dublin cell and they rigged the café with explosives. She then contacted Mick and Mary and lured them there, together with Pat the Chef with the promise of money and the exchange. Mick and Mary were easy to persuade, they thought if they got Callan and presented him to Belfast, they'd be back in the good books.'

'Bloody hell Gruff, what a mess.'

'Here's the kicker Tiger, Mick was shown the firing point where I was going to hiding, sixty minutes before I got there. He was told that there was going to an IRA sniper watching every move of the exchange. If anybody pulled a weapon they'd be shot in the head, if anybody moved from their allocated tables they'd be shot in the head and if anybody fucked up the exchange they'd be...'

'Shot in head.' Tiger finished the sentence.

They totally believed it Tiger and they knew how ruthless their comrades could be. It was a skilful bit of brainwashing by Sheila.

'How could Callan know that he wasn't to do anything stupid?'

'Remember the charade in the Celtic Ross carpark? Well that's when Sheila gave him a quick briefing, he was probably gobsmacked when he saw her, but at least then he knew then that she was a serious player and not some dizzy bird who fancied partying with bikers.'

'She had it all planned from the minute Jane got snatched. What fucking possessed her? Anything else I need to know Gruff?'

'There is something that I don't understand Tiger. The guide, the one who built and showed me to the hide, patted me on the back as he left. We didn't speak and I presumed it was a professional courtesy at the time but now I'm not so sure. I think he may have been a Government deep cover agent within the IRA, but I'll never know now.

'What a fucked up place. I used to love coming here Gruff. Why did she do it? 'What's the plan with Sheila?'

'I don't know why, she won't say, but it's not idealism, so it's probably money, anyway, we are going to take this track up behind the hill I was sitting on earlier I'm going to see if my rifle is still up there.'

'And?'

'And Sheila is coming with me, but she won't be coming back down.'

'Roger that Gruff. Let's crack on then, it'll be light soon.'

~SIXTY ONE~

Tiger and Gruff pulled into a side street outside the 'Corkman,' a small guesthouse on Lee Road to the north of the city. The river Lee ran alongside the road. It was a ten minute drive to the hospital over the Wellington Bridge.

Tiger had picked up a brochure from the Celtic Ross hotel on his arrival with Jane, it was the Tigers ploy, always have a plan B.

The two bedraggled looking men entered the shabby little reception. A counter clerk put down the book he was reading and stood up.

'Morning gentlemen will you be looking for a room then?

'We will,' replied Gruff, quickly adding,' a twin if you have one, en-suite second floor.'

'You're in luck I have just such a room, how long will you be staying?

'Couple of days, maybe three.'

'Certainly Sir and how will you be paying?'

'I'll be using my wife's card if that's okay?' Gruff handed over a Bank of Ireland credit card.

'Ah, Mrs S Brown is it, well it's not usual practice but we're not busy and you look like respectable gentlemen.'

As the clerk filled in the credit form and ran it through the stamping machine Tiger and Gruff looked at each other. Neither man had slept for over forty hours. Gruff had tufts of grass stuck to his black pullover and blood smears on his face and hands. Both men stank of sweat and gunshot residue.

'Here we are Sir your key, you're in room twelve, up the stairs to the right and on the right. Enjoy your stay at the Corkman.

Gruff thanked him and they made their way upstairs, both men stopped as soon as they were out of sight of the clerk and they stood silently. Five minutes passed and the clerk hadn't called the Guards, it was obviously that type of accommodation. They walked quietly along the corridor and opened the door to number twelve.

Tiger took the window bed. He lay down, his head hit the pillow and the Tiger slept.

Epilogue.

Tiger had spent hours at the hospital a lot of them beside Jane's bed as she slowly recovered. She was in a bad way. A broken nose, three broken ribs, a bruised throat and various cuts and lacerations to her arms and wrists meant that she was in intensive care for two days.

The local Guards had interviewed him but as he honestly knew nothing he couldn't answer their questions. They eventually surmised that she had been in the wrong part of town at the wrong time and was beaten up and robbed. Tiger didn't put them straight.

The journey across the Irish Sea and back to Lincolnshire had been a slow and painful journey for Jane, but she was sat in the front seat of the van with the man she loved and a man she adored, that tonic alone made up for the pain.

Two days at Tiger's doing a bit of recuperating himself, was enough for Gruff, he said his goodbyes and he headed south, he would hand the battered looking van back in Slough. The bill for damages would go to a non-existent Mrs S Brown.

Jane took it easy for a week before she felt strong enough to welcome her children back. Their cover story was that Jane had suffered a bad fall whilst they were out walking, Jane had fallen a couple of feet onto rocks. Her Mother had raised a sceptical eyebrow and tried to read Tigers face during the explanation, but he remained impassive and Jane had bravely laughed off the incident as her own fault for being so clumsy.

A fortnight later, Tiger took a call in his study.

'Tiger? Gruff,'

'Now then, what's occurring?' They often dispensed with the pleasantries, especially on the telephone.

'Remember that Irish fella who led me up to the hide in Clonakilty? The one that patted me on the back?'

'Aye, I'm not likely to forget am I? What about him?'

'Well, I was right, he's one of ours. He has no idea who I am, but he's contacted my lot asking for help and were putting together an 'off the books' team to give him some help.'

'Are you asking for my help Gruff?'

Tiger could see through the door into the living room, Jane was sat reading, she looked utterly gorgeous. A sixth sense made her look up at him and she blew him a kiss. Gruff continued.

'How do fancy a quick trip to Belfast next week Tiger. In and out. No drama?'

Tiger smiled and picked up a pen.

THE END

Printed in Great Britain
by Amazon